# A Revolution of Rubies

## Applied Topology Book 6

### Margaret Ball

Galway Publishing

Published by Galway Publishing

ISBN Paperback: 978-1-947648-18-0
ISBN eBook: 978-1-947648-19-7

Printed in the United States of America
Cover art: Cedar Sanderson
Formatting: Polgarus Studio

# A Revolution
## of Rubies

# 1. The Shaimak Rubies

It all started with Aunt Alesia and the dragon rubies, and that dance at the Austrian embassy in Paris.

Purists would go farther back, maybe as far back as the day a couple of years ago when I was concentrating really hard on the Axiom of Choice and accidentally selected several objects out of my kid brother's miscellaneous collections of plastic junk. Without touching them. You could make a case that it all started there.

But I'd been applying topology, and researching further applications of topology, for nearly two and a half years since then without ever causing an international incident. So I blame this one *entirely* on Aunt Alesia.

When Lensky and I agreed that his career would take priority for a while, because I could do my research anywhere that he might be stationed, we'd both envisioned the usual CIA overseas posting. He'd be assigned to some interesting part of the world to collect information and recruit people to bring in more information, preferably not breaking too many laws of the host country too noticeably. We'd set up house wherever he was sent and I would settle down with my books and a stack of blank notepads for a long, quiet period of research.

What we hadn't figured on was that after we successfully retrieved the hostages from East Africa, the entire Operations side of the CIA would become very, very interested in applied topology. And I certainly hadn't figured on being expected to deal with diplomatic social life in Paris, of all places, as part of my service to the Company.

All I had going for me was a decent French accent, a one-month crash course that the CIA called "charm school," and a modestly fashionable wardrobe (also courtesy of the CIA.) That wasn't a whole lot of equipment, linguistic or otherwise, with which to tackle a glittering social life in the fashion capital of the world.

"Cheer up," Lensky said when I whined to him, "you're vastly overestimating the sophistication of State Department social life. It's more like an infinitely boring desert with not nearly enough oases."

"Tell me again about the infinitely boring desert," I suggested under my breath while surveying the ivory and gold ballroom that filled the entire second floor of the Austrian embassy. Men in sober black and white were surrounded by women in a rainbow array of formal gowns, many of them sparkling with enough jewels to rival the GDP of a small country.

This sort of thing had never been hinted at when the CIA funded a grant for me and the other topologists at the Center for Applied Topology. Silly us, we thought we were being supported to continue our research into topological ways to achieve paranormal effects. And for the first couple of years, that was mostly true. Apart from sending Brad Lensky to pass on occasional requests and to try to keep us out of trouble, they'd left us pretty much alone. In the weeks following the bombing and the hostage retrieval this summer, I realized that this was because most of the people in Operations didn't really believe in our paranormal abilities. They'd been too afraid of looking like gullible fools to actually *use* us.

Now, though, the careful people at Langley had realized what an asset they had in the Center, and they were lining up around the block to use us. Their principal interest, to begin with, was in black bag jobs. Every field office in every capital city had a list of places they'd dearly like to bug. Other countries' embassies were high on that list, together with ambassadors' residences, military clubs, private political clubs, you name it. Up to now, they'd had to work with a series of difficult tradeoffs. How hard would it be to break into a given location, and what was the cost if they were caught sneaking around there? Everybody in this business spied on everybody else, but getting caught was not cool and sometimes resulted in embarrassing diplomatic conflicts. Putting your own ambassador on the spot could be a quick ticket out of field work and back home to a basement full of analysts.

Now they thought they could bug every place they'd ever dreamed of, for free – that is, at little or no risk. The theory was simple enough. We – the applied topologists at the Center – could teleport to any place we'd been previously, and we could take passengers. Let a topologist mingle with the legitimate embassy personnel, get invitations to parties at various embassies and other places of interest, then teleport back in the small hours with a technician who would place the bugs. Even if surprised, we could vanish before anybody believed what they were seeing.

There was just one catch. There weren't anywhere *near* as many applied topologists as there were field offices begging for our services.

To be precise, there were exactly four of us: me, Ben Sutherland, Ingrid Thorn, and Colton Edwards.

We did have an infinite set of the magic-enhancing stars that Mr. M. had brought with him from ancient Babylon, but since they could only be deployed by topologists – or Mr. M. himself, of course – that didn't solve the CIA's problem. Too, most of them were not real clear on the whole concept of infinite sets, nor did they find it easy to believe in tiny sparkling points of light that were invisible to anybody but topologists – or Mr. M., of course. The stars didn't really feature in most Company discussions of how to use us.

Lensky tells me there were some nasty scenes, and almost some blood spilled, in the initial discussions of how to divvy up the treasure that we represented. He was in most of those meetings to advise the department heads on how we could best be used, and he took the opportunity to advocate on our behalf before anybody got crazy or cruel notions.

We were going to start in European capitals, because those would be the easiest locales for our untraveled crew to begin with. Postings would consist of one topologist and one partner of the opposite sex, because there were always places a man could go that a woman couldn't, and vice versa.

This worked out nicely for us, as we all had non-topologist partners.

I, of course, was married to Lensky. Just before the diplomatic initiative got started, Ingrid had married our computer expert, Jimmy DiGrazio. Colton had a thing going with Meadow Melendez, the robotics engineer who maintained Mr. M.'s prosthetic body and built the enhancements for it. And Ben was living with his rich girlfriend Annelise, who also worked for the Center as our resident liar. She was an expert at spinning stories to convince people who stumbled across our paranormal work that they hadn't seen what they'd seen, and she looked forward to doing the same, or better, to foreign diplomats.

For our first assignments, they tried to match us with cities that would be relatively easy for us. The Swedish embassy didn't actually have a long list of places they desperately wanted bugged, but Stockholm would be a good place for Ingrid, with her parents' Swedish background, to start work. Colton was assigned to Spain because Meadow was fluent in Spanish. Ben got London, and he swore that Annelise's rich father hadn't influenced anybody to give him the easy English-language assignment. "And besides, Thalia, you got the best posting of all!"

"*Paris*," Ingrid sighed. "While I'm freezing in Stockholm…"

"Paris," Annelise echoed. "Do you realize Paris Fashion Week is just starting? Balmain, Balenciaga, Lanvin…"

"Barcelona is pretty interesting too," Colton said cheerfully. He and Meadow were being sent to the consulate in Barcelona, rather than to Madrid, because the Catalan independence movement was heating up to boiling again after several months at a slow simmer. "I've always wanted to see Sagrada Familia and Parc Güell."

"*I've* always wanted to see *Notre Dame*," Ingrid grumbled. "The Louvre. The Louis Vuitton Museum: they're doing a temporary exhibit of that Icelandic artist's light installations this month."

"Well, you can go look at the Little Mermaid instead," I suggested.

"*Really*, Thalia. That's in Copenhagen, not Stockholm. Why they're sending a cultural illiterate like you abroad at all escapes me."

"I'm a State Department intern taking advantage of this new program to give me a smattering of overseas experience before I settle in to a permanent post," I said, repeating the line we'd all been told to use as an explanation for our joining the various embassies. In most cases the American ambassador didn't know any more than that. Officially, at least. Lensky's agency is very big on plausible deniability.

In fact, I wasn't that thrilled about being sent to Paris. Ingrid could have had it with my best wishes. I'm not exactly the person you would think of in connection with elegant Parisians; ever since graduation I'd managed to use the same little black dress for almost every occasion that demanded something more than T-shirts and jeans. Mom had forced me into ivory satin for the wedding, but apart from that my little-black-dress record was perfect.

The CIA makeover budget did not include jewelry. Fortunately, as a mere intern, I wasn't really expected to compete in that league. My topaz-colored silk sheath with a frill of lighter gold chiffon bursting out from knees to floor was more than adequate for my official position. All the same, I could have used a modest spray of citrines, or something of the sort, to build up my morale. Too bad I couldn't wear my infinite set of stars – well, I could have, but since they were invisible to everybody else they wouldn't have much of an effect. "How am I supposed to compete with *that*?" I groused as a tall brunette wearing a fountain of rubies and diamonds whirled past. "Holy shit," I gasped as her profile came into view. "I don't believe it."

"That kind of language will certainly make you stand out," said Lensky. I ignored him. Men have it so easy; one good dark suit and they could fit in everywhere. I started after the brunette and Lensky grabbed my arm.

"Hey, when they said *mingle*, they didn't mean charge out on the dance floor and trip over people," he said.

"Didn't you recognize her?"

"Who?"

I jerked my chin towards the ruby-bedecked brunette. "Considering she was *Koumbara* at our wedding, I'd think you would remember her. That. Is. My. Aunt. Alesia." She was thirty years older than me and I was willing to swear she didn't own any rubies. What was she doing at the Austrian embassy's ball of the year? For that matter, what was she doing in Paris at all? I'd last seen her sitting at Mom's kitchen table, peeling carrots.

"Let's catch up with her and find out," Lensky suggested, swinging me out onto the dance floor with surprising competence. The man could waltz like a Viennese, something I had not previously discovered during the year and a half we'd known each other. He was even good enough to make up for my awkward steps; the month of makeover-and-training provided before the CIA threw us in at the deep end hadn't been nearly enough to turn me into an expert dancer, but it didn't matter with Lensky taking the lead.

Staying upright through a Viennese waltz was enough of a challenge without trying to look for Alesia. I concentrated on my steps. We turned, dipped, swooped and suddenly backtracked. The music ended with us standing beside Alesia and her partner, a short man with thinning blond hair whom I'd never seen before.

"Thalia, *ma petite!*" Alesia exclaimed. "What brings you here?"

"Funny, I was just about to ask the same question." Up close, I got the full impact of the rubies. The necklace was shaped like two dragon figures, the heads meeting just above the cleavage of Alesia's dress. The eyes were huge rubies surrounded by tiny diamonds, and each of the overlapping scales was set with a smaller ruby. The wings were solid gold accented by wires, with another ruby dangling from each point. The scaled shapes changed subtly with her breathing, suggesting that the scales were attached to something flexible.

"Oh, Daryush and I are old friends," she said. "He was the Cultural Attaché for the Taklanistan embassy in Rome when my dear Georges was posted there, you know. And now he's an ambassador! We were just remembering those happy, happy days."

"Not so happy for all of us," said Daryush in a heavily accented voice, "since you, *ma chére* Alesia, were so devoted to that Georges of yours!" He turned to me. "All of us young men in Rome wished him at the devil, that lucky Georges, monopolizing the loveliest lady in diplomatic circles!"

"Daryush, you will shock my niece," Alesia laughed, "she doesn't know that old people like us ever loved and laughed. This is my little niece Thalia, Daryush."

He clicked his heels, bowed over my hand and just brushed his lips across the knuckles.

"And she is newly married," Alesia went on, "so you mustn't flirt with her, Daryush. Her nice American husband would not understand!"

"But Alesia, *ma belle*, you know my heart is entirely yours!" Daryush protested.

"Do my parents know where you are, Aunt Alesia?"

She shrugged. "I may have said something about going to Paris with my old friend Solange. Or I may not… I believe, actually, I had intended to return to Austin after meeting Solange in New York. But when she was so kind as to invite me back to Paris, how could I refuse?"

The music started again. Daryush, taking my aunt in his arms, whirled back out onto the dance floor. I stayed where I was, frowning.

"Is this going to be a problem?" Lensky asked.

"Oh. No, I don't think so. You never mentioned where you work to Aunt Alesia, did you?"

"Thalia, even your parents don't know who I work for."

"Oh. Right." I have occasionally made fun of the Company's passion for secrecy, but just now it struck me as a very good thing. I wouldn't get many invitations to parties on other embassies' turf if I were identified as a CIA field officer rather than a State Department intern.

Lensky's waltzing style had attracted some attention among the diplomatic wives, so I found that mingling was relatively easy now. The wives wanted to dance with my husband, and offered me up to their escorts in exchange. It worked out reasonably well. The husbands didn't want to dance and neither did I. They fetched me flutes of champagne and little plates of snacks and we chatted amicably enough; they were so grateful that I didn't pine for the dance floor that it was easy to keep them happy. By the end of the evening I had scored invitations for cocktail parties at the Ukrainian and Polish embassies, a reception in honor of Central Asian artists at the Guimet – the Musée National des Arts Asiatiques – and a dinner party at the home of the Egyptian cultural attaché. Not to mention figs wrapped in paper-thin Parma ham, asparagus spears in puff pastry, and Sachertorte under whipped cream. Lensky hadn't done too badly himself: two more dinner parties, a concert and a museum opening.

Aunt Alesia and her date the ambassador were nowhere to be seen. Oh, well. It wasn't like Taklanistan, wherever that might be, was a country of burning interest to the CIA. I could safely leave that to my wayward aunt and concentrate on the Ukrainians, Poles, Egyptians, and whoever Lensky had scooped up.

We decided that we could skip the reception for Central Asian artists, as nobody at the embassy had any desire to bug the Musée Guimet – and if they did, they could walk in there any time; it was a public place. The concert and the museum opening also didn't offer much of interest. We'd be busy enough for the next week dealing with all the other invites.

I fell into bed with a gratifying sense of duty well done. For somebody who doesn't mingle, I thought I had filled out my dance card pretty well on this first excursion. Paris wasn't going to be so bad after all.

I thought that right up until the Friday of the following week, when we returned from our dinner party at the Israeli political officer's home to find Aunt Alesia pacing up and down the marble hall outside our temporary apartment. "Thalia, you have to help me," she burst out as soon as we were inside. "The most terrible thing has happened. The Shaimak Rubies are gone!"

I blinked. "What, that…" I quickly ruled out *insane, extravagant* and *flamboyant*… "that lovely necklace you were wearing at the Austrian embassy ball? How did you lose your rubies, Aunt Alesia?"

"That's just it," she said. "They weren't *my* rubies. They were a loan from dear Daryush."

"Okay, how did you lose *his* rubies?"

"And they aren't his either. They come from the Shaimak ruby mines in Taklanistan. The mines were closed over a century ago, which makes the rubies even more valuable because of their rarity. They are the property of the nation. And those – those *canaille* who took them are blackmailing me!"

When I was so ungenteel as to mutter *Oh shit* at the embassy ball, who knew I was prescient? Because this was a genuine *oh shit* moment if I'd ever seen one.

# 2. Best quality Russian vodka

Meanwhile, in Barcelona, Colton had been having his own problems. And they didn't even seem to be connected with the Catalan independence movement, though that had proved to be a very sticky tar baby indeed for much of the Spanish leadership. The year before, Madrid had overreacted to Catalonia's plans for a referendum on independence, shipping in hundreds of Spanish – not local – Guardia Civil to arrest a dozen Catalan leaders in dawn raids. They had also parked three cruise liners full of more Guardia Civil in the harbors of Barcelona and Tarragona. To everyone's relief, the referendum had gone off without major violence. However, it had hardly settled anything. Barcelona's position was that ninety percent of the people who voted had supported independence and therefore a free Catalonia had the mandate of the people. Madrid's position was that less than half the population of Catalonia had voted, you call that a mandate? And furthermore the referendum had been illegal, unconstitutional and… well, you get the idea.

It was anybody's guess who had thought it would be a good idea to replay the whole mess just one year later. Maybe there had been some hope that the new Catalan President and the new Spanish Prime Minister would be a little calmer and more amenable to reason than their predecessors, and that this referendum would proceed without violence or threats of violence to give everybody a view of what the people really wanted.

The hope was not completely unfounded. Pedro Sanchez, the new Prime Minister, was more tactful about flooding the city with Spanish cops than his predecessor had been: he brought them in by rail, instead of parking a giant cruise liner decorated with twenty-foot-high paintings of Tweety Bird in the middle of Barcelona's harbor. And Quim Torra, the new President of Catalonia, had so far refrained from announcing that his people had plenty of ballots and ballot boxes stashed where the Spanish would never find them. The streets were simmering but so far protests had been peaceful. Catalan flags alternated with Spanish flags on balconies, but since both flags were basically red and yellow stripes the effect was almost harmonious.

At the US consulate, the staff were holding their breath in the hope that (a) the referendum would come off peacefully, or at least (b) that Madrid wouldn't do anything stupid that would embarrass us and force us to rethink our general, rather bland, support of Spanish unity over Catalan separatism.

It was the consul's task to communicate to Madrid that massive dawn arrests of prominent Catalans would constitute "something stupid." It was Colton's and Meadow's task to mingle, circulate, get a sense of the feeling in the street, and get themselves invited into places that our people really wanted to bug.

Diplomatic social life in the run-up to the new referendum was somewhat subdued – well, as subdued as Barcelona ever gets; you can't keep a Catalan down for long, and there were raucous pro- and anti- independence rallies and parties all over the place. But Barcelona's diplomats, such as they were – after all, as a mere provincial capital the city didn't rate the five-star presences that decorated Madrid – were mostly afraid that the one night they went out on the town would be the night the referendum tension spilled over into violence. Rioting. A complete breakdown of civil order. And the ultimate horror: injured diplomats!

The atmosphere dampened their enthusiasm for entertaining, leaving Colton and Madrid plenty of time for sightseeing. That was what got them into trouble. They can't blame this one on the State Department. Oh, they went about it conventionally enough at first: tickets to Parc Güell, a tour of Casa Batlló, standing in the long, long line to get into Sagrada Familia.

That was where they decided to take a small risk. By the time they actually got inside, they were almost late for a reception at the French consulate.

Instead of absorbing the glowing white and gold interior in reverent silence (Meadow) or with guidebook in hand (Colton) they barely got to glance around the place before they had to hustle back and dress up. Colton, whose enthusiasm for Gaudí's architecture had only grown with each place they visited, felt cheated.

He also felt that having stood in line once, not to mention paying for tickets they barely got to use, they were morally entitled to a return visit on their own terms. He'd started thinking along those lines quite early, as soon as he realized that they weren't going to have nearly enough time to explore the place. And he'd picked out a nice, private place behind a spiral staircase, a place that shouldn't have been visible to the tourist crowds surging through the church.

"Nobody will notice us," he promised Meadow. "We'll jump right after it opens, before the place fills up with tourists, and that'll make it even safer."

"I don't know…"

"If you think we're cheating the Catalan Museum Fund," Colton said, "I'll send them an anonymous donation… *after* I get a good look at how those branching columns work. Did you know Gaudí worked out the design by creating a hanging construction of knotted ropes and hanging weights at the pressure points?"

"You may have mentioned it just once or twice," Meadow said. She was beginning to regret having bought Colton that book on Gaudí. Anybody would have thought he, not she, was the engineering major. It was quite enough of a strain to refrain from using her usual pungent language to describe the crowds inside the church. When you added the pressure of being given a crash course in Gaudí's architecture by someone who didn't fully understand it himself… well, sometimes she questioned her sanity in getting personally involved with one of these crazy mathematicians whose "applied topology" looked an awful lot like what Father Hernandez would have considered Satanic magic.

Then Colton hugged her and she decided that as long as she got to wear loose pants and her extra-padded, air-insulated athletic shoes she could probably stand another tour of Sagrada Familia. Maybe this time she'd actually experience the elevated and refined meditative mood that all that white stone and golden stained glass was supposed to induce.

Instead…

"Hello, good morning, cheers, old chap!" burbled the tall, fair-haired, chinless man who'd come around the spiral staircase a split second after they'd materialized in that quiet white space. She *thought* he'd shown up after. The alternative would be… not good. "You come back for another look, eh?"

"I'm sorry," Colton said with his usual automatic courtesy, "I'm afraid I don't recall meeting you." He jammed one hand into his right front pocket and only withdrew it to take the stranger's proffered hand after his stars were safely stashed away again.

"Oh, I am Feodor – Fedya to you," the stranger said. "We have not spoken, but I saw you here yesterday. We both made a big mistake, coming to pay our respects to the masterpiece at such a crowded time, no? And the tickets – so extra-orbitant! Much better to give a little tip to the porter and enjoy Holy Family before the tourists fill up the place!" He winked, placed one finger on the side of his nose, assumed a reverent expression and crossed himself.

Backwards.

"You're Orthodox!" Meadow blurted out. "Russian?"

A flicker of irritation crossed Fedya's face, but almost immediately he replaced it with a toothy grin. "Yes, in Mother Russia the Church is no longer oppressed! We may not pray by your Roman rite, but we can come together in admiring of this work of holiness and great power, can we not! Let us pray that all nations soon be united in peace and amity in the world outside, just as the Holy Spirit unites you and me in this sacred space!" He pressed his palms together and rolled his eyes upwards, then tried to put an arm around Meadow.

"Fedya, *darling*, these nice young Americans will think you are crazy man!" drawled a tall, languid blonde who ambled to Feodor's side and put her arm through his. "Forgive my husband," she said to Colton, "he is too, what, overenthusiastic, yes? But we are both so filled with joy to see at last this city of great architecture."

"How did you know we were American?"

The woman had a low, burbling, intimate laugh. "Why, dressed as you are, and in this tourist attraction, what else could you be? Oh, do forgive my rudeness." She held out one white, perfectly manicured hand, rather as though she expected Colton to kiss it. "Larissa Vasilievna Petrova, from Piter – St. Petersburg, you would say. And this mad scamp is my dear husband Fedya. Now tell me, have you seen –"

Larissa and Fedya appeared to want nothing more than to spend the rest of their holiday with Meadow and Colton. Fedya jabbered around the interior of Sagrada Familia until Meadow had to remind herself that murder was probably even more of a sin if committed on consecrated ground. As for Larissa, she kept snuggling up to Colton with long, sensual wriggles followed by comments about what a pleasure it was to be escorted by *two* gentlemen as tall as she was herself. They only escaped by pleading urgent duties at the consulate, and even then Larissa managed to extort contact information and a promise of another meeting from them.

"There's something fishy about those two," Colton grumbled on the way back. They'd been unable to disentangle themselves until agreeing to meet at a fashionable nightclub that night, and even after that Larissa and her dear Fedya had clung so closely to them that he and Meadow had actually had to go down the stairs and take the Metro back to the consulate. He'd been planning on a significantly quicker and less crowded way to return.

"I think Larissa has a crush on you," Meadow said.

"And what does that make her 'darling Fedya?' The most complaisant husband *ever*?"

"Ah, the Petrova and her partner," said Henry Blevins, the assistant to the Political Officer. "Up to their old tricks again, are they?"

"I wouldn't know," Colton said. "What *are* their tricks? And why are they taking such an interest in us?"

"She said the man was her husband," Meadow contributed.

"Feodor Nikolayevich Ivanov? No, he puts on a very good silly-ass act, but he's not crazy enough to marry a long drink of poison like the Petrova. They do work well together, though. As for why they latched onto you two... I suppose they recognized you, Edwards, from one of the consulate functions, and thought that a green young intern might be naïve enough to take their friendliness at face value. It's just like the Russians to come sniffing around this referendum. Their default position is to encourage separatist movements as a means of weakening the EU, just as our default position is to favor national unity. Why they should take a *particular* interest in State's inner workings just now, though, is... a bit of a mystery, even to me. I'd have thought their time would be better spent fomenting civil unrest. I'd like to put someone more experienced on them, but since they've decided to make up to you..." His voice trailed off and his gaze drifted upwards towards a corner of the ceiling. After a pause that was not quite long enough for Colton and Meadow to excuse themselves, he nodded and resumed speaking. "Yes, you two may as well carry on. You can't do much harm, you don't know anything but our official position, which the President has already stated quite publicly."

"Is there anything else to know?" Colton asked.

Henry Blevins blinked. "If there were, you wouldn't be told. Especially now that you've made contact with a pair of Russian agents. Just go on as if you were the naïve young Americans abroad they take you for – it shouldn't be hard. By all means meet them tonight at – where did they say? Sala Razzmatazz?"

"No, some place called Hotel Dans."

Another sharp nod from Blevins. "Good choice. It's new, not too crowded, popular with you young people. See what you can find out about their mission here, but don't ask so many questions that you make them suspicious."

"This," Colton muttered that night as he and Meadow descended into the Stygian darkness of Hotel Dans, "gives a new meaning to 'not too crowded.' Evidently in diplomatic circles it means, 'you won't step on more than three people at one time.'"

"That's not fair," Meadow said, "your boots are so big you can easily crush any number of people, even at the Broken Spoke."

"I'm not wearing my boots. Wish I were, though. All those stiletto heels are a menace."

Colored lights strobed through the room, allowing them to follow the Russians' cries of welcome to a table easily large enough for one and a half people to sit at comfortably. "Darling Fedya" had already ordered for them. "White Russians," he announced, pushing two creamy drinks towards them.

Meadow took a sip of hers. "That's good," she said, surprised by the sweetness. "What's in it?" She couldn't even tell what color it was; the flashing lights kept changing, showing a sea of green faces that turned to orange, to red, to purple, to blue. Only the black of their clothing stayed the same.

"Oh, just Kahlúa and cream. It is the milkshake for adults," Fedya said. "Come, you two need to catch up with us."

"And vodka," Colton said.

"What?"

"There's vodka in this also. A *lot* of vodka."

"But of course," Larissa trilled, "vodka is mother's milk to us Russians, you know! Finish your drink, Colton. Darling Fedya nurses his drink like a pet kitty-cat, and I want to dance!"

She did? Meadow gazed unenthusiastically on a small dance floor full of writhing black-clad bodies and faces that kept changing color. She missed the Broken Spoke, where you could actually see who you were dancing with. She liked the music there better, too. In fact, at the moment it was hard to think of *any* aspect of Barcelona that she preferred to Texas. Sagrada Familia had been okay, maybe, before it had turned out to be infested with Russians.

"Dancing might work out better before I drink all that vodka," Colton said, setting his glass down and rising. He offered a hand to Larissa and led her out onto the dance floor where too many couples were already gyrating. Meadow took another long sip of her drink.

"This is probably the best milkshake I have ever had," she told Feodor. "I love it!" Okay, that was something good about Barcelona: White Russians. Nobody had ever offered her an exotic alcoholic milkshake like this back home. And Colton had been absolutely right; the coffee liqueur and the sweet cream masked an explosive charge of vodka. "It's just as well they don't allow smoking in here."

"No, is terrible law," Feodor said. "You Americans always talk talk talk about freedom, what about *my* freedom to enjoy a cigarette with my drink? In any truly civilized society…"

Meadow found her mind wandering while Feodor chattered. When his voice finally stopped, she had no idea what he'd just been saying. So she stuck with her original thought, which had only been reinforced by more sips of her drink. "No, it's important for fire prevention. If anybody struck a match and I hiccupped, this place would go up in smoke."

Feodor let go with his odd yipping laugh. Combined with the receding chin, it intensified his resemblance to a coyote. "You are funny girl, Meadow Melendez! Is true, Hotel Dans serves best quality Russian vodka. One hundred and eighty proof."

"Don't you mean eighty proof?"

"No, no. *One hundred eighty.*"

"Christ on a crutch," Meadow said, temporarily forgetting her intensive lessons in polite diplomatic conversation, "that's not vodka, that's a mother-raping explosion waiting to happen!"

Feodor yipped at her again, not in a very nice way. "No, my sweet Larissa is the explosion, and she is happening to your man!"

Meadow squinted through the crowd. Colton's size made him easy to pick out among all the shorter, slighter Spaniards. And Larissa… had apparently forgotten *her* lessons in polite dancing. If she'd ever had any.

Out on the dance floor, Colton felt so hemmed in by other bodies that it took him a while to realize one of the bodies in question was Larissa's. When the music changed from fast to slow she had put her arms around his neck and wordlessly invited him to sway sensuously back and forth with her. He wouldn't have slow-danced with anybody except Meadow back home, but they *had* been ordered to get friendly with this couple and find out what their agenda was. He cooperated until the moment when he realized that only one of Larissa's feet was on the floor; her other leg was winding around him and moving upward. "Is too crowded here," she murmured into his ear. "I know a little room where we can be alone together…"

He put his hands on her shoulders. "Larissa, I hardly know you, but I'm going to save your life."

"What?"

"By putting an end to this *right now*, before my wife kills you." He moved her bodily away from him. She looked over her shoulder and took in the expression on Meadow's face.

"You did not tell you were married," she pouted as they returned to the table.

"But you and Feodor are," Colton pointed out.

"Darling Fedya is very… *understanding.*"

"Fine, that's your business. That isn't the way Americans do marriage."

Larissa's unforced peal of laughter rang through the night club. "Darling Colton, you do not know your compatriots very well, if you believe that!"

By insisting on leaving the Hotel Dans long before Feodor and Larissa were ready to call it a night, Colton and Meadow managed to get themselves out onto a dark street and around a corner into an even darker alley. From there, it was the work of a moment for Colton to whisk them back to their closet-sized apartment on the floor above the consulate offices.

"You idiot!" Blevins berated Colton the next morning. "Whatever possessed you to identify Ms. Melendez as your wife? What happens now if we want to insert you some place as a single man?"

"I guess that won't work out so well now," Colton said equably. "But you didn't really want me to let that – that cut-rate imitation Mata Hari seduce me, did you?"

"You could have gotten out of it without going all Married-Man on her! You… you…"

"We did learn some things last night," Meadow interrupted the tirade. "Do you want to know, or would you rather just keep on with your…" She swallowed the pungent adjectives she wanted to use for Henry Blevins' hissy-fit. "With your critique?"

"What? Anything about their plans?"

"Not that useful," Meadow confessed. "But Feodor is a gambler. While Colton and Larissa were dancing he must have told me about every casino in Barcelona. He's particularly fond of the private poker games at Casino Barcelona."

"Oh, that." Blevins dismissed the information. "We already knew that. But he's clearly been ordered to stay out of the casinos this trip, and anyway we can't risk putting an agent into one of those private games. What if our man lost? But if you'd gone off with the Petrova woman, Edwards, Feodor Nikolayevich might have been off his guard enough to let something slip while he was alone with Ms. Melendez And it all had to fail because of your Puritanical attitudes! You… you…"

Colton took Meadow's hand and told Blevins that was enough. Yes, they'd be at the reception for the incoming Swedish consul that night. Until then, he and Meadow were going to take some personal time.

"As if it will do us any good to get them into the Swedish consulate," Blevins sighed to the chief political officer after they left. "The Swedes really do honor their non-intervention policy in foreign affairs; all that office is concerned with is shipping registrations and trade arrangements. But we could have *used* eyes on Feodor Nikolayevich Ivanov."

"Edwards going off with La Petrova wouldn't have helped us that much," his boss consoled him.

"No, but I bet Ivanov could have been tempted to some indiscretions around the Melendez girl. Look how careless he's already been."

"Hmm. She's not one of the topologists, of course…"

"Classical methods," Blevins said firmly. "We mustn't overlook the basics."

# 3. Black bags and big dogs

I couldn't do anything for Aunt Alesia immediately. It was almost two in the morning, prime time for black bag operations, and we had two of them scheduled back to back. Sheng Williams, the technical officer assigned by the embassy to work with us, was already tapping on the door with his little bag of tricks – and yes, it was black. I asked Brad to see my aunt home and try to find out a little more about her problem, and Sheng to wait in the postage-stamp-sized living room while I changed from my dinner dress into something a little more practical. Brad, rather than the CIA's makeover consultant, had helped me pick out appropriate garments for these little jobs. Now I hung up my rustling taffeta dress and slipped into a pair of lightweight, stretchy pants and a long-sleeved knit top. That was a compromise; I'd be chilly outdoors and overheated inside places that used the kind of exuberant central heating favored by our first involuntary host. But the pants had a convenient pocket for my stars, and the whole outfit would look appropriate if I needed to claim that I'd just slipped out for a night run through Paris. As if I would even consider doing such a thing… oh, well; Americans had a reputation for being health-and-fitness freaks. The story would do in a pinch – that is, if I got pinched.

Sheng pursed his lips in an admiring whistle when I emerged. "That dark red is wonderful with your skin and hair."

"It also reads like black in moonlight or low light conditions, and it doesn't scream, 'I'm dressing up to play spy!'" One of Lensky's better ideas. Oops – Sheng was wearing black cargo pants and T-shirt.

"I need the pockets," he said defensively, patting various small bulges on the outside of his pants.

"Not a problem. Here!" I tossed him the dark red scarf I'd meant to cover my hair with. If I shed a few curly strands on these ops, we'd just have to hope they went unnoticed. After all, if everything went well our hosts would have no reason to look for signs of intrusion. "Loop that around your neck and try to look as if you love exercising after midnight." At least his black T-shirt was loose enough to cover up a soft, slightly pudgy body that would have made a bad joke out of his claims to be a midnight jogger.

Sheng had already been on a daytime test run with me, from this apartment to a closed office in the embassy and back. After the first technical officer that Paris assigned to us screamed and fainted upon being whisked into the Polish embassy, I had refused to teleport anyone into closed locations until they'd already been familiarized with the process.

Oh, the little contretemps at the Polish embassy? No biggie. I didn't even have to abort the mission, just get us out of sight briefly. Fortunately, I always ask to go to the bathroom when I'm a guest at some place of potential interest. I teleported us into the downstairs ladies' room before their security guys got around to looking for the source of the scream. With Technical Officer Screamer (no, I'm not going to embarrass him by publishing his real name) propped up in one stall, I scooched up on the next toilet over and practiced my lines in case anybody asked what I was doing in there with a black bag full of tools. "Ah, answering an emergency plumbing call?"

I didn't need to use the line that time, because the search was cursory. Nobody even looked in the bathrooms. We found out later that the Poles automatically assumed anyone spying on them was from the Russian embassy, and the current political rule was not to try too hard to catch Russians sneaking around because relations between Poland and Russia were fragile enough without their having to respond to an act of aggression. Besides (as the Polish ambassador confided in me later, in fact at the Ukranian's cocktail party) Russia was their best source for top quality vodka, and the Russians could always bug the vodka bottles, couldn't they, if they were all that interested in Polish diplomatic matters?

(I suggested to our handlers that they try bugging vodka bottles instead of making me scurry around darkened embassies with a technical officer who screamed like a little girl. They told me that was technically impossible. I'm not totally convinced.)

Sheng was visibly nervous about our mission – I guessed he was one of those people who's really only happy in a basement full of computers and electronic gadgets – but at least he'd been able to accept the reality of teleportation better than Screaming Geek. Now I took his (sweaty) hand, slipped my free hand into the pocket with the stars, thought about the Brouwer Fixed-Point Theorem, pictured the two glowing surfaces and slid us from one surface to the other via the single point they had in common.

We had time to take just one deep breath before the barking began.

This time I didn't bother with half measures like hiding in a bathroom. We were in the Egyptian cultural attaché's apartment and I already knew there was only one bathroom which the whole family shared. We zipped down a spiraling trail of stars through the in-between and back to the apartment Lensky and I were using.

My legs were shaky; I sat down on the cool marble floor. "That wasn't supposed to happen!"

"No shit, Sherlock," Sheng sniped. "I thought you'd been to a dinner party there."

"I was. Just day before yesterday."

"How did you not notice that he had a dog?"

"He *didn't* have a dog. Not then." I thought back over my briefing. "They told me Egyptians don't like dogs!"

"They don't not like dogs nearly as much as *I* don't like dogs," Sheng groused. Then a puzzled look crossed his face. I had the feeling he was counting negatives on his fingers, trying to figure out what he'd just said. "I thought that monster was going to take a chunk out of my ass."

"You *could* be grateful for the quick reflexes that got us out of there!" Truth be told, I had been possibly a little more alert to the need to exfiltrate quickly than I had been before Screaming Technical Officer fainted on me in the Polish embassy.

We learned later that Said, the cultural attaché, had been dog-sitting for just one night as a favor to a Parisian neighbor of his who'd been called out of town unexpectedly. Just our luck that we tackled Said's apartment on that night.

We never did find out how a fashionable Parisian living in the center of the city managed to keep a dog the size of a small moose as a pet. But then, that wasn't part of the assignment.

By mutual consent, we took a few minutes to steady our nerves before moving on to the pied-a-terre occupied by Ukrainian diplomat Eduard Kravetz. He, thank goodness, was a heavy sleeper and had no wife, no children, no dog, not even a mistress. Sheng snipped and twisted wires and scooted under a table on his back to attach something about the size of two quarters taped together, all to the accompaniment of Kravetz' snoring, and we were back in the apartment before we even had time to get nervous.

Why is it that it takes so much longer to write about problems than successes? Our infiltration of Eduard Kravetz' place had been textbook-perfect. And judging from the amount of floor fluff that had attacked Sheng's nose and mouth while he placed the bug, the Ukranian's cleaning woman was a careless slob who'd never notice a little something extra under the coffee table. Clearly she never swept under there anyway.

But that's how it goes. We hear all too much about the jobs that go wrong, but the things we do well are quiet and smooth and we never get to hear how much use they are. I had some doubts about our bugging of the Ukrainian, actually. He lived alone; if he had acquired the French habit of meeting his friends in cafés, how much conversation would there be for a bug to pick up in his apartment? Oh well, he had given that one cocktail party. Maybe he had a taste for conversing with a dozen other people at the top of his voice while squeezed into a living room barely big enough for a *ménage à trois*. God help whoever tried to disentangle the resulting babble into usable intelligence. Not my problem.

I was just apologizing to Sheng for not being able to give him a lift home – I'd never been to his apartment – when TheSila showed up and, as was her wont, complicated everything.

"Thalia, dear little pet," she purred behind me, "aren't you going to introduce me to your friend?"

"I hadn't planned to, no," I said without turning around. Pretending extreme boredom was one of the few ways I'd found to make the djinn go away.

"Oh, but I insist!" She poured herself around me in a flicker of cold flames. At least she'd chosen to manifest herself in almost-normal guise; apart from the little shivers of flame chasing themselves over her form, she looked like any Oriental odalisque you might encounter in Paris – you know: voluptuous figure spilling out of a skimpy gold-filigreed costume, elaborate henna patterns on much of the exposed skin, huge kohl-rimmed dark eyes.

Okay, so you don't actually see that many scantily dressed Oriental odalisques in Paris. Sheng was stammering, poised awkwardly between the Company's training in diplomatic manners and the natural human desire to scream and run. "TheSila, this is Sheng, a colleague of mine from the embassy," I said tiredly. "Sheng, meet TheSila, an Indian Ocean djinn. Folks, it's late, and tomorrow I have to…" *rescue Aunt Alesia.* Damn. I'd actually forgotten about her for a couple of hours. Now the weight of her problem came crashing down on me again. I wondered whether "darling Daryush" would be understanding about his girlfriend's loss of a national treasure, or whether my next job was going to be springing Aunt Alesia out of a French jail.

Sheng collected himself enough to bow over the hennaed hand that TheSila extended, but his eyes were showing way too much white. Teleportation and unexpected canine encounters had already taken their toll on his self-possession; clearly he wasn't up to discussing life with a djinn from the Indian Ocean.

"TheSila and I met off the coast of Kenya this summer," I said, ruthlessly condensing the multi-chapter detailed version, "and she visited me in Texas afterwards." And she'd been quite enough of a nuisance there without inviting herself along on this assignment. Silly me, I had thought that leaving her blue glass bottle on the mantelpiece of our condo in Austin would guarantee some privacy in Paris.

The trouble was that I hadn't gone the traditional route of trapping her in the bottle, luring her in with the powerfully stinky perfumes she favored and then slamming a cork into the opening. No, I'd done her the favor of *breaking* the bottle somebody else had used to trap her. And then, as a free agent, she'd found a lidless bottle in which to transport herself from East Africa to Austin.

At least that was how I'd thought it worked. Now it seemed that she didn't require the bottle in order to follow me around the world and interfere with my life. Who knew?

And as if that wasn't enough, Mr. M. woke up and joined the party. "What is *she* doing here?" he grumped. "I need my sleep."

Sheng's eyes got even wider, but I didn't feel he was up for an explanation of why we'd been joined by a talking turtle head attached to a robotic snake body. The basic story of Mr. M.'s origins in ancient Babylon and the magic-enhancing stars he'd brought us was already too much for most people to absorb. Adding in the history of how his body got destroyed and Meadow Melendez fixed him up with the present one would definitely overload Sheng.

"*Some* people never do anything *but* sleep," TheSila said, undulating at him. "Where were you when my little pet needed your help?"

"Thalia, do you need my help?"

I yawned theatrically. "I *need* to get some sleep. And Sheng, here, needs to get back to his place."

"Where is Lensky? Has he abandoned you?"

"He's seeing my aunt home." Come to think of it – that had been quite some time ago. What was taking him so long?

Before I had time to work up a good fret, he came bounding up the stairs with his usual excessive energy, and the varied beings crowded into the apartment sorted themselves out. That is: TheSila, in a fit of irritation with Mr. M., started to shift from her human form to her serpentine one. When her shapely legs merged, then grew scales and curled up away from the floor where she'd been pretending to stand, Sheng found his own feet and beat it out of the apartment to save himself from seeing any more disturbing things. Mr. M. went back to sleep on his bookshelf, TheSila condensed herself into a tiny flickering flame on the coffee table, and Brad hugged me and said that

Aunt Alesia's situation was complicated but we could discuss it when she came over for breakfast in the morning. I wasn't satisfied with that, naturally, but I think I fell asleep while demanding that he tell me the details.

# 4. Cuisse de nymphe émue

I woke to sunlight and sprightly breakfast-table chatter.

In French.

*Aunt Alesia.*

I tried closing my eyes again and pretending I wasn't awake, but it wasn't possible for anyone with a pulse to ignore the aromas of warm chocolate and flaky pastry creeping through our little apartment. I ran a comb through my hair, splashed water on my face, threw on a lacy wrapper that had been a wedding gift from Aunt Alesia rather than part of the official makeover wardrobe, and staggered out to join the party.

Aunt Alesia looked a lot better than she had last night; in fact, if I hadn't known better, I would have said she didn't have a care in the world. Granted, the sight of the breakfast table would have cheered anybody up; Brad had evidently gone out for chocolate crêpes, croissants, and a lavish assortment of fruit. Also granted, my aunt had probably enjoyed several more hours of sleep than I'd gotten last night; nobody expected *her* to flit around Paris in the small hours, dodging counter-spies and dogs and calming down nonhuman companions. Still, I would have expected somebody who'd just lost a small fortune in jewelry – and who was being blackmailed over it – to look at least slightly careworn.

Instead, she was exchanging what sounded like society gossip with… Mr. M.

Oh.

I'd been too drowsy to register his voice at first, but now it all made sense. Lensky's French was serviceable, but his accent was terrible; it couldn't have been him I'd heard chatting so fluently with my aunt. That Aunt Alesia had accepted Mr. M. so easily seemed strange, but she did tend to consider herself French and I supposed it was true what they said about the French: speak their language well enough and you were one of them, regardless of race, color, creed… or species. I wouldn't know; my accent was pretty good, but my usable vocabulary fell a long way below the extremely high bar they set for "well enough."

I poured myself a tiny cup of something dark and aromatic that turned out to be melted chocolate, not coffee. While I was staring at it in dismay, Brad patted my hand and gave me a large mug full of milky coffee. "Thank you," I said, pouring my chocolate onto a plate with a croissant on it.

"I like that lace thing on you," he said. "Always have. That color's good for you. What do you call it? Cream? Pink?"

"*Cuisse de nymphe émue*," Aunt Alesia said, interrupting what I thought were Mr. M.'s scandalous accounts of the goings-on between the Swiss ambassador and any number of ladies who were no better than they should be. And I'd thought the Swiss were boring bankers! Maybe Mr. M. should be in charge of the Paris field office. "He is right, Thalia. You should wear that color more often."

"I don't dare," I said, dipping my croissant in the puddle of melted chocolate. "I'd be sure to spill something on it." The chocolate tried to drip off the croissant as I spoke, but I rescued it with a quick-moving tongue. One foodstuff that seldom gets away from me is chocolate.

After I'd finished the croissant and sipped about half of my large-economy-sized mug of coffee, I felt better able to cope with the world. "You're pretty cheerful this morning, Aunt Alesia. Did you find the necklace, then?" While ingesting chocolate and caffeine I'd managed to convince myself that had to be the explanation for the sunny atmosphere at the breakfast table.

"No, but everything is going to be all right." Aunt Alesia's rings flashed in the morning sunlight as she straightened her empty croissant plate a quarter of an inch. I noted with some envy that it really was empty. How does anybody eat a croissant without dropping a single flaky pastry crumb? "I'm going to get it back," she went on. "It's quite simple really. The thieves made contact with me again. All they want is for you to place one little bug in the Taklanistan embassy."

"*What?*"

"Yes, isn't it wonderful that the solution is so simple? I can take you with me to call on Daryush; then you'll be able to do the same thing you've been doing at all these other places. Just teleport back in later and place the bug. You don't even have to ask your technical officer to help; they've given it to me." She opened her pearl-covered clutch and brought out a small plastic bag with something that looked like an American dime inside it. "As soon as they hear it working, they've promised to return the necklace to me so that I can give it back to Daryush. If we get started at once, he'll never even have to know that they were missing very briefly."

"Aunt Alesia, I can't do that."

"Thalia, from what I hear, you've already been doing similar things all over Paris."

I gave Brad a dirty look. What had possessed him to babble CIA business to my flibbertigibbet aunt?

"Hey, it wasn't me," he said. "Your turtle-snake buddy must have spilled the beans while they were doing all that gossiping in French."

Mr. M. raised his head. "*I* am proud of your achievements, Thalia."

I caught sight of a flickering blue flame out of the corner of my eye and winced in anticipation. A moment later TheSila had poured her almost-human form between Aunt Alesia and the sideboard.

"Aunt Alesia," I said firmly, trying to ignore the appearance of TheSila, "I do – what I do – in the service of my country. It's my patriotic duty. That duty does *not* extend to spying on my country's friends for the benefit of unknown thieves and blackmailers." Although it did extend to spying on my country's friends at the behest of the CIA. As far as I could tell, the only countries the CIA *didn't* want to spy on were the other Anglophone countries – Great Britain, Australia, New Zealand, Canada. Other allies were fair game.

If I allowed myself to think about it too much, my moral position could get kind of wobbly.

"Family before clan," TheSila said, "clan before tribe, tribe before country, country before the world. That is the natural order of things, Thalia-my-pet."

"Do you not wish to help your aunt?" Mr. M. gave me a dirty look. He and Aunt Alesia must have bonded over all that salacious gossip.

"But they're not *unknown* thieves and blackmailers," Aunt Alesia said, "it is obvious who they must be. The Religious Liberation Party of Taklanistan."

"The who?" My coffee was getting cold; I downed it anyway. I was going to need extra caffeine to keep up with all these people and non-people.

"An outlawed political party," Lensky said. "They were the principal opposition to the incumbent party, until they were banned last year."

"And why should I help the Religious Liberation Party?"

"You shouldn't," Lensky said over my aunt's cry of, "To help *me*, Thalia!"


In Barcelona, Meadow Melendez was having a similarly unprofitable conversation with the American political officer and his assistant.

"Those two Russians have become persons of considerable interest. Our agent in the Russian embassy says they have definitely been sent here to make mischief within the Catalan separatist movement, and we need to know exactly what their plans are."

"Then why don't you ask your agent in the Russian embassy?"

"Those two don't work out of the embassy. They pretend to have no connection with official Russian business. Of course we all know they're doing their government's bidding, but they do keep up a pretty good pretense of separation. No, we need someone to engage them directly, and that's what you're going to do."

"Me?"

"You."

"What the…. I mean, what? Yesterday you were gibbering with rage because Colton told them we were married. You acted like that had ruined a year's work for you guys."

Blevins cleared his throat. "Yes. Well. That *was* an unwelcome surprise, but now we've figured out how we can work with it. You're unhappy in your marriage and just one small nudge from being unfaithful to Colton."

"What, before we're even actually married? Thanks a lot!"

"As far as the Russian agents are concerned, you *are* married, remember? I'm just trying to plan a reasonable scenario within the new limitations."

"Look, Henry," Meadow said in her most reasonable voice, "this scenario of yours is not going to fly." Her voice started to rise. "Married or not, there is *no* [expletive] way I would *ever* [obscenity] cheat on Colton, and furthermore there is no conceivable circumstance in which I would allow that chinless Russian clown to [double-barreled profanity] paw me!"

Henry Blevins actually took two short steps back. He shot his boss a pleading glance.

"It's fiction, Ms. Melendez," the Political Officer said patiently. "You do understand the concept of fiction?"

"I'm a robotics engineer." She folded her arms. "We deal in reality."

"Not any more," the Political Officer told her. "While you're seconded to our consulate by the CIA, you're a spy, and like all other spies, you deal in more or less plausible fiction."

Meadow glowered. "This particular one is highly implausible."

"We'll talk again after lunch," the Political Officer told her. He felt it was time to retreat and regroup. He, personally, intended to have one of those three-martini-lunches so popular with American businessmen in an earlier and less namby-pamby age. And while he was doing that, young Blevins here could get together with Meadow's partner Colton and explain the concept of fiction.

***

In Paris, I too was having some difficulties.

"That is a very pretty bug," Sheng said when I showed him the explosive contents of Aunt Alesia's purse – sorry, I kept thinking of the thing as an unexploded bomb rather than a bug. "Voice-activated, I presume. And it's even smaller than the ones the technical division gives *me*. How come a proscribed political party from a Central Asian 'stan can get their hands on better technology than the Paris office of our own agency?"

"I haven't a clue," I said, feeling a faint ray of hope. "Maybe they didn't. Maybe somebody sold them a dud and this doesn't actually pick up anything." No, that wouldn't help, would it? Aunt Alesia had been told she would get the rubies back *after* Hormuz Rakhim, the RLP representative in Paris, heard conversations from the Taklan embassy. And we needed to make that happen soon. Aunt Alesia had already accepted Daryush's invitation to a reception and dinner at the Canadian embassy, just a couple of days from now. He would be expecting her to wear those rubies. If we couldn't retrieve them before that party, Aunt Alesia would have to come down with a very believable, very bad illness.

She had already expressed her unwillingness to fake anything that involved vomiting or other unattractive physical expressions. A broken leg was also out; she pointed out that she'd have to wear a cast for weeks, and this would interfere with her social life – especially with dancing.

I was beginning to lose patience. But Aunt Alesia's approval had been the sole bright spot in my home life back when my father's favorite subject had been my physical and moral shortcomings. I was still determined to do my best for her.

"Sheng, I need your help. Can you take this thing apart, figure how it works, and put it back together? *Today?*" I wanted him to do a little more than that, but there was no point in going into the details unless he thought he could do that much for starters.

His eyes brightened. "I thought you'd never ask."

It turned out that when assigned to Paris, he'd insisted on having a basement room at the embassy that he could fit up as a mini-lab. One of the frustrating aspects of his job, he said, was that he spent so much time doing black bag jobs and was hardly ever asked to whip up new spy gadgets in his lab.

Engineers. I don't understand them. He didn't find being teleported into the Ukrainian's apartment exhilarating, but he was *thrilled* at the prospect of poring over a device so tiny that he would have to look at it under a microscope. Oh, okay, under a magnifying glass. A super-powerful one.

"Good. Just a couple more things…" I explained what else I needed. He looked doubtful, but promised to do his best.

In Barcelona, Meadow was still having a tough time with the Political Officer's plans for her.

"What do you mean, seduce Fedya? I don't do seduction."

"Moral objections?"

"Practical ones. *Look* at me! Did you ever see anyone *less* seductive?"

"Oh, I am looking at you. And the more I look, the more I think you're just what we need. You just need a few wardrobe adjustments… Fedya is a boob man."

"*All* men are boob men. Why do you think I dress like this? I want them to talk to me, not to my chest!"

"Ah, a few attitude adjustments too, maybe."

Sheng came through with everything I could wish for. Well before dinner, no less. I would never understand engineers, but I was impressed by his ability to do complex technical work in the daytime. Also, it explained a lot. He was a morning person; I am more of a mornings-ought-to-be-abolished person. Sneaking into houses and offices at two a.m. was probably an offense against his internal clock, whereas I didn't mind the hours nearly as much as I minded getting up the next morning.

I'd been thinking – and making use of Lensky's brains and political knowledge as well – while Sheng worked. We agreed that the only person in Paris who would benefit from bugging the Taklanistan ambassador was the representative of the Religious Liberation Party. At least, he was the most likely candidate; the others trailed a long, long way behind. The doddering relics from the Cold War always suspected Russia when there was mischief afoot, but Lensky said the Russians had no reason to spy on Daryush Burkhan. They already had the president of Taklanistan under their thumb – he needed their military to help guard his border with Afghanistan – and an ambassador who plotted against the interests of the president would suffer a fatal accident in short order. Ergashi, the president, had already disposed of most of his opposition in that way.

"Then how come Hormuz Rakhim is still running around loose in Paris?" That was the name of the RLP leader who represented his cause to anyone in the French government who might help him.

Lensky heaved a sigh. "He may not be – not for long, anyway. He's the third man they've sent here since the party was banned in Taklanistan. They keep getting into, um, accidents."

"Sheesh. How do they keep getting volunteers for the job?"

"It's more of a grass-roots organization than most political parties. Cut off one head, ten more potential leaders spring up… Ah, I meant that metaphorically. Ergashi isn't a savage, he doesn't have his enemies beheaded. He just… arranges fatal accidents for them."

"Oh. How… civilized."

"He's what we have to work with, and his interests align with American interests in Central Asia." Lensky was uncharacteristically short with me. I suspected that he wasn't totally happy with our country's support of this dictator.

All I had to do now was get into the Taklanistan embassy. Aunt Alesia helped with that, at least. She took me with her on a surprise visit to Daryush. It was a very *short* surprise visit. He had meetings lined up, and she was eager to get out of there before the subject of the Shaimak Rubies came up; he might have thought she'd come to return them. As it was, he looked confused when we departed after just fifteen minutes of polite conversation. Oh well, if I could get the necklace back Aunt Alesia would calm down enough to convince him her flying visit had been perfectly natural. Her attitude that having been married to a French diplomat turned her into a Frenchwoman might be slightly insane, but her social skills were impeccable. It was, I thought, entirely possible that insanity helped with navigating Parisian society. Anyway, the visit had been long enough for me to get a fix on the women's lounge on the first floor – another reason for Daryush's confusion; he probably didn't have many visitors who needed to go to the bathroom ten seconds after he greeted them. Sheng and I could teleport into that room in the small hours and sneak out to place the bug.

Apart from Aunt Alesia's calling me before afternoon tea at the British embassy, before dinner for herself and her friend Solange with the Austrian cultural attaché and before the reception for visiting artists at the Belgian embassy, the rest of the day went smoothly. Evidently being distracted with worry wasn't putting much of a crimp in my aunt's social life. Having no engagements myself, I napped between telephone calls and invited Brad to cook dinner. Last winter he had displayed a surprising talent for cooking, mostly Italian, and I exploited him whenever possible. Eating out at the kind of French restaurants he chose was a three-hour affair that didn't start until after eight o'clock, and I didn't have the energy to combine one of those excursions with doing an unauthorized black bag job with Sheng. Also, I was hoping he would go to sleep before Sheng came over. It would be better for both of us, I thought, if he could plead total ignorance of an intrusion into the Taklanistan embassy which the CIA had neither requested nor desired.

That part worked out well. A pasta dinner in itself wasn't enough to make Brad sleepy, but sufficient and satisfying exercise afterwards did the trick. It also left me glowing with good cheer and confidence; not a bad side-effect. Everything was looking good; there were even some chocolate cookies hidden in the back of the pantry in case I needed to boost my blood sugar later. Sheng turned up exactly on time. I let him in before he had time to ring the doorbell, we teleported into the ladies' lounge and he found an excellent way to hide the bug in the ambassador's study. Did I feel guilty about undercutting an ally like this? Not very, especially when I contemplated the president of Taklanistan's way of dealing with his competition. Besides, Sheng had made sure that the Religious Liberation Party wouldn't get to hear very much of the conversation in Daryush's study.

There wasn't much point in listening now; I was pretty sure that whatever the strange customs of Taklanistan, getting out of bed at three in the morning to have political conversations wasn't one of them.

I didn't actually hear anything until the middle of the next afternoon, when we got back from a lavish lunch with the Danish trade officer that had been pretty much a dead loss as far as the Company was concerned; even the CIA, with its penchant for listening in on everybody and anybody, couldn't work up much excitement about bugging the Danes. However, Lensky had flirted outrageously with the wife of a junior Russian diplomat and with the lady who represented Bulgarian trade interests in Paris. Both of those could result in useful invitations, and I was happy to know that Brad would have to get me included in the invitations when and if they happened. Both the Russian and the Bulgarian had been the sort of tall, blonde, very calm women who had been Brad's type. Before he met me. I trusted him, of course... But it hadn't been fun observing the flirtations.

After Lensky declared his intention of taking a nap after the multi-course mid-day meal, with all those toasts in Danish aquavit, I tiptoed into the living room. Putting in earbuds, I opened my iPad and typed in the combination of letters and numbers that Sheng had given me. That was the first modification he'd made for me; he'd figured out the frequency the bug was using and arranged for it to send to my iPad as well as to Hormuz Rakhim of the Religious Liberation Party.

The ambassador was actually in his office. The quality of the signal wasn't that great – it was strangely muffled – but based on the fact that the other party to the conversation said nothing except to repeat the last few sounds Daryush had made whenever he stopped for breath, I thought that maybe he was dictating letters to his secretary. Good. That should make Rakhim happy. I hoped the letters weren't about anything important; that would make *me* happy. Even Sheng hadn't been able to arrange to pass the bug's signal through a Taklan-to-English translation program, so all I could do was hope while I listened intently for clues.

I jumped about a mile and a half when Brad spoke from the bedroom door. "Do I want to know why you're listening to a program in a Farsi dialect?"

"I was using earbuds!"

He ambled into the room and picked up the cord dangling from my head. "Thalia. You forgot to plug them into the iPad."

"Oh." No wonder the sound quality had been so bad; I'd been listening to my iPad with earbuds blocking my ears. I pulled them out and realized that in an effort to hear better, I'd turned the sound up so high that Lensky could hardly have avoided hearing it in the bedroom. I shut the iPad down.

"Sorry to disturb you. Ah... what do you mean, a Farsi dialect?" I thought the ambassador had been speaking Taklan. Wasn't Farsi what they spoke in Iraq? No. Iran, that was it. "I didn't know what they were saying."

"Farsi," Lensky said, "with some interesting vowel and consonant shifts and a *lot* of Russian loan words." He sat down facing me. "The kind of dialect you find in certain parts of Central Asia... such as Taklanistan. Thalia, you bugged their embassy for your aunt, didn't you?"

"Uh... not for very long."

"What is that supposed to mean? Either you bugged it or you didn't." He looked very sad. "I suppose you went out after I fell asleep last night? With Sheng?"

He had been known to get quite unreasonable on a few occasions when I'd been, perfectly innocently, hanging out with Ben Sutherland, who was my best friend after Lensky. But this was beyond unreasonable. "Brad. You can't be jealous of *Sheng!*"

"I'm not," he said. "Just disappointed. Last night... I didn't realize that all that enthusiasm you displayed was just an attempt to tire me out so that I'd fall asleep early. I hope it wasn't too much effort for you, faking it like that."

"Brad! I didn't fake anything! Yes, I wanted to make sure you went to sleep before I had to..."

"Sneak out?"

"If you want to put it that way. But..." Dammit, I was blushing. "Look at it this way: we didn't do anything I didn't enjoy too. In fact, up until just a minute ago I was thinking that I ought to, um, take the initiative more often. It was... unexpectedly rewarding."

"Apart from making it easy for you to sneak out?"

"Yes!" Words weren't doing it; I jumped up from the couch, circled behind his chair and put my arms around him from behind. "And you ought to know that without being told. Didn't I show you, last night?"

"I guess I do know it," he grumbled, turning to hold me. "But Thalia, this kind of thing makes it very difficult for me as a CIA field officer."

I wasn't as worried about that as a truly good and loyal wife ought to have been, because now I was sitting on his lap and his grumbling was interrupted by frequent stops to kiss me. "They'll never have to know."

"Do you think they won't find out about the bugging? Eventually?"

"I didn't sign my name, and the device isn't one of theirs. In fact, Sheng complained that the bugs they supply aren't as good as this one. And besides, there isn't going to be any 'eventually.'" I explained one of the other things I'd asked Sheng to do.

"Oh. Well. There's no way of making sure that happens." He wasn't ready to give up grumbling quite yet. "And if it does, that puts a lot of time pressure on retrieving the jewels."

"Agreed," I said with regret. "I've told Aunt Alesia she needs to leave a message for the blackmailers *right away* telling them that the job they asked for is done – they've got some intricate system of dead drops for her to use, don't ask me how it works."

"See, that's the trouble with you going out on your own like this. That kind of job is what field officers are *for*: inconspicuous surveillance, following, tracking back from dead drops."

I decided not to point out that if I'd asked him for help, he would have vetoed the entire plan. We'd argued long enough. Besides, I still had one card up my sleeve – and it was another one that he wouldn't approve of my playing. I hoped it wouldn't be necessary to take drastic steps to recover the rubies.

# 5. Meadow is shocked out of her sandals

After Meadow had a chance to talk it over with Colton, she agreed to go along with the Barcelona political officer's plan. To a certain extent.

"I'm no good at fluttering my eyelashes," she said glumly.

"Would you like a fan?"

"I don't think I could flutter that either."

"It won't make any difference," said Colton, sounding pretty glum himself as he surveyed the dress Henry Blevins had come up with for Meadow. Low-cut would have been a charitable description; the cut seemed explicitly designed to persuade an onlooker that she might suffer a major wardrobe malfunction at any moment. "Not in that dress."

"You don't like it?"

"I love it," Colton said. "And it's not just the cut. Let's face it, this Blevins jerk has a better color sense than either of us. You look as if you're glowing with an inner radiance. We should put him in charge of your entire wardrobe."

"Inner radiance, my [expletive] left foot. If I'm glowing, it's with embarrassment."

"I'd prefer that you weren't going to wear it in public," Colton admitted, "but once this is over, you can wear it for me in private. And take it off for me in private."

That suggestion cheered Meadow up to such an extent that she actually listened without swearing to Henry Blevins' instruction in the art of almost seducing a man.

"The first step is getting alone with him," Blevins said, "and that shouldn't be difficult. The only thing our Fedya would find more attractive than you in that dress is a poker hand with a royal flush, and the Petrova woman, for all her faults, has been remarkably effective at keeping Fedya away from the cards on this trip. He'll maneuver to get you separated from Colton."

"What if he doesn't?" Meadow wasn't nearly as entranced by her appearance as the two men seemed to be.

"He will," Blevins said confidently, "especially with Colton's help."

"You expect Colton to pimp me out to this [obscenity] Russian?" Meadow started to stand up, glowering.

"Language, language, Meadow!" Blevins said. "Remember your lessons from charm school."

"If you're referring to the indoctrination I had to go through before coming overseas," Meadow said, increasing the force of her glower, "I find 'charm school' an extremely inaccurate [profanity] description."

Blevins sighed. "Just clean up your language, okay? We're trying to lure Fedya into indiscretions, not curl his hair. As for Colton's help, all I was thinking was that he can pretend to be falling for Larissa Petrova's moves. Then, don't you see, she'll be working for us without knowing it; she'll want to detach Colton, leaving you to Fedya."

"I'd rather be left to an inebriated octopus," Meadow grumbled, but that night she wore the dress to a cozy dinner for four in the apartment the Russians had found for Feodor and Larissa.

It was significantly nicer than the place where she and Colton had been stashed.

"Two birds with one stone," Colton said on the way over. "Once I've been there, I can teleport back some time when those two are out and bug the bejesus out of – I mean, bug the place. You're a bad influence on me, Meadow; I never used to swear."

"Cussing is an advanced form of punctuation," said Meadow, who certainly used it that way.

The dinner consisted of Catalan *tapas* sent in from a neighborhood restaurant and washed down with icy Russian vodka. Meadow nibbled her way through crisp little potato cubes with creamy garlic sauce, deep-fried baby squid, and a pizza-like concoction topped with sardines, green peppers, eggplant, and onion. "*Coca de Samfaina*," said Fedya of the pizza. He offered her a bowl of small rubbery-looking things sloshing around in a thick red liquid. Meadow tried to move away; the bowl was tilting dangerously while Fedya tried to look down the front of her dress. "And you must try these *Cargols a la Launa* – snails in a spicy tomato sauce."

Meadow shuddered, refrained from saying that she would rather eat pencil erasers, and washed down two of the snails with a long sip of icy vodka. Setting down her glass, she viewed the clear liquid with increased respect. In college she had prided herself on being immune to keg parties and the blandishments of her fellow engineering students. But this vodka was to beer as a high explosive bomb was to a string of sparklers. And when you got down to it, engineering students didn't really know how to blandish, did they? Unlike this Russian agent, who was simultaneously pressing the snails in hot sauce and the fried shrimp with lemon upon her, sneaking glances down her dress, and chatting about the pleasures of meeting a beautiful woman who was also so intelligent. What exactly, he wanted to know, did she do as a robotics engineer?

The vodka, if not the blandishments, had softened Meadow up to the point where she accepted more snails and launched into a discussion of her latest augmentations to Mr. M's prosthetic snakebot body.

Colton stepped on her sandaled foot, and this time he was wearing his big clumping boots. Meadow suppressed a curse, but she got the message. She backpedaled to a general discussion of the challenges of hyper-miniaturization in robotics, and by the way, had Fedya seen the latest videos from Boston Dynamics?

"They've got a bipedal robot now. They call it 'Atlas,' though that might be a reference to the weight of the backpack it has to carry with all its power supplies and processors. Still, it's impressive. It can do a two-legged jump – you know, feet more or less together – from one narrow box to another one. It can do a jump *and* a 180 degree turn in one move. And it can do a backwards somersault!"

"Fascinating!" the Russian said. Sounding anything but fascinated. "And how unusual to meet a lovely young woman who interests herself in such matters. Have you no lighter interests? Dancing, sports, fashion?"

The good thing about the snails was that they took a long time to chew, giving Meadow time to evade Fedya's attempt to steer the conversation into more personal channels. She had a lot more to say about bi-pedal robots, the complex system of feedback loops that would be necessary to support one that actually walked on two feet, and the fact that Boston Dynamics had not yet released any videos showing Atlas walking.

Fedya's eyes glazed over as she talked, then brightened again when Larissa stood and announced that she and Colton were going out to the terrace to inspect her rooftop garden.

"Only a little hobby," she purred, taking Colton's arm and pressing it against her body, "but a comfort to those of us who are so far from home. I take a little earth from the public gardens in Piter and add it to the potting soil wherever we make our temporary home, so that we have always a little of Mother Russia with us. Do tell me, Colton, how you deal with being stationed so far from home? Do you not find your life cold and lonely at times?"

Colton's reply, if any, was swallowed by a closing door.

"Alone at last," Fedya breathed, leaning so close to Meadow that she could feel his breath on the exposed portion of her chest. Which was most of it.

She scooted her chair back a few inches. Misunderstanding the gesture, he took her hand and stood as if to help her to her feet.

Meadow *sat*. She might have let the Political Officer dress her up like a piece of enticing meat, she might have sipped enough vodka to go to her head thanks to the Russians' incessant toasts, but she reckoned that she still had one thing going for her: inertia.

"Thank you, I'm perfectly happy right here," she said when Fedya's chivalrous gesture changed to a definite tug.

He sank down beside her again, and Meadow sent up a brief prayer of thanks that the man could take a hint.

Too soon, as it turned out. "If you are worried about Larissa," he murmured, breathing into her ear this time, "there is not absolutely any need. We understand each other, Larissa and I, and I promise you she does not spoil my sport."

"Well, bully for her, but it doesn't happen to be *my* sport," Meadow said. She wriggled but failed to dislodge Fedya's arm, which had somehow crept round her shoulders while he was distracting her by babbling about sports. She felt this nonsense had gone quite far enough. The Russian wasn't babbling secrets, just corny seduction lines. The Political Officer couldn't expect her to actually sleep with him in the pursuit of his secrets, could he? Well, yes, he might. That piece of slime Blevins almost certainly would. Too bad: in that case they – and Fedya – were doomed to disappointment.

"But we always retire to more comfortable chairs after dining," Fedya said. "It is a Russian custom, and very civilized. Why are you Americans always sitting upright as if you expected the inquisitors to question you? You need to relax and learn to behave like a sophisticated European, little Meadow. Let me teach you…"

She turned her head just fast enough that his kiss landed on her jaw rather than her lips. It was disconcerting to find that he didn't act in the least discomposed, but simply trailed light kisses over her cheek as though that had been his goal all along. "That is better, isn't it, my lovely girl?"

"No," Meadow said, "it isn't. And I'm not your girl." She squirmed away from him and scrubbed at her cheek with one hand.

"No need to play coy." His arm tightened painfully around her shoulders. "Larissa has taken care of the jealous husband for us. I promise you that we shall be quite alone." He laughed quietly. "And in any case, what are you going to do, little girl? Are you going to make yourself invisible, like when you popped out of the empty air at Sagrada Familia?"

So that was it. Larissa and Fedya weren't after them for mere political secrets; they had a hint of Colton's special abilities, and they wanted to know more. Meadow thanked her lucky stars that it was only a hint. They couldn't understand much if they thought it was invisibility rather than teleportation, or that Meadow rather than Colton was the mastermind.

Perhaps Fedya was simply generalizing from his own situation. Meadow would have bet that Larissa could spot him thirty I.Q. points and still tie him into knots.

In which case, *she* could spot him at least sixty points, and it was time she applied her brains to the job instead of letting him paw her. Meadow lifted Fedya's exploring hand and put it firmly back on his lap. "You want to know my secrets," she said, "then trade. A secret for a secret. What are you really doing here in Barcelona?"

Fedya laughed. "Is it not obvious? We are observing the great art, we are dancing, we are enjoying some of the best food in Europe. Larissa is shopping. Mother Russia has my undying devotion –" he kissed his hand and made a vague gesture towards the east – "but our motherland has not yet recovered from the years of Communism. She is poor and cold and dark and the food – the food that we ordinary people get—is, to be honest, *terrible*."

Meadow thought that might be the first honest thing he'd said in the course of their short acquaintance.

"Ah, but you are far too intelligent to waste your time playing the tourist," she said, making a mental note of one more lie for her next confession back home. "It's obvious even to a woman that your presence has something to do with the referendum."

Fedya chuckled. "Maybe so, maybe so… but who talks money and politics when a beautiful woman is present?"

"I do," Meadow pointed out. "Anyway, I'm not beautiful. Money?"

"A woman," Fedya backtracked, "whose secret of invisibility would be worth a great deal to Mother Russia – more, even, than the proper outcome of this referendum. I have some discretion in how to use the sums entrusted to me."

"What sums? And what do they have to do with the referendum?"

"Oh, we are merely observing the course of events for our country," Fedya parried, moving in on her again. "And *I* do not mean to waste this precious time on politics."

"And you've as good as admitted," Meadow said, twisting in her chair to evade Fedya's hands, "that you're here to influence events in favor of your country."

"Now, why should you think my country cares about a tiny, tiny corner of Spain? Stop playing, darling Meadow—aah!" The hand that had plunged down the front of her dress was returned to him with a twist that Meadow devoutly hoped had sprained something. She followed that up with an elbow to his face and a full-throated scream for Colton, who came crashing into the room seconds later.

"You did *what?*" Henry Blevins all but screeched when they reported to him the next morning.

"I found out that Fedya's got money to burn in Barcelona," Meadow said. "And he practically admitted that he's here to make sure this referendum has 'the proper outcome,' meaning, whatever his masters in Russia want."

Blevins made a disgusted gesture. "In other words, you barely got started before you put on your frightened virgin act and screwed everything up."

"If you want pillow talk," Meadow said with a scowl, "you should go out on the street and find someone who's willing to let you be her pimp. It shouldn't be that hard. I'm sure you've found women like that for your personal use, because I can't imagine you could get a woman any other way."

"Meadow, be nice," Colton said under his breath.

"There's nothing 'nice' about the situation!" Meadow flared up at him.

"I'm sure we can work this out in a civilized manner," Colton said, not sounding all that sure.

Blevins grinned. "Sure we can! I've just had a brilliant idea. Meadow, we can fix this after all. Now listen carefully, here's the tack I want you to take. You're a virtuous wife who was shocked out of her sandals by that pass. Also, you'd had a little too much vodka and Fedya, being a Russian, didn't understand how much effect his national drink could have on a nice American girl. Now, in the sober light of day, you're terribly sorry you overreacted and—"

"But I'm not," Meadow interrupted. "If I'm sorry for anything, it's that Colton hauled me out of there before I could punch him in the jaw. Do you realize where the son of a bitch grabbed me?"

"If anybody gets to punch him out," Colton grumbled, "it's me."

"I think I can guess," Blevins said, his eyes straying south from her face.

"Ah – it's not about how you really feel, Meadow."

"I can take care of myself," Meadow told Colton.

"But you don't have to, not now," he said. "Let me take care of you just once, okay?"

"*I* know," Meadow said, brightening. "Let's *both* of us punch him!"

Henry Blevins cleared his throat. "Kids, you need to focus. And Meadow, you need to understand that we're creating fiction. Let's try again. You are so innocent you had no idea what Fedya was leading up to and you decked him—"

"Sprained his wrist," Meadow corrected. "Oh, and gave him a bloody nose."

"That's my girl!" Colton said with admiration.

"Whatever." If his hair weren't thinning prematurely, Blevins thought, he just might yank some of it out. Wasn't this big lunk supposed to be a mathematician? Couldn't mathematicians concentrate better than this? "Meadow, don't you have any acting ability whatsoever? You need to convey that you're terribly sorry about last night's little contretemps and that you understand now Fedya meant nothing improper, you're just unfamiliar with sophisticated European society."

"Since when is boob-grabbing a sign of sophistication?"

"Stop interrupting and learn your lines! Then, after his ego is adequately soothed, you hint that you and Colton are somewhat cash-strapped, bad investments, gambling, whatever, and you're *definitely* interested in the financial arrangement he hinted at if he can help you out without spoiling his other plans. Try to get him to say just what those plans are."

Maybe, just maybe, with enough intensive rehearsal – and another inappropriately low-cut dress – the girl would be able to pull it off. It had to help that any red-blooded man would experience a rush of blood *away* from his brain at the sight of her neckline. Which was a somewhat inappropriate term, wasn't it, considering that the line in question was a long, long way from her neck.

# 6. Catch me if you can

By midnight we still hadn't heard from the ruby thieves, and Aunt Alesia's serene confidence in my problem-solving abilities had been replaced by a jittery attack of nerves and the conviction that bugging the Taklan embassy had been only the first in a series of increasing demands that would end up with Daryush not speaking to her and both of us imprisoned for life. She seemed to regard these two outcomes as equally calamitous.

I had spent the evening sitting in her suite in her friend Solange's town house, holding her shaking hands and waiting for the return of the rubies. "And when it comes to that, Thalia," she said tearfully, reverting to the subject of prison, "you must go to the American embassy and confess everything to them! Take it from me, American prisons are infinitely better than French prisons."

I eyed her doubtfully. My fluttery, pseudo-French aunt had displayed a surprising range of experiences that she'd never hinted at when she was living with my parents. But, *French prisons*? "And when exactly were you ever in jail here?"

"I saw *Catch Me if You Can*," she said impatiently. "Such a nice, well-spoken young man, and look how they treated him."

"Hmm." That had been a movie about a con man, hadn't it? One who came to a bad end, but then reformed? I wasted a few brain cells thinking about Lenski's older brother Alexi, a compulsive gambler who'd come to his own end in the Delaware River. Might the shock of a French prison have inspired him to mend his ways?

Water a very long way under the bridge, that, and not something I needed to be thinking about now. I was just trying to avoid the observation that my own life was rapidly turning into something that could have been titled *Catch Me if You Can.*

But then, I had far more resources than a con man's tools of impersonation and obfuscation. I hoped.

"If we haven't heard by morning," Alesia said, "I shall—I shall—"

Leave another message to be ignored?

In any case, we didn't have a lot of time to wait around for a response; the Canadian reception and dinner was in two days. Possibly I had been too optimistic with the parameters I'd given Sheng. I rang for the maid who took care of Solange's guests, procured some hot milk for my aunt, and settled her in her bedroom with a spicy book of diplomatic memoirs that had her chuckling with delight and telling me the names of the real people who were thinly disguised under pseudonyms in the book.

Then I went out to the sitting-room portion of her suite and called Sheng. It was late enough that he was grumpy about being woken up, but he cheered up when I explained that I wasn't going to ask him to come out on a black bag job tonight.

"I'm not going in there to leave anything," I explained, "I'm going to retrieve something. You've already done more than enough for me on this project, Sheng, and I'm awfully grateful, but I don't have to ask you for anything more than information this time."

He had the information I'd asked for, but it still took too long to get off the phone with him; as soon as I made it clear that I didn't require his services as a Technical Officer this time, he started fretting that he shouldn't let me go in there alone.

"With any luck, I won't even have to go inside the suite," I said. If the rubies were in the room safe, as they ought to be, I should be able to duplicate the neat little telekinetic shift by which I'd once provided Lensky with access to the contents of a target's safe. And this time would be easier; I wouldn't have to put anything back into the safe when I was done.

"You won't get that lucky. I feel it in my bones. I should be with you."

"If it is necessary to go inside, two people are twice as likely as one to get caught," I pointed out. "It won't do you any good to ask to see a representative of the American embassy if you're caught with your hands on a priceless national treasure. And if certainly won't do your career with the Company any good if somebody from the embassy has to bail you out in the small hours of the morning." Did French jails even let you have a telephone call, let alone allowing your friends to make bail at all hours? I felt a brief moment of regret that I hadn't had time to learn just a little about the workings of the criminal justice system in this country. Then I shook my head and told myself to get on with it. The best way not to suffer from my ignorance on that subject was not to get entangled with it in the first place. In short – don't get caught. Always a good plan, and it really should be my motto. How did you say that in Latin?

"If you stay where you are, he'll never know you had anything to do with it," I interrupted Sheng's plaints that my husband would kill him if he learned Sheng had allowed me to go on this little errand. "You're in far more danger if you come with me. Remember, I have all sorts of ways to avoid problems that you don't have." True, that, and it made it even stranger that I was so frequently caught in the middle of a problem. My guardian angel must have a habit of snoozing on the job. "Look, Sheng, I really have to get going. I promise I'll call you again when it's done."

"Well, do it fast for pity's sake," Sheng said, reverting to his usual grouchy style. "I won't get a wink of sleep until I know you're safe home."

He had accomplished a work of art in the few hours he'd spent with the bug that Aunt Alicia's blackmailers had given her. Not only had he made it broadcast to my iPad as well as to the blackmailers, but he'd also been able to piggyback on the signal they were receiving and identify its location. The Hotel-Spa Eiffel was one of the most famous luxury hotels in Paris, and it was conveniently located in the 7th Arondissement where most foreign embassies made their home. I'd been imagining the Religious Liberation Party as a group of bomb-throwing men with long beards, skulking somewhere in one of the suburbs outside the Périphérique. By contrast, infiltrating this place should be a piece of cake.

Sheng had even furnished me with the name of a bellhop who was on the Paris office's list of part-time agents and generally helpful citizens. If he was working tonight, this job would be a piece of cake with chocolate icing.

Jacques-Henri was on the job, and his only problem about letting me into the suite was that he, too, felt it was not safe when Hormuz Rakhim was sleeping in the bedroom. Why couldn't I sneak in there at a reasonable hour like two in the afternoon, when everybody who was anybody would be out enjoying a six-course lunch?

I was afraid we didn't have time to wait until the middle of tomorrow afternoon, but I didn't spell that out to the middle-aged bellhop whose face was prematurely creased with worry. "Operational requirements," I said, trying to sound like Lensky when he was trying to sound as if he'd answered a question but hadn't actually said anything. Apparently it worked, because his face relaxed fractionally.

"You *are* a pro, then," he said. "You'll forgive me wondering…"

A gesture at my dress, which looked more suitable for a black-tie dinner than for a black bag job.

"Protective coloration," I said. "I'd be noticed in a New York minute if I tried creeping around this place in a black jumpsuit and a mask."

"I get that. But you look so *young*…"

I dimpled and smiled up at him as if I'd just received the greatest compliment of my life. "Dear boy, how charming of you to say that!"

Well, it wasn't exactly going to build his confidence if I told him I was going to be twenty-five in a couple of weeks, was it? Better to pretend I was well over thirty and just flattered to pieces to be called young.

Maybe it would have been simpler if I'd skipped the human element and gone straight for picking Hormuz Rakhim's lock, using Ben's developments in the field of remote manipulation of small objects in metric spaces. But I hadn't worked on that enough to have anything like his delicate touch, and anyway this was a modern hotel that used key cards and optical sensors. I don't like sending my mind out into devices that use electricity, they can't be trusted.

Oh well. I'd finally reassured Jacques-Henri enough to get him to open the door and tiptoe away, leaving me to my work. I sidled inside, closed the door with infinite gentleness, and sank down cross-legged on the carpet to search for the hotel's room safe.

Theoretically this kind of work could have been done from outside the suite, which was what I'd been hoping for initially. But when I'd made my plans, I'd had no idea how busy a fashionable Parisian hotel could be in the middle of the night. The spiffiest place I'd ever stayed in Texas had been the time my parents took us all to Schlitterbahn (I think it was an attempt to wear out my brothers), and that New Braunfels hotel had been full of other parents shepherding their offspring through the water park and falling into bed exhausted after supper. This was *Paris*, and it appeared to give New York pretty good competition for the label of "the city that never sleeps." It had been tricky enough for Jacques-Henri and me to find a moment alone when he could slip me into the room. (Oh, he'd had a plan for how to do that without surprising the other paying customers, but the plan involved my using much more of his girlfriend's cosmetics and much less of my dress than I was comfortable with.) Anyway – it had quickly become clear to me that sitting on the floor of the hotel corridor and focusing on multiple metric three-spaces for long minutes was not going to work out. Too, people passing in the hallway might be curious about why the gaudiest National Treasure ever created by a jeweler suddenly appeared out of nowhere in my lap. Working in Rakhim's living room seemed safer; only one person to worry about, and he was asleep.

Since the first development of a Safe Space algorithm blending metric movement with telekinesis, I'd done enough of this kind of work for Lensky to give me a pretty good idea of where hotels liked to stash these little boxes. Yes… I sensed it by the total stillness of air inside it. The safe was probably built into the closet in Rakhim's bedroom. I held my breath and built a complex stack of topological mappings and identities in my head: a standard 3D space defined by three perpendicular axes, the curving planes of two sets obeying the Brouwer Fixed-Point Theorem and touching at just one point, a second three-space with slightly twisted axes… I gave the whole construct a gentle tug. Something stirred in the other room, in the locked space within the safe, and fell back again with a barely audible chime of fine metal links and springs falling against each other.

This was a much bigger job than moving two wedding rings, the only jewelry I'd ever abstracted from a safe before. (Don't even ask; of course I put them back!) I'd need to deploy some serious mental muscle for this job. I reached into one of the deep pockets concealed in the side seams of the dress and felt the little stars bouncing off my palm, fizzing and tingling and ready to go. A deep breath, and I selected just a few of them to add to the already complex mathematical construct in my head. Eyes closed, I sent them flying through grids and sliding along curving planes, forming themselves like an outer skin around the necklace…

The jewelry fell into my lap. At the same time a hand came down on my shoulder. I had the brief impression that my heart stopped. As soon as I could move again, I gathered my legs under me, but it was too late to run. It was even too late to teleport, now that this man had my shoulder in a firm, if not exactly friendly, grip.

I twisted my head up and saw a faint, light oval above me. The bottom half of it was oddly fuzzy…

A voice command brought up some lights and the oval resolved into the bearded face of a man who looked just faintly familiar. As I stared, the familiarity came into focus. If the leader of the Religious Liberation Party wasn't a brother of the Taklan ambassador to Paris, he had to be something like a double cousin of his. Paste a curly blond beard and round wire-rimmed spectacles on Daryush, and he could have been this man's twin.

"I see you are struck dumb by the consciousness of your guilt," said a deep, amused voice. "Come, let us sit down and discuss the matter in a civilized manner."

He let go of my shoulder and slipped one hand under my elbow to help me stand up. Very gentlemanly, except that at the same time his other hand relieved me of the Shaimak Rubies. I could escape now – but without the rubies. "Tell me, little one, what made you think you had the skills to steal a national treasure of Taklanistan from *me*?"

I sat on the chair he offered me, facing his couch, and found my breath.

Finally. "Don't you think 'steal' is an unnecessarily pejorative word in this context? Shall we discuss how you came into possession of the Shaimak Rubies?"

"I do not consider it theft," he said, "to remove them from the custody of the ambassador's current paramour. Should a national treasure, a defining example of Taklan gold-working and stone-setting arts, be passed around to whatever woman Daryush choses to bed on any given night?"

"That's my Aunt Alesia you're talking about," I said, "and she is nobody's paramour. She and Daryush are old friends from his days with the embassy in Rome, if you must know, when her husband was stationed there with the French embassy."

Hormuz Rakhim – for it must have been him – nodded gravely. "I would not insult any woman; I retract the word. All the same, you must agree that it is inappropriate for Daryush to lend his… ah… lady friend something that is so valuable, and that is the property of the nation."

I couldn't really argue with that; it was exactly what I'd thought when Aunt Alesia told me how that extravaganza of gold wire and precious stones came to be around her neck. "It is not the property of the RLP either, though, is it?"

"What do you know about the Religious Liberation Party?"

Precious little, when I thought it over. "Um – banned in Taklanistan since, um, a year or so ago. Hardly the people I'd expect to be speaking for the nation. Why didn't you take your beef to Daryush himself?"

"Because," said Rakhim, "I prefer my head attached to my shoulders, and my heart beating within my chest. Have you any idea how many leaders of the opposition have experienced fatal accidents under the presidency of Jahandar Ergashi?"

Of course I didn't, so I moved the focus of the conversation slightly.

"One does not expect somebody who's afraid of assassination to take a suite at the Hotel-Spa Eiffel," I countered. "Under your own name, too! What were you thinking?"

"Perhaps I was curious to see what kind of … people… Ergashi would send after me."

"Well, that lets me out! I've never even met this Ergot-whats-it guy. I'm only here to retrieve that necklace so that my aunt can return it to Daryush… and I wouldn't have had to come if *you* had honored your agreement. Speaking of *gentlemen*," I said, laying on the sarcasm with a trowel. "You told my aunt you would return the necklace if she performed a certain task for you. That task has been done; give me the necklace, and call it even."

Hormuz Rakhim's lips curled just slightly upward; you could, if sufficiently optimistic, have called it a smile. "Your aunt is in quite a hurry, is she not? I had intended to return it in the morning."

"I can save you the trouble," I said, holding out my hand as though I really expected him to drop the Shaimak Rubies into it.

"Ah, but now there is an additional item on the account," he said. "I wish to know who it is that comes to invade my privacy and disturb my sleep. You are not, I think, an innocent young lady whose only concern is for her aunt. Such young ladies do not break into my rooms like thieves in the night – more is the pity. I could be very hospitable to a pretty girl who is so eager for my company."

"That would *not* be me," I said, beginning to picture two curved shapes that met at a single point. It might be wise to start visualizing the Brouwer Fixed-Point Theorem, just in case I was forced to teleport to freedom. Sleeping with Hormuz Rakhim would definitely be too high a price to pay for those rubies. Aunt Alesia wouldn't blame me for failure on those grounds.

But somehow, I didn't feel he was really going to try and exact that price. There was something off about the whole situation.

Hormuz sighed. "Yes, I suspected that was the case. You can still earn the rubies from me, nameless little miss. All I ask is your name, your position within the American government, and your ear for one little, little hour."

"Why?" Despite the purring voice and the double-entendres, I still didn't get the feeling that Hormuz was all that interested in me as a woman. I can usually tell when somebody's just talking up that line to put me off balance, and that was definitely the almost asexual vibe I was getting from him.

"Your ambassador refuses to receive me," he said, and I blinked in surprise. "I understand; your country sides with the incumbent government in

Taklanistan, and his openly receiving a leader of the opposition party might cause President Ergashi to doubt that support. You are young, American, and I suspect you are connected with the embassy or you would not have dared this exploit."

"You got that right," I said. "But I'm not exactly a substitute for the ambassador. I'm just a State Department intern, being shuffled around to experience a bit of diplomatic life before they slot me into a permanent posting."

"But you *are* with the State Department, and you *are* presently posted in Paris. You are, Miss…"

"Kostis," I said, giving him my maiden name. He might already have some associations with Brad's name; I still hadn't found out how my husband happened to recognize the Taklan dialect of Farsi. It seemed safer not to identify myself as Mrs. Lensky. "Thalia Kostis."

"A lovely name for an even lovelier lady," Hormuz said, and pulled off the difficult trick of appearing to bow while seated on a low couch. "You, Miss Kostis, are an American; you have the ear of your State Department…"

"Not so much," I said. There was no point in encouraging expectations I couldn't meet. "Did you miss the part about being a very junior intern?"

"But I am sure you will soon rise to greater things," Hormuz said, "as long as there are no embarrassing incidents to mar your career. Such as, for instance, having to be retrieved from the Paris *gendarmerie* after a charge of breaking into a hotel room. Oh, and attempted jewel theft," he added, as if that was just a minor afterthought.

That wasn't as strong a threat as it might have been, because the consequences of his calling the cops wouldn't be anywhere near as bad as he thought. I still planned to teleport to safety the moment things looked desperate. And even if he did manage to get me arrested, and the cops managed to keep me arrested, the CIA didn't take nearly as negative a view of these matters as the State Department did; after all, breaking the laws of foreign countries was in our job description.

And finally, my real career was research in applied topology, which I could do despite any weight of official disapproval.

Those were a lot of things for a slightly argumentative person like me to keep to myself; for a long moment I was fully occupied by not saying any of them. Long enough that Hormuz shifted position, betraying slight unease for the first time. "I have no desire to ruin your career, Miss Kostis," he said finally. "All I want is to talk frankly with an American representative. Let us discuss my poor country and the challenges confronting her – and us – at home and abroad. I hope to persuade you to a more balanced view of the disagreement between my people and the incumbent government, that is all; to make you see that we are not totally unreasonable. And in any case, whether you are persuaded or not, you shall take the rubies and go free in one hour. You have my word for that."

I could see little or no downside for me in agreeing. If he was lying and intended to hold on to the rubies, I'd be no worse off in an hour than I was now. And if he was telling the truth, I would be able to return with not only the Shaimak Rubies but, perhaps even more valuable, some insight into the plans of a major political player in Taklanistan. That might be enough to make the State Department willing to overlook the fact that I'd acted without orders.

Okay, so it wasn't like getting a one-on-one with Vladimir Putin, but to be honest, a tiny Central Asian country like Taklanistan was probably more in my league.

There followed one of the most interesting and surprising hours of my life. Hormuz Rakhim had clearly put time and thought into his political positions and those of the party he claimed to represent. I had to agree with him when he condemned President Ergashi's persecution of Muslims in Taklanistan. It went far beyond banning the Religious Liberation Party, Rakhim told me. Most members of his party were Muslim, he admitted, but he insisted that they believed in freedom for all to practice whatever their faith might be. "It is written, 'There is no compulsion in Islam,'" he told me. "But there is much compulsion in Ergashi's rule." He spoke of pious Muslim men being forced to shave their beards, of the closing of mosques, of attacks on modest women who covered their heads according to Islamic custom. Ergashi had even claimed, he said, that the veil was not part of Taklan culture, which was completely inaccurate: before the Bolsheviks took over Taklanistan, nearly all women wore a veil called the *faranji*. It was banned by the Soviets, and now that his country was free of the Soviet oppression Ergashi was trying to re-create the worst features of Communist rule. There had been a time, he said wistfully, when America was the ally of people fighting to throw off the yoke of Communism.

"In America," I said, "Ergashi's actions would never be tolerated." I wasn't really equipped to discuss U.S. foreign policy and how the end of the Cold War might have changed it; I wasn't even born when the Berlin Wall came down and ended an era. But I did know the Bill of Rights. "Our Constitution guarantees freedom of religion, speech, the press, and..." Maybe I didn't know it quite as well as I'd thought; I couldn't remember the fourth freedom guaranteed by the First Amendment. In Texas people talked a lot more about the Second Amendment.

"Ah, if only Taklanistan had the benefit of your Constitution, your Bill of Rights!" Hormuz exclaimed. "We are a poor country, and the people are held back by ignorance; yet when my co-religionists try to establish schools, they are shut down by a government that prefers to keep its people ignorant and poor." He went on to talk about his dreams for Taklanistan, his plans for improving its infrastructure, health care, trade – and most of all, it seemed to me, for combating Russian influence over the country.

"Even now," he said, as if marveling over the fact, "more than twenty-five years after we declared our independence from the so-called Soviet Union, there are Russian troops stationed on Taklan soil and commanding Taklan soldiers! While the great powers of the world allow such oppression of the new republics of Central Asia, how can we possibly take our place as equal members of the world community?"

A fair question. I promised to do what I could towards getting him a meeting with somebody more important than me. That probably sounded better to him than it should have; I still hadn't properly conveyed to him that the third under-secretary in charge of signing requisitions for toilet paper outranked me at the embassy. Still, it was true that I would do my best, and what more could he ask of me?

I left by the door, carrying the jewelry in a discreet padded box in my left-hand pocket, the one that wasn't carrying my stars. I ducked into a convenient hallway niche and called Sheng to tell him it was done and I was all right. Then I teleported back to the tiny apartment the embassy had given Brad and me. I aimed right for the kitchen, because I was feeling just a little bit shaky and thought I might need to raise my blood sugar.

Someone had left the lights on in the living room. Before even checking the refrigerator, I walked into the living room to flip the switch and had another *Oh shit* moment.

Brad hadn't been asleep while I was exploring Paris by night.

# 7. Mata Hari had nothing to do with it

This time Colton and Meadow arranged to meet the Russians at Parc Güell. It was a pleasant autumn day and since entrance to the park was strictly controlled, there was no danger of running into mobs of protestors, either pro- or anti- independence. That didn't weigh as heavily with Meadow as did the open-air setting. Surely it would be hard for Fedya to corner her in a sculpture park?

Half an hour after meeting at the entrance gate, she had to revise that assumption. Merely staying out of the fantastically shaped buildings flanking the entrance hadn't been nearly enough to deter the enthusiastic Russian. Between the entrance and the main terrace, high on a hill overlooking the city, there was a maze of winding paths through flowery hillsides and under stone-built arches leaning into the earth. Colton, blast him, got all interested in the shapes of the arches and the guidebook's statements about how they supported the roadway above them, and the next thing she knew he and Larissa were off to admire the vaults supported by branching arches while Fedya led her along the garden path and chattered interminably about flowers she'd never heard of. She half suspected him of making up their names on the spot: surely there wasn't really a Spanish flower called "Dragon Tooth Cavity?"

"But there should be," Fedya protested when she called him on it. "Could anything better describe this... this object? With its long greenish-ivory central cone, broken off at the top to reveal a dark and menacing interior?...

In any case, I am sure the proper names of the plants are not nearly as amusing as those I, Fedya Nikolayevich Ivanov, can invent!"

Meadow laughed and liked the Russian better than she had since he first forced their acquaintance. At least on this flowery path she didn't have to waste energy defending her virtue; she could get right down to the business of subtly eliciting Russian plans for the upcoming referendum.

How did one do *subtle*? She wondered. In the School of Engineering, shouting, "You got the [obscenity] variables backwards, halfwit!" and slamming the door was considered a gentle way of hinting that someone might have made a slight mistake in their calculations. The CIA officers charged with teaching her the art of polite conversation had been at pains to impress upon her that these manners weren't acceptable in diplomatic circles. The trouble was, they hadn't given her a lot of examples of what *was* acceptable. She was pretty much flying by the seat of her pants, here.

"So, Fedya, everybody in Barcelona seems to be getting more and more tense as the referendum comes closer." It was – what? – five days out, now? Whatever the Russians were up to, wouldn't they have to show their hand soon? "I suppose you and Larissa will be too busy for any more social excursions until that's over."

"Oh, no," Fedya said with his toothy grin, "this referendum is extra-specially Spain's problem, not ours. We would be happy to join you for more sight-seeing, perhaps a trip to the beach or a picnic, tomorrow or the next day."

"Perhaps we could visit another nightclub?"

"Certainly. Tonight? Tomorrow night?"

"I'm afraid we have tiresome embassy duties tonight and tomorrow," Meadow said. To infuse her voice with the right flavor of regret, she pretended to herself that she and Colton were going to have to attend meetings explaining the political history of Catalonia from its founding to the present day. "Perhaps Saturday night?" The referendum was to take place on Sunday.

"Ah, what a pity," Fedya said, "Larissa will be free on Saturday, but I too have… tiresome political duties."

Meadow widened her eyes. "Why, Fedya Nikolayevich, I thought you were only here to observe events!" She thought using his patronymic, the way she'd been told Russians did, was a nice touch suggesting that she was open to a less formal relationship. "But I should have known," she sighed, leaning a little on his arm, "they would hardly waste a man of your intelligence and talents as a mere observer. What are you really going to do?" *Laying it on kind of thick, aren't you?*

But Fedya didn't laugh at her. She almost wished he had, instead of smiling and stroking her arm. "Let us just say that I shall spend the funds entrusted to me in the way most beneficial to the motherland."

"And you can't spend them until Saturday night?" At last she felt like she was getting somewhere.

"It is not wise," said Fedya solemnly, "to entrust the proletariat with cash beyond their immediate needs. To act sooner than Saturday night would be to risk my country's money being drunk up unproductively before the referendum even begins." He patted her arm again, with slow, lingering gestures that he probably thought were seductive. "Or were you suggesting I might invest in… something else?"

"You did suggest that we might find it, ah, financially rewarding to share our new technology with you," Meadow said, trying to bat her eyelashes and feeling as though she was merely blinking furiously. "My husband would disapprove, I fear… but then, he will also disapprove should he learn how much I lost at Bingo Laietana last night."

"Oh, you should not go there," Fedya said, suddenly all attention. "Casino Barcelona is *the* place in this city… Furthermore, it is the only place where you can legally play poker."

"Oh, poker is too complicated for poor little me," Meadow said, trying really hard not to throw up in her mouth. "I prefer a pure game of chance, like roulette."

"No, no, there is no such thing as pure game of chance," Fedya expostulated, "you are only choosing to lose money to the house, odds in anything like roulette always favor the house. Now with poker, on the other hand, an astute player can beat the house."

Meadow looked up at him, eyes wide. "Oh, is that how you and Larissa can afford such a spacious apartment? How clever you must be! I could never do anything like that. In fact, I have no idea how I am going to replace the money I lost before Colton finds out… unless…?" She flapped her eyelashes some more.

"I can hardly expend funds entrusted to us by our country to rescue a foreign woman," Fedya said.

There was a brief pause.

"*Unless…*"

"Unless?"

"Some expenditure might be approved… if I could bring this new technology of yours back to my country. Show me again how you appeared from nowhere?"

Meadow bit her lip and looked around. She'd been so intent on her task that she hadn't noticed Fedya gradually leading her farther and farther from the tourist sights of the park. She had no idea where they were now.

Worse, she had no idea where Colton was either.

"I, I can't actually…."

Fedya bared his teeth. For once, the effect was neither silly nor friendly. "Meadow, are you trying to sell me something you do not possess? Is Colton the only one who has the technology?"

"You don't think they'd tell the secrets to a *girl*, do you?" Meadow parried.

"Larissa is every bit as technologically accomplished as I am. More, probably."

Meadow found that easy to believe.

"I am disappointed, but not surprised, to find that American women are not up to the standard of Russian women. Well, it does not matter. Colton might not be willing to give your American technical secrets to Larissa, he might balk at selling them to settle your gambling debts, but I am quite sure he will give them up to get *you* back."

Fedya grabbed Meadow's wrist and twisted it up behind her back. He was stronger than he had appeared. *Much* stronger. She filled her lungs and gave one despairing shout for Colton before she felt something round and hard poking into her other side. "Shout again, and I'll shoot you," Fedya panted.

"I understand gut wounds are extremely painful."

"You wouldn't dare!"

"I would much rather trade you undamaged. It is neater that way. But if I bring the secret of invisibility home, I shall be a national hero. I am willing to dare more than you can imagine to get that status. No more travelling at the end of Larissa's leash – no more silly rules about staying out of the casinos – the man who gives Russia this gift can do whatever he wants!"

Colton stepped out of the air just behind the Russian. He brought one of the large, rounded stones from the vaults down on the back of Fedya's head.

Larissa, running down the path towards them, screamed.

A little farther away, two of the Guardia Civil shouted and started towards the scene.

Colton grabbed Meadow's arm and they turned sideways and vanished.


Brad was on the phone when I walked into the living room. He turned his head and took the phone away from his ear for a moment.

"*You!*"

He didn't sound exactly delighted to see me. But then, he'd sounded exactly the same on the May night when I'd turned up outside his motel room, just before the end of his first trip to Austin. And that time – well, a few minutes later – he'd been very happy about my visit. Dared I hope that this would work out equally well?

Then he returned to his conversation.

"Abort that. Abort *everything*. She's here, and not even injured. Tell everybody they can stand down. No, I can't tell them in person, it would take too long to get there and anyway I have something I need to do here. Oh, one thing. You might check and make sure the Hotel-Spa Eiffel isn't on fire. With these mathematical maniacs you never know."

He put the phone down and turned to me. "*Now. You!*"

It didn't sound like a delighted welcome was hovering in the near future. His face was red and that vein on his left temple was jumping like a demented worm.

"How *dare* you take off on another of your missions without even warning me? And into the rooms of the RLP leader in Paris, no less! Do you have any idea what I've been going through? What I've done? Do you even care, or am I just a convenient escort for those rare occasions when you *don't* enjoy the illusion that you can fix everything all by yourself?"

"Brad, I—"

"Do you realize that the RLP *beheads* people who interfere with them? Why couldn't you wait until morning to see if your trick with the blackmailers worked? Why did you lie to me – again—about your plans? Why did you put your aunt's peace of mind above *mine*?"

"It wasn't like—"

"Why did you embroil Sheng Williams, who up to now was a perfectly good technical officer? Now he's been compromised and will probably lose his job. For that matter, I'm going to lose mine too, not that *you* care about little details like that!"

I had never seen him so fluent before. By contrast, he was practically tongue-tied when talking about important matters, like telling me he loved me or asking me to marry him. Now I couldn't get a word in edgewise. I had perfectly good answers to at least half his questions, but it didn't look like I was going to be allowed to give them. Besides, now I had questions of my own.

Finally I gave up trying to speak and just backed away from the fury of his tirade. It was just dumb luck that the couch was right behind me. The seat hit me in the back of the knees. I fell back onto some extremely overstuffed cushions, got my feet under me in time to forestall sliding off in a total loss of whatever dignity I still possessed, and looked up at him, trying to decide where to start.

At this point, the noise he was making inspired Mr. M. and TheSila to join the discussion. Mr. M. buzzed into the room at head-height; ever since he'd mastered topological flight he preferred that mode of transport to slithering along the floor, where he might be stepped on.

"Do you dare to threaten the Daughter of Stars?" he demanded.

TheSila undulated into the room, gradually solidifying her form from a shapely column of flame to a curvaceous and scantily clad odalisque with just a hint of fire beneath her "skin."

"*So* provincial, Lensky," she breathed. "My little pet Thalia's method of retrieving the rubies is a time-honored technique among spies. Only consider Mata Hari."

"Mr.M., he's not going to hurt me, and this isn't your fight. *Please* go back to sleep!"

I turned to TheSila. "And I'll thank you not to cast aspersions on my methods. If I understand your meaning, let me assure you that nothing of *that* sort occurred."

Lensky had to put his big foot in it then. "Don't you have a bottle to go into?" he demanded of TheSila.

"I do not. I am a free agent now."

"Well, just wait a few minutes. If I can find a corkscrew, it won't take me long to empty a nice bottle for you."

TheSila gave an offended *huff* and made herself invisible. Finally, a chance to talk sensibly? No, the man was just getting his second wind.

"Of all the crazy stuff you've ever pulled, Thalia –"

"What do you mean, you're going to lose your job?" I asked before he could get properly launched on another tirade.

I said it very quietly; he had to stop yelling in order to hear me.

"What?"

I repeated the question, and he sat down opposite me, wiping his brow. "For the last half hour," he said, "I have been calling in every favor I ever had with the Company, plus some I didn't have, plus promising a few miracles that I'm totally unable to deliver, plus browbeating the ambassador and most of his staff, all to get a force together to raid the Hotel-Spa Eiffel and rescue you – *if* you were still alive. *If* I wasn't going to receive your head as a present from the RLP. *If* we weren't going to discover your headless body dumped somewhere in Paris. *If* Hormuz Rakhim hadn't already disappeared with you before sending his ransom demands. All of which I would have met," he added, slightly more calmly, "up to and including high treason. That's how much you meant to me."

*Meant.* Past tense. Suddenly I felt colder and more terrified than I had been at any other time that night. Including when Hormuz Rakhim's hand fell on my shoulder and yanked me out of the remnants of my topological application to retrieve the jewels.

Was this going to be the fight that destroyed our relationship?

And had it already done so?

I might have been feeling my way, in total darkness, through the mangrove swamps of the Island of Devils. Only this time I had no hope of teleporting myself out of trouble.

This time there was no way to go but forward, and I had no clue if that really was a way out.

"Why do you think you're going to lose your job?"

"Weren't you listening? I've been using every scrap of influence I ever had, or ever will have, to get the Company and the embassy and the Paris gendarmerie to come with me to raid the Hotel-Spa Eiffel. For a personal mission. For a crazy girl whom nobody sent into danger, who put *herself* in danger, who isn't even an accredited CIA or State Department employee."

That distracted me momentarily. "I'm not?" They sure had been treating me like I was. Like a serf, really, ordered here and there to use my paranormal abilities to get them whatever they wanted.

Brad scrubbed one big hand over his face. "It doesn't make any difference. I'd be in just as much trouble if I'd tried to organize a team to extract the ambassador himself."

I doubted that, but it wasn't worth arguing about. There were more important things to settle. "Why were you so worried?"

He sighed deeply. "Why wouldn't I be? Look. I woke up at three-thirty and you weren't in the bed. I went looking for you, to tell you to come back and go to sleep. It didn't take long to figure out that you weren't even in the apartment."

"I told you after dinner that I was going over to see Aunt Alesia. She was going crazy, waiting for someone to return the rubies."

"And at what point, exactly, did you decide that her peace of mind was more important than mine?"

"It wasn't like that! I had a very good reason for being in a hurry, myself, to get the necklace back."

"Yeah, sure," he said with heavy sarcasm. "You always have a very good reason for every crazy thing you do."

I swallowed, hard, and clamped down on my incipient hysteria. Somewhere, deep within, a terrified Thalia was wailing that I'd destroyed the best thing in my life, that you couldn't fix what had been broken so badly, and that no amount of talking would put it back.

Would put Brad and me back together.

But talking seemed like the only tool I had. Sex wasn't going to distract him this time, and anyway, it seemed creepy to try and use sex to get out from under this. He deserved a full explanation. After that – if he was still done with me and the problems I'd caused him –

I couldn't think about that now, or the hysterical Thalia inside me would get the upper hand.

The only way to go was forward.

I plunged into it.

"By mid-afternoon tomorrow, or at the latest tomorrow night, the bug I put in the Taklan ambassador's study is going to stop working. *You* should know that, I told you how Sheng Williams set it up. It only depends on how much they talk in the study. I don't understand exactly, but there was some micro-circuit that was only activated when someone was talking, and he separated it from its… um… its heat bathtub?" That seemed wrong. I wished I had Sheng there to explain what he'd done.

"The technical term," Lensky said, "is 'heat *sink*. Do continue; you cannot imagine the depth of my interest."

"Look, I thought that twenty-four hours or so would be long enough to convince the RLP that Aunt Alesia had done what they wanted and get them to return the necklace. Only Daryush didn't go into his study until afternoon – you know that too, you caught me listening to him."

"It seems," he said grimly, "to be the only way I ever do find out anything about your activities – by catching you. This time I called your Aunt Alesia and woke her up. She said she didn't know where you'd gone, but she knew you'd called Sheng Williams first. So I woke *him* up." He took a deep breath. For the first time, I noticed that his hands were shaking. He really had been afraid for me. I was deeply sorry about that. But I didn't think he would forgive me if I tried to explain why I hadn't told him what I was going to do. If I'd told him to his face, he would have found some way to stop me. And if I'd told him from Aunt Alesia's, he would probably have raised hell at the Hotel-Spa Eiffel while I was still looking for Jacques-Henri. I really didn't see how I could have told him and still accomplished my mission.

He wasn't going to be open to that line of argument, though.

"Thalia, don't you have any idea what it did to me when I learned you'd gone off to infiltrate a bunch of cold-blooded killers who make a habit of beheading anybody who annoys them?"

As a description of Hormuz Rakhim, that seemed grossly unfair to me. "I don't think Hormuz is like that at all."

Lensky raised his eyes to the ceiling and groaned. "She's on first-name terms with the worst one of them all!"

He sounded more resigned and annoyed than furious, now. Perhaps I was making progress.

"If he's the worst RLP member you can name, they can't be as much of a threat as you're making out," I said. Perhaps he'd feel better when he understood how perfectly innocuous my time spent with Hormuz had been. "He did catch me trying to sneak the jewels out of his room safe – no, that's not quite accurate. I had already extracted them when he caught me."

"Thalia, will you for the love of God forget about perfect accuracy and just *tell me what he did to you*? The longer you beat about the bush, the worse I think it must have been. You're just pretending to be all right because you don't want to upset me, aren't you? What did he do? Whatever it was, you don't have to be ashamed to tell me, I love you, I will always love you no matter what happens."

Okay, that was a lot less scary than he'd sounded a few minutes ago. He'd quit using the past tense with words like 'love'. Now I just had to explain that he was definitely barking up the wrong tree. "He didn't do a damned thing to me," I said firmly. "He just wanted to talk. He said that catching me in his room was the closest he'd come to an interview with someone from the State Department since he'd arrived in Paris, and all he wanted was to put his point of view to me in the hope that I'd convey it to my superiors."

Lensky groaned again. "Is it too much to hope that you had the elementary caution not to tell him that you work for the CIA, not the State Department?"

"No, dammit, it's *not* too much!" I snapped. I was beginning to feel a bit annoyed myself. On *top* of the guilt. "But I did tell him I was just an intern. He wasn't going to believe I was anybody important anyway, you know. I'm not old enough to pass as a high-ranking diplomat."

"Not to mention that high-ranking diplomats don't usually do black bag jobs. Well, put me out of my misery: what happened after that? And tell me *everything*."

"We talked, that's all. He explained that he and the rest of his party only wanted religious freedom for everybody in Taklanistan."

"The hell they do," Lensky snapped, "they want to kill everybody who doesn't subscribe to their version of Islam."

"That's not what he said, and not what he sounded like, and I'm not totally hopeless at reading people, Brad!" Finally, I was beginning to feel back on first-name terms with him. I remembered something Hormuz had said right at the beginning of our talk. "He even said it was written in the Koran that there is no compulsion in Islam."

"A lot of things are written in the Koran," Lensky said. "You should read it some time. It's possible to use it to justify anything from religious tolerance to killing all heretics and infidels, and I have to tell you, Thalia, that the track record of the RLP leans considerably to the latter interpretation."

"Then maybe Hormuz Rakhim is just the leader they need to persuade them otherwise. Most of what he said sounded perfectly reasonable to me. He said that Ergashi – the president of Taklanistan, you know –"

"I do know who the president of Taklanistan is, thank you very much."

"Well, he said that Ergashi had been closing mosques based on his personal whims—"

"Oh, it's more than that—"

"*Will* you stop interrupting? He also talked about mobs forcibly shaving men with beards, which apparently is a big deal to Muslims – like the Amish, I guess – and tearing the veils off modest Muslim women, and Ergashi's administration didn't do anything about the mobs because most of them were incited by his police in the first place."

"So he spent what, an hour telling you about the poor, unhappy Muslims of Taklanistan and their sad plight?"

"No, that was all he said about that. It wasn't a complaint-fest. We talked about education and Ergashi closing down schools for political incorrectness, and how the country needs infrastructure, and how Taklanistan still hasn't really defined its own national identity even though it's been like twenty-five years since they declared their independence from the Soviets—"

"Twenty-seven."

"*Now* who's insisting on perfect accuracy? Twenty-five, twenty-seven, it's been way too long to justify their still being oppressed by having Russian troops in their country!"

Brad sighed but didn't say anything.

"Look, would you like it if our president went around closing schools and churches and oppressing Christians? What if we hadn't been able to get properly married because St. Elias Church had been shut down?"

"I wouldn't like it," Brad admitted, "but it hasn't happened and it isn't going to happen, no matter what lunatic gets elected president, because America is a constitutional republic and no one man has the kind of power Ergashi wields."

"Yes. He said he envied us that, and that he wanted Taklanistan to have a Bill of Rights, only one that was appropriate for Muslim countries. He talked about something called the Cairo Declaration of Human Rights. *And*," I said triumphantly, "he gave me back the Shaimak Rubies after we'd finished talking!" I pulled the long padded box out of my pocket, flipped it open and held the necklace up in all its fragile, trembling, sparkling glory. Of course," I had to admit, "he was under the illusion that the bug we hid in the embassy is going to continue working. But when it fails, even if they find somebody to retrieve it, Sheng assured me that it'll look like a natural failure due to shoddy workmanship. I'm going to give the necklace to Aunt Alesia in the morning… no, I'd better just show her, and then we'll go together to return it to the ambassador. She's just crazy enough to try and keep the things for the next formal ball instead of giving them straight back to the owner before anything else h-happens."

Brad actually chuckled. "It *is* difficult when the people you love go off and do crazy things, isn't it, Thalia?"

The irony was not lost on me, but the shakes that had started in Rakhim's suite were starting to overwhelm me now. "Y-yes. It is. And I'm so, so sorry you w-went through all this, Brad! I d-didn't mean you to be h-hurt. I never do, you know."

"I know," he said. He left his chair, joined me on the couch and wrapped his arms around me. "We'll get past this, Thalia. We'll talk more in the morning, after I deal with my boss and the State Department."

"After *w-we* deal w-with them," I said. "I'll ex—ex— tell them it was all my fault."

"That's debatable." He put one hand under my chin and raised my face until I met his eyes, and then I knew he still loved me, and nothing else really mattered. "Why are you starting to shake, love? *Was* there something you feel you can't tell me?"

"Just t-tele—too much travel," I managed to say. Shaking and stammering were usually my first symptoms; having trouble with multi-syllable words was the next. I didn't really think tonight's teleporting across town and back was doing it, though. What was really giving me the shakes was the double dose of adrenalin, first when Hormuz caught me and then when I found Brad waiting for me in the living room. But I didn't want to admit how scared of Rakhim I'd been at first. "N-need food."

Brad laughed. "That, at least, I can take care of! Do you want a sandwich, or—"

"There are chocolate c-cookies in the p-pantry."

# 8. The same zip code as a poker game

The next morning was one of those times in my life which I would prefer to pass over in dignified silence, or at least with only a brief recapitulation. Suffice it to say that quite a number of people were very unhappy with us. I might have been their principal target, but Lensky was second on the list, and poor Sheng Williams was third. I got the distinct impression, too, that they would have snatched Aunt Alesia out of Solange's town house and dragged her in to be upbraided if they hadn't been concerned about causing an international incident. We had, the ambassador informed us – yes, the collection of people yelling at us went that far up the chain of command – anyway, he felt we had already come far too close to causing an international embarrassment and a diplomatic crisis all by ourselves, and the best that he could hope for now was for the entire episode to pass without calling further attention to our various misdemeanors and shortcomings.

He was willing to leave the initial critique at that, but the high-ranking guy from State who attended via a supposedly secure teleconferencing system was rather more expansive. And when he got through with us, Lensky's boss at Langley got into the conference and tore a few more strips off Lensky.

The upshot was that a trusted member of the embassy staff would be tasked with returning the Shaimak Rubies to the Taklan ambassador, with a note supposedly from Aunt Alesia saying that recent burglaries in Paris had made her nervous about being entrusted with this national treasure and she hoped dear Daryush would forgive her returning his extraordinarily generous loan. Aunt Alesia wasn't going to be allowed to write the note, but she would get to sign it.

Sheng Williams had displayed a degree of initiative far above his pay grade and even farther above what his *new* pay grade was going to be; he was busted down from Technical Officer to Polygraph Technician. And they would have placed him lower than that, Lensky told me quietly after the teleconference, if the Department of Technical Operations hadn't raised hell about being deprived of his skills. "He'll be stuck in an office in Langley, probably giving new job applicants the routine polygraph, for a few months until all this blows over. Then they'll quietly reinstate him. Really, a few months of boring duty isn't much of a punishment. They're usually a lot harder than that on loose cannons."

I was glad I hadn't gotten Sheng into more trouble, but not terribly reassured for Lensky and myself. In an unguarded moment last night Lensky had said that my picture appeared in the dictionary definition of 'loose cannon.' And as my handler, if not as my husband, he was going to be almost as unpopular as I was for not ensuring that an inexperienced intern didn't get herself into trouble.

"But I didn't get into trouble!" I protested when he said that. "Everything worked out just fine – at least it would have if—"

I looked at his expression, swallowed what I'd been going to say, and shut up. It wasn't fair, was it, to blame him for having been so afraid for me that he woke up half the embassy? "It was my fault," I said, more quietly now. "Everything was. They shouldn't censure you at all; if I hadn't gone off on my own, you wouldn't have done anything to upset them."

"Thalia, it doesn't work that way," he told me. "I'm the case officer; it's my responsibility to see that none of my people go off on crazy tangents." He put an arm around me and hugged me tightly. "Although how they expect me to manage mathematicians as if they were normal people does escape me."

Then it was our turn to be called back into the ambassador's office, berated some more, and informed about our own fate.

I, the ambassador said sternly, deserved nothing better than to be expelled from the internship program and sent home in disgrace. (Oh, right. The

Company hadn't exactly explained how few of us had the special qualifications required for this program. As far as he was concerned, I could and probably should be replaced by somebody who looked better, dressed better, and did only what she was ordered to.)

As it happened, however (he said with a sour look) the consulate in Barcelona had informed him that they had an urgent need for my services. I was, therefore, to proceed to Barcelona by the next plane out of Orly Airport, to which I would be escorted after a fifteen-minute stop at our apartment to pack up my things. Furthermore, much against his personal recommendations, it had been decided that due to the fact of our marriage, this officer (giving Lensky the kind of look generally bestowed upon day-old fish) was to accompany me and continue to act as my handler, to which job he trusted that Mr. Lensky would bring more dedication and competence than had been displayed during our stay in Paris, blah blah blah. Lensky's neck slowly turned red as the ambassador blathered on, but otherwise he presented an admirable picture of calm and self-discipline under difficult circumstances.

Rather more of me turned red, but that didn't matter; I was only an intern.

"What do you suppose happened in Barcelona, for Colton and Meadow to call in reinforcements?" I speculated while we were throwing our clothes into suitcases.

"The request didn't come from them," said Lensky, who has this spooky spook's ability to know more about any situation than he's supposed to have been told. "The consul-general in Barcelona contacted Harrison – my boss – and requested an immediate replacement. Colton and Meadow are on their way to Santiago."

"What, the pilgrimage place?" Even I had heard of Santiago Compostela. It was, like, the Lourdes of Spain, wasn't it?

"Santiago, *Chile*," Lensky clarified.

I was impressed. "They must have screwed up even worse than we did."

"I'm not sure that's possible." Lensky picked up my big suitcase, his suitcase, and a backpack that I'd bought to hold the overflow after a few trivial little purchases. "How can we be leaving here with so much more than we brought?"

"Brad, it's *Paris*. You didn't expect me not to buy any souvenirs at all?"

"As long as you didn't saddle us with another four-foot masterpiece of native art, I guess I'm okay with it."

That was a totally unjustified dig about this mask I was stuck with. I'd picked it up on our last assignment, in East Africa, shortly before coming across the street in Mombasa where woodworkers mass-produced masks identical to my treasured purchase. Now I couldn't get rid of the thing. Our agent in Mombasa had shipped it to America along with the possessions we really wanted to get back, and Brad insisted on giving it a prominent place in the Austin condo just so he could keep teasing me about it.

The next day, in Barcelona, the consul added the vital details required for us to fully understand the situation. *He* hadn't been kept in the dark regarding applied topology, and he'd been trying to use Colton to find out more about a pair of Russian agents who were sniffing around Barcelona in the run-up to the referendum. In fact, he'd been perfectly happy when the Russians caught a hint of Colton's paranormal abilities and suddenly wanted to make Meadow and Colton their new best friends.

He got a bit vague about what happened next, but I got the impression that he'd tried to get Meadow to act seductive with the Russian man, Feodor Nikolayevich Ivanov aka Fedya (why do Russians have such a superfluity of names?) in order to worm out his secrets. And that this had worked exactly as well as anyone who knew her would expect. What had they been thinking, sending Meadow of all people out to bat her eyelashes? We were here to do *applied topology*, not to set honey-traps.

"She did have that month of training before being assigned here," the consul said defensively, "and she didn't have to do that much. Feodor is known to have a penchant for young women who are, um, spectacularly well-endowed. All we asked her to do was to wear a dress that wouldn't hide the fact."

Yeah, right. I was willing to bet that they'd asked for a great deal more than that.

"Well. I'm clearly not the right person to carry on where Meadow left off," I pointed out. "I can't bat my eyelashes worth a damn, and anyway I don't have anything like her, ah, natural advantages." They should have requested Annelise and Ben; she was an expert on men, and he could have quietly protected her. I guessed they hadn't annoyed anyone in London yet.

"So I see," he said, sweeping his eyes over me very quickly. "No, we're reverting to the first plan, dangling paranormal abilities in front of them."

"You want me to teleport in front of Feo…" oh, I was never going to get all those syllables right… "Fedya?"

"Not you," the consul said, "him." He nodded at Lensky. "And not in front of Fedya. He's going to tackle the other Russian – Larissa Vasilievna Petrova. She's pretending to be Fedya's wife, but that's never slowed her down in going after anybody who takes her fancy."

"And you expect Brad to do that?" I was liking this assignment less and less.

"I expect the hints that he has paranormal abilities to do it," the consul said impatiently. "All *you* have to do is make yourself invisible – you *can* do that much, can't you? – and stay with them in order to give Lensky a few special effects to whet the Petrova's interest."

It all sounded unnecessarily complicated to me.

"Why don't I just get invited to their apartment, mark it, and teleport back when they're out to place a few bugs? That's what we've been doing in Paris, and it's worked just fine." Oh, with a couple of tiny exceptions, but there was no need to go into those.

"No time," said the consul. "The referendum is on Sunday. Your predecessors thought that Feodor Nikolayevich had been given a large sum of money which he meant to pass out on the night before the referendum – effectively, hiring thugs to make trouble – but they couldn't find out what *kind* of trouble he plans to make, or where the hired thugs are supposed to meet him."

"I could still try getting invited to their apartment, and then teleport in and steal the money. Wouldn't that work?"

"Too risky," said the consul, "and we might not be able to pull it off in time. They're bound to be more cautious about letting anybody close to them as the date of the referendum approaches. Even that about the money is only guesswork, but it's supported by the way the Russians are behaving."

"Splashing it about generously?" Lensky guessed.

"Quite the reverse. Larissa Vasilievna is keeping her partner on an extremely short leash, this trip. Normally Feodor Nikolayevich hits the casinos whenever he's flush with cash – he's particularly fond of the private poker games hosted at Casino Barcelona – but this time he hasn't even been allowed to get within the same *barri* as a pack of cards."

For once, Lensky looked as confused as I felt.

"Oh. Local slang for a neighborhood. You might say, uh, he hasn't even been in the same zip code as a card game."

I suggested that a known weakness like gambling might provide a useful entry point, and both the consul and Lensky came down hard on me.

"*You*," the consul said, giving me his best steely glare, "they warned me about you. No mischief-making, no independent initiatives, no acting like a loose cannon. You will do *exactly* and *only* as told, is that clear?"

I nodded. Meaning yes, it was clear to me what they wanted. *Not* meaning yes, I would act like an idiot with no mind of my own just because they told me to.

Lensky's objection was more personal. "You're not getting anywhere near a casino," Lensky said. "Remember what happened to Aleksi?"

Well, for me it was ancient history, and somebody else's history at that. But for Lensky, his older brother's death shortly after an unfortunate gambling interaction with a Jersey gang was an unhealed wound. He went white to the lips at the bare suggestion that Fedya's gambling habit might be useful to us, and I nodded again. This time meaning yes, I remembered about Aleksi, and yes, I would respect Lensky's prejudices and stay away from Casino Barcelona. If possible.

The consul had made sure that Brad and I received invitations to every social event in diplomatic circles between today and the referendum. Our job was simply to show up at the events until we lucked into one that the Russians actually attended; then Lensky was supposed to scrape acquaintance with Larissa and imitate a man too intoxicated by her charms to hide his paranormal abilities, while I stayed in the background and worked the special effects.

I wasn't thrilled with the plan. While Lensky stayed for more details on the political situation, I excused myself to unpack in the minuscule apartment over the consular offices. As I moved my clothes from the suitcase to a closet where the wrinkles might shake out before the upcoming cocktail party, TheSila slithered out from between the folds of my topaz dance dress and commiserated with me. "It is always a mistake to send your man out to attract other women."

"I trust Brad. Absolutely. This is just a – a political maneuver." I shook out the topaz silk and slid it onto a padded hanger.

"It makes them think that you do not care if they amuse themselves elsewhere."

"Brad knows better."

"Yes, well, even if they do not *think* it, they *do* think it," TheSila announced with an air of profound meaning. She spotted an empty raku vase and glided into it, compressing her flaming person until she appeared to be no more than a cluster of flowers emerging from the vase.

Extremely vibrant flowers. I hoped that she would tone it down a bit after dark.

Mr. M. slipped over the edge of the suitcase and undulated along the bed.

"I suppose you want to give me the benefit of your advice too," I said.

"It is unfortunate," he said, "that this fool of a consul does not wish to take advantage of your talents."

"Oh, he does. He just wants me to make it look as though Brad is doing everything." And I really didn't mind that. Considering how often I get in trouble for doing something perfectly sensible with topology, I was fine with somebody else getting blamed this time if we frightened the neighbors or blew our cover or whatever. It was the rest of the setup that made me unhappy. Was I supposed to act the meek little wife who tagged along behind hubby and didn't even object to him loving up some Russian enchantress? If so, I certainly hoped Brad wasn't stupid enough to take that act at face value.

"I was not thinking of your showier abilities," Mr. M. said. "This situation seems to me to call out for some of your subtler applications. *Small object manipulation*," he said pointedly. "You are very good with objects like – to take just one absolutely random example – *playing cards.*"

I slumped down on the edge of the bed and closed the suitcase on my collection of Paris souvenirs. "The consensus of opinion seems to be that I should stay away from Casino Barcelona," I said grumpily.

"Ah, but you are also supposed to keep an eye on the Russians," Mr. M. said. "And if it should happen that Lensky takes Larissa Vasilievna Petrova to some place without her so-called husband, who will keep tabs on Feodor Nikolayevich Ivanov?"

"I think you *like* all these triple-barreled Russian names," I said, still grumpy.

Mr. M. preened in the dressing-table mirror. "They have a certain resonance... Nothing to compare with Babylonian names, but at least they are not as awkward and ungraceful as the ones you Americans choose. But this is beside the point. According to the consul, Feodor Nikolayevich is drawn to the casinos as a moth to the flame. Should he take advantage of Larissa Vasilievna's inattention to pursue his favorite avocation, would it not be your duty to follow him and to make what profit you could from the situation? You would not have *initiated* the casino visit, so you could hardly be criticized for using too much *initiative.*"

I had a feeling that this line of argument would not be fully persuasive to the consul, but then... you know, the thing about permission and forgiveness? Mr. M. and I discussed the idea a bit more – always in purely hypothetical terms, mind you. We had a plan of action worked out by the time Brad came bounding off the little birdcage elevator, ready to change and take me out for tapas before the cocktail party. I mean, of course, a purely hypothetical plan of action. About what I *could* do if certain circumstances *happened* to arise.

Brad and I had tapas at the little bar around the corner from our apartment and watched the waiters there running around in circles. The place wasn't that busy, but the owner had a toddler – an adorable black-eyed moppet with an inextinguishable lust for freedom. We discovered that on the evenings when her mother dropped her off at the bar to get a couple of hours' peace, the two waiters and the bartender had a second job heading off the kid's attempts to hurl herself into the street. Once I even saw the cook running after her, scooping the little girl up with one hand while the other waved a skewer of something flaming.

After that, we stood around at the Brazilian consulate making conversation with other low-ranking diplomatic types and not spotting Fedya or Larissa. Then we went back to the neighborhood bar for a second series of tapas rounds. I did like the Catalan approach to food: plenty of it, in savory bite-sized pieces, and there was always a new dish circulating. The little girl had gone to bed by now, so the place was somewhat calmer, if not so entertaining.

"You'd better teleport yourself twenty miles out and back to burn off some of that," Brad said around ten-thirty, looking at the empty plates stacked all over our table.

"Can't, I haven't been anywhere yet. How about we go for a walk instead?"

Barcelona is a very fine city for strolling around at night. It was warmer than Paris – winter probably came later, and lay more lightly upon the land, in this Mediterranean city – and everybody else in the city appeared to be doing the same thing, strolling along the broad streets and greeting friends and showing off their best clothes. And the walk was quite relaxing. By the time we returned to the apartment I was beginning to think that I could do with a pleasant few days here, and if we never made contact with the Russians, well, nobody could expect us to succeed every time, could they? Maybe tomorrow I'd take one of those tours of Art Nouveau houses. I'd heard that Casa Batlló was something really special.

# 9. Getting to first base in Barcelona

Casa Batlló was everything it was talked up to be, and then some. From the front it looked rather sinister, with a façade of white shapes that made me think of a wide mouth full of bones. But inside, it was pure delight: curving walls, doors carved into the shapes of wooden trees that bore circles of glass "fruit," pearly ceilings that mimicked nautilus shells. I snickered a little over the picture in the guidebook that showed it filled with totally unsuitable, stodgy old-fashioned furniture. I would have bet the first owner was a bit alarmed by the interior but was afraid to say so for fear of being thought a Philistine, so he tried to tame it with gigantic overstuffed sofas and dark, dark tables.

I scored a cute souvenir – a little ceramic model of the house, wavy tiled roof and all – and came back to the apartment feeling just a tad guilty over abandoning Lensky, who'd announced his intention of spending the day hanging out in various cafes the Russian agents had patronized at one time or another.

I felt less guilty when we compared results. He had no sightings to report, only kidneys awash in coffee. I had the little model house and a guidebook full of pictures. "You should have come sightseeing with me," I told him. "Who knows, maybe Larissa and Fedya are doing the tourist thing too."

"It's Friday already," Lensky said.

"What, Russians don't go sightseeing on Fridays?"

"The referendum is on Sunday. We have a day and a half left to find out what they're up to and stop them. Get dressed, we're going to a dinner-dance hosted by the Romanian consulate. It used to be an Iron Curtain country, maybe the Russians will drop by in a salute to old alliances."

I thought "occupation" was a better word than "alliance" for Romania's past relationship with Russia, but decided not to say so. Lensky was grumpy enough already. My feet were already complaining about the prospect of dancing after a day of walking around Barcelona's stone-paved streets and buildings, but the prospect of wearing the topaz silk again helped me to ignore them. As for Lensky, I thought he might have picked the evening's entertainment more to cheer himself up than because he really hoped to encounter Fedya and Larissa. He would get to use his Romanian (souvenir of a foreign posting before we met) and, with any luck, to show off his amazing ballroom dancing skills.

"Were the waltz and mazurka part of your training at the Farm?" I asked while we were dressing for dinner. "Because we never learned anything like that in the one-month crash course the Company put us through before sending us abroad." Even if that course had been nicknamed 'charm school,' there'd been precious little that was charming about it.

"No, that was Aleksi," Lensky said. For once, pronouncing his dead brother's name didn't bring on the usual cloud of gloom. "He tried to take on the duties of a father towards me when ours died… but his notions of fatherhood were somewhat eccentric. When I was in middle school, he told me that ballroom dancing was one of the absolutely necessary skills for a Polish gentleman to master. He wanted me to learn to ride and use a cavalry saber as well, but fortunately we couldn't afford horseback riding lessons. He taught me to dance himself." He laughed; an unusual sound when he was talking about Aleksi. "Of course, I had to take the girl's part while he led. I don't think it occurred to either of us that when I actually danced with a girl, I would be the one leading, not following. My first few experiences were… well, you remember when we were getting married, and I kept trying to put the ring on your left hand and you kept shoving your right hand at me?"

I did. Lensky's solipsistic view of the matter had been that the Greek Orthodox church got everything backwards and on the wrong side. (He didn't like the way we crossed ourselves either.) Evidently he'd been more flexible about dancing; in Paris he'd demonstrated that he could lead perfectly well, even with an imperfect partner like me.

The evening started well, on this note of pleasant reminiscence. For Brad it became even better after the dessert course, when we spotted Fedya and Larissa among the crowd of late arrivals who'd been invited for the dance but not for the dinner. They weren't hard to spot: two tall, blond people in a sea of mostly short and dark locals. (I'm told that there are actually tall Spaniards. And blond Spaniards. And male Spaniards who don't try to pinch your bottom. All I can say is, I can't verify any of that from my experience in Barcelona.)

Tonight, it seemed, I wasn't going to benefit much from Brad's dancing skills: he was using them to dazzle Larissa, while I bumped around the floor with various Spanish diplomats who enjoyed the unusual experience of having an American dance partner who was shorter than they were. Some toes got stepped on, my bottom got pinched more than once (and not always by my partner) and I was extremely happy when a new man bowed over my hand and suggested we sit the next dance out together.

It was Fedya Niko-whatsit in person, toothy chinless grin and flamboyant manners and all. He complained to me in dramatic fashion that my husband was monopolizing his beautiful Larissa, and asked if he was in the habit of neglecting me so shamelessly.

I tried for a forlorn sniffle but it turned into a snicker, and I had to admit that I was just fine with sitting down and not dancing for a while. "At least this way no one is trying to pinch me."

Fedya took that as evidence that I didn't care for dancing. Which was actually kind of true, although Brad's performance at the Viennese embassy in Paris had opened my eyes to new possibilities along those lines. Being whirled around the dance floor by a strong, confident partner was a universe away from my previous experience of dances, which had mostly consisted of everybody wriggling and swaying and doing their own thing to the beat.

I watched Brad and Larissa dipping and gliding around the floor and didn't have to fake a slightly forlorn expression. She was actually taller than he was, but somehow she managed to nestle her face against his neck anyway. And the rest of her moved in ways that any man standing that close to her would have to find seductive.

He'd once told me, during one of our moments of shouting and throwing things at each other, that he couldn't understand how I'd gotten under his skin to begin with: I wasn't even his type, he'd said, before me he'd always dated tall, restful blondes. That crack hadn't bothered me unduly at the time, because immediately afterwards he'd displayed a degree of enthusiasm that convinced me I was his type now, whatever he'd thought in the past. But now…

Larissa was definitely blonde. And tall. Two strikes. "Fedya?"

"Yes?"

"Would you say that Larissa is restful?"

Fedya spluttered with an attempt to swallow his laughter. "My angel, Larissa is anything but restful!"

Well, that was something, anyway.

"A night with her would exhaust the strongest and bravest man!"

Oh.

I nibbled one fingernail and tried not to look as fretful as I felt.

Brad and Larissa were no longer even in sight. Maybe they'd ducked into one of the curtained alcoves scattered along the walls, where he would be… *persuasive*… in his efforts to find out the Russian plans. I wondered exactly how persuasive he was willing to be, and probably looked even more fretful. In any case, Fedya too had noticed their disappearance. And his response, rather than what you'd expect of a wronged husband, was that it would serve our wandering spouses right if we found some entertainment more amusing than waiting for them.

I gave him a suspicious glance, but his hand wasn't anywhere near my bottom.

In the next moment he used the magic word.

*Casino.*

Well…

It wasn't like Brad had needed me running applications of topology to get

Larissa interested in him. Her interests were probably much earthier. I glanced over the crowded room again. Still no Brad and no Larissa.

And I hadn't mentioned the casino; Fedya had.

It was practically my duty to follow up on this, the first possible crack in the Russians' reserve. The consul had said that Larissa was preventing Fedya from sneaking off to gamble. Ergo, encouraging him to gamble was tantamount to supporting American interests. Especially if he just happened to lose the money he'd been given for purposes of fomenting unrest.

Although both Brad and the consul had been extremely negative about this way of getting close to the Russians, there were factors clouding their judgment. In Brad's case, the mention of private poker games had opened the old wound of Aleksi's death, making it impossible for him to be completely rational on the subject. And in the consul's case, he hadn't been briefed about some of my less dramatic topological skills in the realm of small object manipulation. As Mr. M. had hinted, it was practically my patriotic duty to deploy those skills in support of our interests abroad. Wasn't it?

Not to mention that it would serve Brad right if I solved the Russia problem all by myself while he was off being *persuasive* with that blonde menace.

I made my excuses to one of our hosts, pleading a sudden headache, and I may have given him the impression that Fedya Nikolayevich had offered to escort me home and would be right back. I didn't actually say that in so many words, so I didn't have to fight the urge to touch my face that Brad says always tells him when I'm lying.

Another bit of luck, here: as a CIA field officer Brad was used to operating with a copious supply of cash for bribes, payments, and persuasion. And on this European venture he'd trained me to carry a lot more cash than I would normally be comfortable with, just in case I needed to do some of the bribing et cetera. My yellow silk evening bag actually contained what should be more than enough for an opening stake in a private poker game.

After the opening, of course, the other players would supply my needs.

***

"You shouldn't have waited up for me," I told Brad as soon as I walked into the apartment, several hours later. "Didn't Mr. Enescu give you my message?"

"He said that Fedya Nikolayevich was escorting you home." Brad's face was dark with anger. "Naturally I left as soon as I heard that; what were you thinking about, Thalia, to come home alone with that – that Russian two-timer?"

"Obviously, I didn't come home with him," I pointed out, "Mr. Enescu must have got the message mixed up. And anybody who's been sneaking off into corners with that Larissa has one hell of a nerve calling anybody else a two-timer!"

Brad's face darkened even farther. I was impressed. "She was my *assignment*, Thalia."

"Oh? And did she give you a good grade for your performance this evening?" I hadn't planned on having this particular fight with Brad, but it seemed his disappearance with Larissa had bothered me more than I liked to admit.

"Leaving abruptly to save you did not improve the relationship. You may have spoiled everything, Thalia! I was just gaining her trust…"

"Oh, is that what you call it? We called it getting to first base when I was in high school! Or did you make it all the way to second in one of those conveniently curtained little alcoves?" Okay, that might not have been entirely fair, but I didn't feel Brad was playing fair either. It was really beyond the limit, accusing me of spoiling everything when in fact I had just, brilliantly, spiked the Russians' guns. I would have to rise above bickering and explain that to Brad. But I needed a moment to cool off. "Look, can we table this fight and continue it after I've had a shower? I want to get the smoke out of my hair."

He sniffed. "An excellent idea. Where have you been going that smoking was allowed, anyway?"

"It wasn't allowed, that was the whole problem. I had to walk through a mob of nicotine addicts in the street to get in, and again when I left." I pulled down the zip of the topaz sheath and stepped out of it.

"To get in where, exactly?"

But I'd made my escape into the tiny bathroom, and I used the time-honored evasion. "Can't hear you when the water's running!"

After washing off the smoke, I tied the sash of my bathrobe carefully before stepping out of the bathroom. Discussions like the one we'd been having tended to degenerate into yelling, throwing things, and Brad trying to shake me. It was disconcerting if my bathrobe fell off during those parts of the discussion. Put me off my game.

This time, though, I came out of the shower and started talking before he had a chance to yell. "I have solved the Russian problem," I told him as soon as I was out. "Don't you want to know how?"

"What, the entire Russian problem? They're no longer our geopolitical enemies?"

"Sarcasm is not becoming to you. You know what I meant. Fedya is not going to foment any subversive actions whatsoever come Sunday."

"Oh, did he pinkie pinkie promise you?"

"Remember what I just said about sarcasm?" It would serve him right if I left him to wonder just what I had done. But – oh, all right; I was feeling proud of myself, and I wanted to boast. "We went to Casino Barcelona," I said, "and we got into a private poker game. You know all that Russian money that he was going to hand out to selected thugs tomorrow, on the eve of the referendum? I *think* the plan was to hire people posing as pro-independence supporters to start violence at the polling places that would tempt Madrid to overreact and arrest everybody, thus leading to district-wide riots and an immediate declaration of Catalonia's independence. With luck, he could even have provided the spark for a nasty little civil war. But it doesn't really matter now, because he doesn't have enough money left to buy a box of matches, let alone starting a political conflagration. I won it all."

"You. Did. What?"

I repeated my statement. "Trust me, he is *broke*. I had to give him the cab fare to get home."

Lensky grabbed my yellow evening bag and upended it. A compact and my favorite comb fell out, and then a couple of one-euro coins bounced on the floor. "Thalia, this does not look like the proceeds of a successful night at the casino."

"Of course it doesn't," I said, somewhat impatiently. "I didn't want to be mugged for my winnings on the way out, did I? Besides, I didn't feel like it was really my money. It was just a by-product of the covert operation. I cashed in my chips and asked the cashier to send a check for the total to the Fundació Joan Salvador Gavina. It's a children's shelter."

"Which you knew about how?"

"Asked people about worthwhile charities. While I was winning their money. It seemed to make them feel better about losing to me."

"And did it also make you feel better about cheating them? I assume you did cheat?"

"Naturally. I couldn't risk losing, could I? That would have gotten you in trouble."

There was a grinding sound that I couldn't immediately identify. Oh – Brad's teeth.

"You really shouldn't do that," I told him. "It's bad for the enamel."

That was when he really lost it and started yelling at me. "Are you out of your mind? You were specifically told to stay away from the casinos."

"The consul wasn't aware of my special skills."

"Special skills, my ass! People with 'special skills' like you used get killed for this kind of stunt. Look what happened to Aleksi!"

Why couldn't he let me enjoy the evening's triumph? "Yes, well, as you may have failed to observe, I am not your brother!"

"No, you're my wife, and is it too much for me to hope that you will occasionally heed an occasional mild and perfectly rational request to *stay out of danger*?"

"Brad, please calm down!" How dare he assume that I would be as stupid as his brother had evidently been? I was sorely tempted to punctuate that request by breaking something, but there weren't any suitably fragile ornaments within reach. Instead I put my arms around him and lowered my voice, trying to get us out of shout-and-scream mode. "Aleksi was addicted to gambling. I'm not. Playing poker was a tool to achieve what we were asked to do here, nothing more. I'll be perfectly happy if I never have to enter another casino."

Eventually Brad admitted there was some justice to my point of view. Besides, he said, he was extremely happy not to have to spend any more time with Larissa Vasilievna Petrova. Apparently she'd gone all slinky and seductive and – according to him – embarrassed him terribly while giving no clue whatsoever about their plans for the referendum.

"So, not your type after all?"

"What?"

"You told me once that before me, you only dated tall blondes."

"Oh, for the love of… Thalia, I don't have a 'type.' What I have now is *you*, and you are all I want, always and forever."

He took me to bed then and expanded on this theme until I fell asleep, quite happy, and with no more worries about the Russian agent.

Our employers, come Monday, were not nearly as grateful as I felt they should have been.

# 10. Pomegranate seeds

Before things in Taklanistan blew up – and roped Brad and me in – I had nothing to do, suddenly, but laze around my parents' back yard and try to explain to my family why I was back in Austin while my husband remained overseas.

"I don't get it," Andy said after my first-pass, succinct explanation. "They sent you home in disgrace for fixing their problem?"

"Apparently I didn't do it in an appropriately diplomatic fashion." I lay back on the lawn chair, put one arm over my eyes and listened to the chatter of cicadas in the back yard and the clatter of dishes in the kitchen. The condo had been surprisingly lonely without Lensky in it; I'd surprised Mom and myself by coming over for dinner when it wasn't even a Friday night. Being totally convinced (not without reason) of my uselessness in a kitchen, she'd shooed my kid brother and me out into the back yard while she cooked.

I'd been whisked from a nippy autumn in Paris, to a gentler Mediterranean version in Barcelona, and now back to the brutal Texas version that still hadn't let go of summer. We usually had a few cool days in October, but this wasn't one of them. The heat was enervating, and in any case I didn't know what to do with myself. Lying back and listening to the cicadas was more attractive than pulling up my socks and getting on with the pure mathematics research that was supposed to be my raison d'être.

That relaxed attitude probably wouldn't survive my first meeting with Dr. Verrick, the Director who'd been left without any research fellows to direct after the CIA decided they had a use for us overseas. That meeting wouldn't happen until he found out I was back, though, and I was in no hurry to announce my return. I was daunted by the prospect of being the only researcher at the Center, and hence the only recipient of Dr. Verrick's views on the proper behavior for topologists (in brief: doing topology, applying topology, and ignoring everything else in the world).

There was really a lot to be said for my parents' back yard on a warm weekday afternoon heading gently for evening.

The clatter in the kitchen diminished slowly. I recognized the rhythm of Mom's cooking: there would be a quiet spell while stuff was simmering on the stove, baking in the oven, coming to completion in the crockpot. A few minutes later she came out to join us, carrying a shirt and her small sewing box. "Andros, hang this up, it's got all its buttons now."

Andros – or Andy, as he preferred to be called now – looked at the shirt in some surprise. "Mom, these buttons are *blue*."

"What do you have against blue?"

"Well, this morning it had all white buttons, except for the one that was missing."

Mom waved her free hand. "I couldn't match that missing button, so I took them all off and replaced them with the blue ones. What do you care? They go with the blue and white stripes, don't they? Besides, blue is better. Protection against the *vaskania*."

"Mo-om! Nobody believes in the evil eye any more," I protested without bothering to sit up. "Come on, even *you* don't really believe that stuff, do you?"

"Oh, so now you're smarter than Father Niketas, Thalia?"

I shut up. I knew better than to keep arguing once Mom brought the entire Greek Orthodox church in on her side.

Andy took the shirt and ambled off to hang it up, or (more likely) to drop it on a chair in his room. If he could find one that wasn't already festooned foot-deep with clothing.

Mom settled into his chair, which creaked ominously but, like everything else in the household, knew better than to give her any grief. "A good boy," she said, casually waving her hand towards Andy and over my supine body. The needle she'd used to sew on the new buttons still dangled from a length of thread in her hand.

"Mom," I said, staring upward at the mosaic of leaves against the evening sky, "that won't work. Even if I were pregnant, which I'm not, there are plenty of better ways to find out the sex of the baby than watching to see if a needle swings back and forth or around in circles over my stomach. For heaven's sake, there were better ways back when *you* were pregnant!"

My mother's eyes brightened. "Oh, so you know already! Is it a boy or a girl?"

I thought back over what I'd just said. Apparently it had been subject to Mom Editing, in which the parts she didn't want to hear were deleted and she claimed I had really meant whatever parts of the sentence were left. "Neither! I mean, I'm not pregnant!"

"Didn't you come back so you could have the baby at home?"

Her fantasy skills were reaching a level that would have been envied by Annelise, the receptionist we'd hired because she was so good at convincing outsiders they hadn't seen anything unusual about us. "I got *sent* back," I said now, and not for the first time, "because the State Department didn't like the way I handled the problem they wanted us to solve."

"My little girl," Mom said happily, "an important person in the Department of the State! Who'd ever have imagined it?"

You see what I mean about Mom Editing? I decided not to argue with her on this one, though. I was not fond of reliving the Barcelona consul's views on what I still thought had been a perfectly reasonable way to squelch Russian meddling with the independence referendum. He wasn't even grateful that the referendum had gone off peacefully, with a record three-quarters of the population voting and most of them coming down solidly on the side of independence from Spain. The State Department would have preferred the opposite result.

"But I don't see," she went on, less happily, "why they have to separate you from your husband. How can he be expected to help you make a baby when he is in Berlin and you are here?"

Freed of the responsibility of looking after me, Brad had been sent to Berlin to assist Annelise and Ben in doing something tricky there after their London assignment.

Given that I took the Pill religiously, Brad didn't actually have much less chance of impregnating me from Berlin than if he'd been here. However, pointing that out would just focus Mom's attention on me. "I wish he were here too." Not getting pregnant could have been a lot more fun with his participation.

"I will write to my Congressman," Mom decided. "I will explain to him that it is against God's holy will to separate husband and wife in this way. *And* we will have yogurt and pomegranates with honey for dessert tonight."

I love that thing Mom does with yogurt, pomegranates and honey, especially on hot days like this one. So I didn't point out that if she was hoping for results, it might be smarter to wait until Brad was back home before plying me with fertility-enhancing recipes. Besides, it wasn't like any number of pomegranate seeds was going to overpower the Pill.

Over dinner my father, who'd been watching the news while Mom and I dished up, filled us all in on world affairs. Since the explosive winter when we'd finally convinced him to give up verbally abusing Andy, he had taken up politics and foreign affairs as his new topics. Neither Andy nor my two older brothers followed current events outside of sports, and I am as apolitical as you can be while still having a pulse. Thus, the new subject gave him much the same pleasure as the old subject had: he was free to rant interminably and tell us all what the great powers of the world were doing wrong.

I privately applauded the new Dad. Maybe he was still boring and bossy, but it was a lot less irritating hearing his opinion on Angela Merkel's missteps than being treated to a scorching exposition of my own shortcomings. Andy favored the change even more strongly, to the point where he actually paid attention. Not much, just enough attention to encourage Dad's harangues about how world leaders ought to be acting.

Dad hardly needed much encouragement, and he was repetitive enough so you didn't really need to listen all that carefully. Or maybe it was world events that were repetitive. Tonight's monologue certainly went over familiar material. The NATO countries were unhappy with the President, there was violence in Africa, a Republican senator had been implicated in a sex scandal and a Democratic congressman was trying to explain why his freezer had been full of plastic-wrapped bundles of cash. The usual. But as Dad expatiated on the wickedness, folly and corruption of those in high places, he mentioned one name that caught my attention.

"Wait, what was that, Dad? *Who* was assassinated?"

"Jahandar Ergashi," my father said. "You wouldn't know who he is, but—"

"The president of Taklanistan!" Less than two weeks ago, I had been sitting in a luxury Paris hotel, listening to Hormuz Rakhim's litany of complaints against this man.

Dad looked annoyed and I mentally kicked myself for raining on his parade. "That is correct. But, of course, you do not understand the international implications of this event!"

A chance to retrieve the situation. "No, I'm sure I don't," I said, as humbly as I could. "Explain it to me?"

I chewed, swallowed and nodded while Dad went on about martial law, US and UN pressure on Taklanistan to hold elections, the Chinese border with Taklanistan, the Russian border with Taklanistan, the Afghan border with Taklanistan… CNN must have put up a map to illustrate their story. I didn't have to pretend ignorance here. Geography isn't exactly my strong point. Who would have guessed a little, landlocked country in Central Asia would have had so many internationally important borders?

Well, Brad would, of course, but that's not a fair comparison; the man knows way too much about far too many obscure places. He even knew that the Taklans spoke a dialect of Farsi that was loaded with Russian words.

I didn't get a chance to air that bit of esoteric information, though, because my phone rang. Dad disapproves of people accepting phone calls when he's talking – which basically rules out the entire evening – but even he had to bow to the Greek imperative of Honoring Your Husband. Which was a good thing, because I wasn't nearly interested enough in keeping my father happy to pass up a phone call from Brad.

And that was how I found out, before I'd even had to explain myself to Dr. Verrick at the Center, that I was back in the game.

# 11. A dialect with its own army and navy

For once the government did something moderately intelligent. Instead of going directly to Taklanistan, I flew to Berlin first, where Brad and Ben met me. Then we all three boarded a flight for Merzadeh, the capital of Taklanistan.

Come to think of it, there probably weren't any direct flights from Austin to Merzadeh. So, maybe it was luck rather than intelligent planning. Whatever. I wasn't going to quarrel with it. Although I would have liked some time to recover from jet lag with Brad in Berlin, being on an airplane with him was definitely my second choice.

I wondered if I'd have suffered from jet lag if I'd teleported? One of these days – if the CIA ever gave us a chance to do actual research again – we really needed to do some serious work on establishing the distances we could teleport and the amount of immediate feeding required to stave off shock at a given distance. Up to now nobody from the Center had teleported more than three hundred miles. And we were strongly disinclined to try extending our range from that to something that would cover a transatlantic flight. What happened if we ran out of energy in the middle of a Brouwer teleportation? Would we wind up in the ocean?

Ben and I discussed that, off and on, on the way to Merzadeh. Being on three very long flights within six days had greatly increased my interest in figuring out if we could substitute teleportation for mechanical travel. If nothing else, Brower teleportation didn't *vibrate*. Or expose us to the toxic soup of airborne viruses inside most jetliners.

However, as Ben pointed out in an atypical display of caution, there were a lot of intermediate steps we needed to try out as we moved from teleporting across three hundred miles of Texas to attempting five thousand miles across an ocean. Also, we needed to establish destinations. Which meant traveling to multiple places by conventional means. Which would require not only time but financial support from the CIA.

I was tired enough to let all those reasonable objections shut down the research project for the time being. By the time we were halfway to Merzadeh the thing I wanted most in life was to *not* be on something that vibrated and could fall out of the sky without warning. But failing that, I was much too tired to plan a teleportation research program. Dozing against Brad's shoulder was an acceptable second choice.

He and Ben, not having started off already jet-lagged from a transatlantic trip, talked over the situation in Taklanistan during the flight. I paid attention when I could stay alert, but I'll freely admit that was not very much of the time, and hence my understanding of the geopolitical situation may have been less than perfect.

From what I did take in, I gathered that matters in Taklanistan had not been great before the assassination of President Ergashi, and they'd been on a quick downhill run to hell since then. The incumbent government hadn't stopped with declaring martial law; they'd also arrested a number of Religious Liberation Party leaders and had issued new anti-Islamic decrees. There were protests in the streets that made Barcelona's referendum protests seem like a tea party. Taklans of any political persuasion, it seemed, did not need bribing to get violent about their politics.

Against this troubled backdrop, international problems were heating up. Some Taklan construction workers had encountered armed Afghan drug traffickers on the border. Two workers were dead and the others had been kidnapped. The Russians, rather than helping retrieve the kidnapped Taklans, were talking about pulling out of the few posts they still manned along that border.

"Isn't that a good thing?" I asked, rubbing my eyes and trying to stay focused. "Hormuz was indignant about the fact that his country is still occupied by Russia after more than twenty-five years."

"A handful of officers commanding poorly trained Taklan troops in a few isolated border posts," Brad said, "is not what most people would call an 'occupation.' The Taklans cannot protect that border without help, and most of them appreciate that fact. And *please*, Thalia, try not to talk about 'Hormuz' when we get there. My wife being on first-name terms with a vicious, unprincipled opposition leader is exactly the kind of thing that could blow up into an international incident."

One of these days we were going to have to discuss things like Brad's taking such a prejudiced view against people he had never met. I had actually talked with Hormuz, and he had struck me as anything but vicious and unprincipled. I wasn't sure the same thing could be said for the president – I mean, the *late* president of Taklanistan, Jahandar Ergashi. But I fell asleep again while trying to formulate my objections to Brad's attitude.

Our arrival at Merzadeh International Airport compared favorably, as far as I was concerned, with my airport experiences in Europe. The building itself was small, dilapidated, and plagued with draughts where pre-fabbed sections failed to come together properly. But we were met as soon as we left the plane by a security officer who asked us to step aside, out of the main stream of returning Taklans and a few American and European trekkers. While the other foreigners lined up to be interviewed by a single tired-looking clerk behind a shabby desk with peeling varnish, we were escorted to a comfortable lounge. Here a man who identified himself as a Taklan station officer welcomed us to the country and ushered us to the other side of the barriers.

"You are being met?" he asked, looking somewhat dubiously at the sea of Taklans with a few signs for "InterAsia Trekking" and "Central Asian Cultural Tour," bobbing in the crowd.

"There may have been some… difficulties… at the embassy," Lensky said.

The station officer gave a sharp bark of laughter. "And why not? There are difficulties everywhere, now. You will forgive that I leave you here?"

And that was it for the formalities. There were no stamps on our passports (I kind of regretted that part) and there was no official record of our being in the country at all. "The Company has a good relationship with the government here," Brad murmured to me, in partial explanation.

For the first time, then, I'd been received by a foreign government as a CIA representative. It seemed rather a shame that there was no record of the event, but I supposed we shouldn't complain about things going smoothly. If my limited experience in Europe was any guide, there would be plenty of problems ahead without looking for unnecessary ones.

Our good luck continued; our baggage was the first to be unloaded, and by the time we'd collected all our bits and pieces our ride had appeared.

Gary Shields had been the lone CIA case officer stationed in Taklanistan up to our arrival. Thankfully, he didn't seem offended at having three new people dumped on him. Mostly he looked *tired.* A lean, dark man with what looked like permanent five o'clock shadow, he introduced himself, picked up some suitcases, and led the way to his car while telling Brad how glad he was to have somebody to share the work.

"Not that there'll be much actual intelligence work," he said while piling our baggage into the back of his car, "if present trends continue. Mostly I'm helping out the remaining embassy staff, the ones who haven't been evacuated yet. I'm short on agents anyway. One was shot in the street right after the assassination, when the Presidential Guard was trigger-happy, and another one has taken his family to the country. It's getting ugly, and I can sure use somebody who speaks the language to help us make new contacts."

"I wouldn't quite claim that," Brad said. "But I did study Farsi when I was first with the Company, and I can pick out some of the Russian loan words in the Taklan dialect because they're similar to the same words in Polish. I should be able to get up to speed in this dialect pretty fast."

"Language, not dialect!" Gary said, laughing. "Remember what they taught us? A language is a dialect with its own army and navy."

"Taklanistan doesn't have a navy," Brad riposted. "So is Taklan half a language?"

I was more interested in this glimpse of Brad's past than in the debate. "You studied Farsi?" That explained how he'd caught me eavesdropping in Paris.

"And Arabic."

"Trying for one of the really interesting posts, were you?" Gary Shields perked up a bit. "And instead, it got you dumped here."

"The funny-language salary bonus didn't hurt, either," Brad said. He looked at me. "That was back when I was still paying off Pam's tuition for that cosmetician course."

An explanation of sorts, but I suspected his attraction to trouble spots had something to do with the choice of languages to study.

"And," he said, turning his attention back to Gary, "it appears that Taklanistan may be more 'interesting' than any of us anticipated. Can you fill us in on what's happening? I gave them – "he nodded at Ben and me – "a quick overview on the plane, but we'd all like to hear your expert assessment of the situation."

Gary glanced at me, swaying on my feet and almost overbalanced by the shoulder bag I'd stuffed with warm clothing back in the heat of a Texas October. "Your wife looks as tired as I feel. I'll tell you what I can on the way to the apartment, then why don't I leave you folks to unpack and relax for a bit, and we can do the rest over dinner?"

Sounded like a brilliant plan to me. I wasn't quite sure what time it was, or what day, but *later* sounded like a good time to try and be intelligent again; a whole lot better than *now*.

The way to the CIA apartment led through city streets more attractive than I'd anticipated. The main shopping street was lined with shops showing off goods behind plate-glass windows. "Cheap Chinese imports," Gary said dismissively, but at least the shops looked bright and cheerful. He told me that the music blaring from boom boxes was mostly Persian pop.

"Ah, they haven't discovered iPods and earbuds?"

"They *like* using the boom boxes," Gary said with a slight shudder. "More sociable, you know, sharing your music with the neighbors."

After a few crowded blocks he turned off Akbaital Street and onto a broad, tree-lined avenue called Kalot Rushan Street. This was a mostly residential neighborhood of old, crumbling buildings in soft colors, none more than three stories high. The apartment was in one of those buildings, and it was big enough for all of us: three bedrooms, a tiny kitchen, and a living-dining area dominated by a massive table that almost blocked the way into the kitchen. "I've been sharing with some embassy people," Gary explained, "but they pulled strings and got themselves evacuated right after the assassination."

"You didn't want to go with them?"

He looked surprised. "Oh, hell, no. This is the best time to be here. If the Company can deliver, we'll be able to write our own ticket with State for all of Central Asia." What we were supposed to deliver, I gathered while unpacking a few essentials, was a peaceful election that came out the way the State Department wanted it to: with Ergashi's party still in power.

"Not so different from Barcelona, then."

Brad looked grim. "Except that the referendum there did not turn out the way State wanted it."

"You win some, you lose some." That sounded too frivolous. "I mean… we can't, and shouldn't, interfere with people's desire for freedom." And that sounded way too pompous. I gave up trying to sound any way at all and took a nap before dinner.

That meal was considerably later than any of us had anticipated. But it was worth waiting for. When Gary did return to the apartment, he was followed by two boys with their arms full of cardboard boxes. He opened the boxes on the dining table to reveal rice flecked with bright flowers and nuts, tiny balls of ground meat stuck with almonds, grilled peppers and eggplant, some kind of spiced meat on skewers, and flaky sweet pastries that tasted kind of like Mom's baklava might have, if she'd made it with pistachios.

"I've been grabbing a bite to eat downtown," he told us, "but I thought your first night here deserved something better."

Over lukewarm beer from the laboring box-like refrigerator, he told us that the remaining State Department representatives were too busy to offer us any guidance: negotiating to get the kidnapped workers back, persuading the Taklans not to overreact, the Russians not to pull out. Trying to get the government to tone down its repressive measures.

"And what," Brad asked, "is the State Department doing to persuade the RLP not to gin up violence in the streets?"

The tired lines in Gary's face sank in a little deeper. "That," he said, "they feel is *our* job. And I can tell you, it's hell making contact with any of those people. I had a meeting with Suhrob Abdulin, one of their top men, just ten days ago. I'd hoped to find out where his headquarters were so I could get a technical officer out to bug them, but his security was just too damned good."

He described the setup for the meeting, and it did indeed sound daunting. He'd had to wait on a street corner for a car to pick him up; when the car arrived, the driver and a guard searched him in minute and embarrassing detail, including using electronic signal detectors. "It was a good thing I hadn't tried to plant a GPS tracker; they'd have found it for sure, and I'd probably be dead now." Crouched on the floor in the back of the car, a blanket over his head, he'd tried to keep track of directions and distances but had been completely lost after over an hour of apparently random driving around the city. He'd exited the car in front of a plain white bungalow that could have been in any lower middle class neighborhood. After a brief and unsatisfactory talk with Abdulin the whole thing with the car had been repeated and he was dropped off several miles from the original pickup location to find his own way home.

"This Abdulin, he's the head of the RLP?" Lensky asked.

"Was." If Gary looked any more tired, he'd be able to pass for a corpse. "He was arrested two days later; I guess the security wasn't quite good enough after all. Now we've got to make contact with a new man – I hear it's to be somebody who's been out of the country for a while. He may be returning to run as their candidate in the upcoming election."

"How does a banned political party get to run a candidate?" I asked.

Gary shook his head. "State has been leaning on Ergashi – oh, sorry, *Jamal* Ergashi, the old man's son—to let the RLP run openly against the PTK, the ruling party that is, the Party of Taklanistan. Told him his regime will have more legitimacy if he is seen to have won a fair and free election. You can judge how well that's gone over by the fact that Abdulin was arrested and has now disappeared."

"*Would* Jamal Ergashi win a fair and free election?" Brad asked. "Or is that an irrelevant question?"

"State hasn't given up on the project yet. As long as Ergashi's people control the polling stations, I think he can count on 'winning.' The US official position is that a show of leniency now will pay him back in more international support afterwards, and that he doesn't really risk anything by lightening up on the opposition. That's probably true; they'll make sure that something happens to the ballot boxes in neighborhoods where the vote might go against Ergashi."

All that lovely food had helped me wake up for a while, but now I was beginning to sag again. Ben, however looked as if somebody had lit him up from inside. As soon as I excused myself from the table, leaving Brad and Gary to their spook talk, he followed me to the bedroom Brad and I had chosen.

"Go away." I yawned. "I'm tired. Go call Annelise – Why isn't she with you, by the way? Still bugging the Berliners? Can she even do that without your help?"

"It's too dangerous here," Ben said. "I wouldn't let her come."

I blinked at that. I hadn't thought anybody in the world could be more overprotective than Brad, and yet *I* was here.

"You're a technical agent," Ben said impatiently, sitting down on the bed while I put stuff in drawers. "*I'm* a technical agent. It's our job to be here. Annelise didn't sign on for any of this spook stuff."

"Technical agent? Is that what they've decided to call us?"

He lay back on the bed, hands locked behind his head, and bounced gently. "Pretty good mattress you guys have. Better than mine... They're still debating what title to give us."

"Oh well, if we're picking titles I'm voting for Wonder Woman."

"Doesn't work for me."

"Don't be sexist."

"Don't distract me, Thalia. Don't you see, this is a perfect chance to show the Company how valuable we can be. When Gary makes contact with this new RLP guy, I'll ride along to the meeting. Then I'll be able to teleport back and bug the house!"

I had to admit that was a pretty good idea, but I thought he could go chat with Gary about it and leave me alone. I wanted to get between the sheets of that bed and wait for Brad or sleep, whichever happened first. Ben was in the way, so I chased him out of the room before digging out my nightgown.

# 12. Varieties of sudden death

For once, Brad was happy about an idea for utilizing our paranormal skills. All right, mostly he was happy about the fact that Ben, not I, would be the logical choice to accompany him into danger. He rubbed that in a bit too much, in my opinion. "Face it, Thalia, these fanatics have no respect for women. Whoever the new guy is, you can be sure he would not understand my dragging a girl along to a serious political meeting. Remember how the al-Shabaab prisoners and defectors in Mogadishu wouldn't talk to you? Same kind of situation here. You're just going to have to sit back and let us handle it."

What I remembered about Mogadishu was that after the local CIA office refused to let me sit in on interrogations, I'd gone off and talked to another mere female and had gleaned more useful information than all of Brad's and Ben's formal interrogations had produced. I would have loved to pull the same trick again, but didn't see much chance of it. Meeting the terrorist leader's ex-wife in Mogadishu had been pure dumb luck; there hadn't been any clever moves I could repeat. Too, this was a different situation. We weren't trying to rescue hostages, just keeping back channels open for political discussions with both sides of what might yet turn into a civil war.

The only useful thing I could think to do while we waited was to fill in Ben on what I'd learned in Paris about the Ergashi regime and its opposition. We had found a good place to hang out, the Moskva Chaikhana. It had a dark but comfortable interior with patterned felt blankets decorating the walls and shining, unused samovars in niches. It was just a few blocks down Kalot Rushan from our apartment, at the intersection with Akbaital Street. We'd learned that they didn't mind us sitting by a window and enjoying the panorama of the commercial district for as long as we liked, as long as we kept ordering tea and pastries. I was happy to order plenty of snacks to go with the tea; they had these little fried dumplings with spiced mutton, flat bread pockets stuffed with fried onions, honeyed puff pastry full of ground pistachios, braided strips of dough deep-fried and covered with powdered sugar…

"I'm going to have to do more teleporting to burn off all these calories," I said happily on the day that I discovered they had a version of *pilita* (those last things I mentioned, the deep-fried dough braids) that came dunked in melted chocolate.

"Mm-hmm." The Moskva Chaikhana's great attraction for Ben was its excellent wi-fi. He would have been happy to move in there just so he could Skype with Annelise 24/7. Sadly for him, the place was only open fourteen hours a day, and some of those hours overlapped with night in Berlin. Now he reluctantly broke off the connection so that Annelise could get something done besides chatting with him. "You can't teleport to and from here. It'd upset the locals."

"I know that. Maybe I can get Brad to take me out into the country some time so I can teleport back. I'm getting twitchy with nothing to do." I sighed and signaled the waiter for another little cup of tea to wash down the chocolate thingies.

"So, you can brief me some more on the Religious Liberation Party."

Somewhere around the crowded tables in the back, a head snapped around. Slightly too late, Ben lowered his voice.

"I think I've already told you everything I found out in Paris," I said. "They don't like the regime's persecution of Muslims, arbitrary closing of schools that try to educate Muslims, ditto closing of mosques. And Gary Shields has confirmed that all those things really are happening."

"Um. He has a slightly different take on it, though."

"Well, he would, wouldn't he? The State Department has already decided that we're aligned with the incumbent government. The regime claims all the dirty tricks they're pulling are anti-terrorism measures, so naturally that's what Gary calls them. But it looks an awful lot like religious persecution to Hor—to the guy I talked to in Paris." I'd decided it would be better not to use his name outside of the apartment.

"Looks like that to me too," Ben agreed, "but why isn't the regime also persecuting Christians?"

"There aren't that many? *I* don't know. I have a feeling, though, that if you-know-who hadn't been assassinated, they would have been next on his list. Remember what Gary told us, just before the assassination he issued a decree that media outlets had to refer to him by his official title."

Ben grinned. "And it was a mouthful. How did it go again?"

I picked up my phone and tapped in the search term. "'The Founder of Peace and National Unity, Leader of the Nation, President of the Republic of Taklanistan, His Excellency Jahandar Ergashi.' Sounds like a personality cult on its way to becoming a state religion, doesn't it?"

"Gotta admit… Is the son going after the same title?"

"Not yet. But then, he hasn't been elected yet. Or simply named President. I'm not sure which he's planning on."

"Neither," said Ben, "is anybody else. Isn't that why we're here?"

"Theoretically, but nobody's asked us to bug the Presidential Palace yet."

"And I'm happy they haven't. Remember what Gary said about the Presidential Guard being trigger-happy? The last thing I want is to surprise some nervous eighteen-year-old with a machine gun while I'm watching a technical officer install bugs in that place."

"Well, we're safe for a while. They don't even have any tech officers here; they'll have to fly somebody in." I stuffed the phone back in my right front pocket. I was experimenting with keeping it in proximity to my collection of magic-enhancing stars, hoping that the little guys would be inspired to do some battery-enhancing magic that would spare me having to plug the thing into a charger every night – in a country where, just to make matters worse, electricity was off as much as it was on. So far the stars didn't seem to have gotten the idea. I would probably have to think of some topological analogy to persuade them to transfer power. "And I'll tell you what, Ben, I'm not nearly as sure as the State Department that Jamal Ergashi *should* be elected. Religious persecution, arresting the opposition, collaborating in a *de facto* Russian occupation of the border... Just because he *says* he wants to stop the drug trade doesn't seem like enough reason to support the Ergashi dynasty over an opposing party that's all about improving education and infrastructure."

Ben nodded slowly. "All right. Given what you've told me so far, I don't like it much more than you do. But what do you want to do about it? Take our marbles – or stars – and go home?"

"Not yet." I propped my chin on my hands and scowled at the table top. "We just got here. Let's see what happens next."

What happened next was a tumult of running steps in the street, a crackle of gunfire, shouts and screams. Our glass-topped table beside the window suddenly seemed like a very undesirable piece of real estate. I dropped a handful of ergashis on the table. (Yes, that's what the currency was called. See what I mean about a personality cult?) Ben and I retreated to the back of the café. The unisex bathroom was empty; we ducked in there, closed but didn't lock the door, and used Brouwer teleportation to return to the apartment.

"Ah, there you are," Brad said when we appeared in the living room. "I meant to tell you two, don't go out today, things are heating up in the streets."

"We noticed." He was being remarkably calm about my having just been in close proximity to a riot; perhaps he was getting used to the idea. I enjoyed that notion very briefly before he returned to his telephone conversation. He was speaking English, so either it was an overseas call or he was talking to Gary or somebody else at the embassy. And he was hunched over the phone and murmuring into it, so it was something he didn't want us to overhear. Ben flopped down on the cushioned bamboo frame we were using as a couch, pulled out his own phone and started reading. I headed for the kitchen, banged my hip at the usual spot where a corner of that blasted table stuck out – I was developing a permanent bruise there – and got myself a bottle of water. I didn't really need it, but it was an excuse to sit down at the table where I might be able to hear something.

Lensky gave us both a dirty look and retreated into our bedroom, closing the door behind him. So much for eavesdropping – and so much, too, for his newfound calmness about my activities. He was simply too absorbed in whatever he was doing to take time out for yelling at me.

When he rejoined us, a few minutes later, he certainly looked as if he'd like to yell at me. He didn't say anything about the riot, though. It turned out that something completely different was bothering him.

"Gary says that his agent's reports have been confirmed." Now he looked less angry and more like somebody who'd just bitten into a lemon. When he was expecting a nice, soft, ripe apricot.

"About?" I sipped water and regretted having left the Moskva Chaikhana so precipitately. The contents of the refrigerator suggested we were having beer and beer for lunch, with beer for dessert. I could have ordered a couple of plates of those spiced mutton dumplings and those onion triangle pies, and picked up some late melons at the market...

"The identity of the RLP candidate. He's being brought in from Paris."

I almost dropped my water bottle. "Brad! Not..."

"Yeah," he said sourly. "Your old buddy, Hormuz Rakhim."

I started to grin. "*Really*. And is Gary going to meet with him? Or are you? Either way—"

"Yes, I figured that out already," Lensky said, and the lemon-sucking look got even more pronounced. "You get to come with me instead of Ben, because that's more plausible. We were having trouble figuring out how to account for one of us wanting to bring Ben along. If I take you to the meeting, it's easy. My wife wants to renew her acquaintance with an old friend from Paris."

"See, it really was for the best that I met with him at the Hotel Eiffel, even if you were slightly annoyed with me at the time!" I was all but bouncing on my chair. So much for his sexist assumption that no RLP leader would bother talking to a mere female! Hormuz had already found me worth talking to! "Now I'm the one topologist that you have a perfect excuse for bringing to the meeting! When is it going to be?"

Lensky rolled his eyes. "Anybody would think you were looking forward to seeing the man again, Thalia!"

"Why shouldn't I? Our last encounter was perfectly pleasant and civilized." I was beyond pleased by this turn of events. Now Lensky would talk to Hormuz for himself, and hopefully he'd get over his prejudiced view of the man and his party. Everything I learned about Taklanistan made me think that Hormuz and the RLP offered the country a brighter future than the repressive government of the PTK. Now I had a shot at changing other people's minds, starting with my husband's. I couldn't wait for him to enjoy the same kind of calm, civilized, enlightened discussion that I'd had with Hormuz Rakhim.

A dark flame flickered into existence, growing and taking a familiar form. "I am glad to see your husband grows wise enough to use the power of women, little pet. You will extract concessions from this man that he can only dream of."

Well, I'd already learned that she didn't need a bottle to follow me around and interfere with my life. "Shut up, TheSila. Talking like that will only change his mind."

"Hmmph! What mind? We are speaking of a man." But thank goodness, after getting huffy she dematerialized again, before Brad had time to worry about her hyper-sexualized views.

"Remind me to save the next bottle of wine we empty," he grumbled. "That Oriental sex maniac needs to be *contained*."

"Yes, well, good luck with that project."

I had to admit that the process of getting to the meeting was anything but calm and civilized. We followed the lengthy protocol Gary had described, beginning with being picked up on a street corner, searched in *very* uncivilized detail, and shoved down into the back of a car under a blanket. Only this time, the hour-long meandering ride around the city was enlivened at its beginning by machine-gun fire, squealing tires, turns so fast I thought the car was going to spin out, and bone-rattling abrupt stops. That night Brad said that I had nothing to complain about; *he* had gone through the same thing with the added disadvantage of being at the bottom of the heap on the car floor, and had I ever noticed how sharp my elbows were?

"I guess Mom was right," I told him in response to that last complaint.

"About what?"

I heaved a mournful sigh. "She warned me that romance would fade after our wedding day. There was a time when you wouldn't have complained about having me lying on top of you."

"Ah, that would have been a time when I was in a position to make the most of the situation," he said, gathering me in his arms, "rather than in the extremely cramped circumstances of our recent experience. Let me demonstrate…"

But that pleasant interlude was still in the future when we made our ungraceful exits from the car, and Brad's mind was more on the fact that I'd accidentally planted a foot on his ribs while extricating myself from the back seat and the blanket.

This time we were in front of one of the hideous grey towers of apartments put up by the Soviets during their time of control over the capital. Any numbers that might have helped identify the building had either fallen off long ago or had been removed by security-conscious RLP members, as had the street sign.

While our driver urged me into the building with the butt of his gun, I reflected that it was a good thing that the only GPS system we'd brought with us resided between my ears. Because we weren't exactly being received as trusted, honored guests, were we? That aborted shoot-out at the start of the ride had clearly made as much of an impression on the driver and his buddy as it had on me.

The two Taklans showed us the door to the stairwell.

"Twelve floor," one of them said in broken English, and I groaned. Silently.

Oh, there were elevators, but they weren't working; from the rusty look of their little birdcage compartments, they might not have functioned since the collapse of the Soviet Union.

I wasn't totally surprised when Brad told me quietly, on the interminable climb to the twelfth floor, that the front-seat conversation had been in Taklan and that it was mostly a debate on whether to just kill us and dump us in the river rather than even risk taking us to see Hormuz. They thought we might have leaked our meeting plans to the government and enabled the trap that so nearly got all of us killed.

"Why didn't they kill us?"

"Two reasons." Brad had that lemon-sucking expression again. "The river is inconveniently far across town."

"And?"

"And," he said, very reluctantly indeed, "they thought Rakhim might be unhappy if you were killed before he got another chance to see you."

I really am a nice person; I didn't gloat when he admitted that my presence for this meeting just might have been what saved both our lives. Well, I didn't gloat explicitly or out loud, anyway.

I had to save my breath for climbing stairs.

The building seemed to be little more than a collection of metal boxes, stacked way too high. "I wonder how this place would fare in an earthquake?" Brad speculated somewhere around the eighth floor.

"Why?"

"Taklanistan, especially the bit around the capital, is notoriously earthquake-prone," he informed me. "There's a reason why none of the older buildings are more than three stories high."

Oh.

Given that we were headed for the twelfth floor of a very shoddily constructed apartment building, I rather wished Brad hadn't brought the subject up. Now I could add earthquake collapse to the varieties of sudden death this meeting offered, right after being killed by the government or being killed by our escorts.

You can see why I was reassured by the warmth of our reception, once we made it up all the flights of stairs to the apartment Hormuz was using.

"Miss Kostis, what a pleasure to see you again! Don't tell me the State Department has transferred such a lovely young intern to my poor, war-torn country?" He took both my hands and nodded to our escort over my shoulder. "Latifi, Rasulov, you can wait downstairs. I have no fear of our guests."

"Actually," I said, feeling slightly awkward, "it's Mrs. Lensky, not Miss

Kostis. And I wanted to go wherever my husband happened to be sent."

"Please, be seated. Allow me to offer you what poor hospitality I can."

The room was traditionally furnished, dominated by a knee-high table covered with embroidered cloths. Bowls of dried fruit and nuts were set out in the center; Hormuz indicated that we were supposed to sit on the edges of the table and help ourselves to the refreshments.

He favored Lensky with a nod and – after I reclaimed my hands – a brief handshake, but kept his attention on me. "At the time of our pleasant conversation in Paris I did not realize you were married, but I should have guessed as much. Even Americans are not so slow in matters of the heart as to leave so fair a flower unplucked for long." He darted a measuring look at my husband.

I could sense a nasty growl starting deep in Brad's throat, so I stepped on his foot. "We are both very happy to have the chance of another chat with you. Is it true that you plan to run against Jahandar Ergashi's son?" I took a dried apricot. It had a complex flavor, smoky and sweet.

"Insh'Allah," Hormuz said, placing his right hand on his heart and bowing slightly. "If there *are* elections, Allah may have a role for me to play in them. At present it seems more likely that the tyrant's son will seek to continue the tyranny unchecked. Does your country approve of that?"

"We do not," Brad said with a bit of a snap. "We are attempting to persuade Jamal Ergashi that his international standing will only be enhanced by his holding open elections as soon as possible."

Hormuz's lips curved very slightly. "Only if he wins."

I investigated a bowl of walnuts.

"Judging from the trap that almost killed us on the way here," Brad said, "he's planning to run unopposed. How do you propose to surface long enough to file your candidacy?"

"All will proceed as Allah wishes," Hormuz said. "If it is His will that I serve as president of Taklanistan, He will make the way clear before me. If not—" He spread his hands and shrugged. "Perhaps it is His will that I become another martyr to our cause. But please, I am a poor host. Mrs. Lensky, let us drink tea together, to celebrate your gracing my humble apartment with your lovely presence." He smiled at me, but his eyes slid sidewise to take in Brad's expression. He indicated a stack of small bowls without handles. I took one; he picked up a brass carafe and poured rich, sweet-smelling tea into my cup.

"I apologize for our drab surroundings," he said. "This is not exactly the Hotel-Spa Eiffel, where we spent such a pleasant hour together."

"What made it pleasant was the company and the conversation, not the furniture," I said over another incipient growl from Brad. "I hope you will be willing to share your vision for Taklanistan with my husband, who is in a much better position than I to advocate for your cause."

"Ah, yes," Hormuz said, rather more sharply than before, "we all know that in the Third World, your CIA decides who is to be the leader of a country! But I think they have already chosen Jamal Ergashi, have they not?"

Brad cleared his throat. "It is up to the people of Taklanistan to choose their leader. We only wish to make sure they have a chance to do so," he said. "I would be happy to hear your views… and plans."

There was nothing new to me in the political landscape Hormuz proceeded to describe – or, at least, tried to describe. Brad's questions and interruptions were just short of being openly rude.

"You claim to be the party for education, but isn't it true that the only schools your party has opened have been religious schools?"

Hormuz spread his hands and smiled sweetly. "What other type of school would you expect good Muslims to open? I am told that even in your own country, church-sponsored schools are tolerated, even encouraged."

I did not quite dig an elbow into my husband's ribs; he was seated just that little bit too far away from me. "He's got you there, Brad. My husband went to parochial school," I told Hormuz.

It was the same with other areas of discussion.

"Infrastructure investment? In what, specifically?"

"Our first priority will be the improvement of bridges and roads, to make trade easier."

"A good road network will certainly make life easier for the characters presently enabling drugs to flow from Afghanistan into Russia. Are they paying for it?"

"Brad, you sound like a prosecuting attorney."

"Shut up, Thalia."

"Do not be concerned for me, dear Miss – Mrs. Lensky." Hormuz patted my hand; Brad growled; I kicked him. "I can weather a few sharp questions from anybody who may have it in his power to help my country. American aid for our infrastructure projects, Mr. Lensky, would both expedite them tremendously and put to death the story that our party receives financing from drug traffickers."

When we were safely back at our own apartment – having been spared earthquakes – I got after Brad for being both hostile and persnickety with Hormuz Rakhim. "He's a good man, trying to do the best for his country, and it looks as if he is very likely going to get killed in the attempt. Did you *have* to be like that?"

"Like what? You mean, objecting to his oily flattery of *my wife*?"

"Oh, don't be silly. He didn't mean any of that, he was just teasing you."

"And you know that how?"

"Gaydar."

"Now *you're* being silly. His party has been demanding the death penalty for gays."

"He may be so deep in the closet he doesn't even know it himself. Or maybe he's asexual. But Brad, I *can* tell when a man is interested in me and when he isn't. And it's not just me, I don't think; it's women in general. I mean, Hormuz was so far from being interested that he was, like, in a different country. I bet your researchers can't dig up a single woman that he's ever been involved with."

"No, based on today it appears that he prefers to go after married women."

"No. He doesn't. He didn't. I don't know why he was trying to get a rise out of you, but trust me— you, not I, were the center of his attention today." I thought that over for a moment. "Maybe he's attracted to *you*."

Brad didn't think much of that theory. He changed the subject to complaining about all the bruises my knees and elbows had inflicted on him during those two long trips on the floor of a car, and, well, you already know how that discussion ended.

# 13. A civil war waiting to happen

While his wife slept, Kambiz Yuldashev labored over the wording of the most important letter he would ever write.

Physically, it was not impressive: a small rectangle of flimsy, yellowish paper which he filled with downward-slanting capital letters. He suspected the spelling was also not impressive, but he dared not take time to look up every word in his tiny Taklan-English phrasebook. Tahmina would not sleep forever, and for her own protection she must not know until later about the dangerous step he was taking.

His hands sweated so much that his first two attempts at a note started to dissolve before he was halfway through printing his message. Finally he thought of slipping a piece of newspaper over the water-soluble paper, and the third version began to take shape.

He had too much to convey, and too little space, and his English was not good. It would have been infinitely easier if he had been able to write in Taklan, or even in Russian. But the one man he had positively identified as a CIA officer, the one called Gary, was a typical American - ignorant of all languages except his own. And he dared not leave a message that would have to go through a translator. He knew, if the CIA did not, just how little their local translators could be trusted. Any information that passed through such a route would reach Rakhim before it reached the CIA. What happened to defectors from the RLP was well known. And what would happen to Tahmina, after the knock on their door revealed her husband's head in a plastic shopping bag?

Sweat dripped from Yuldashev's forehead, blurring two words on the flimsy water-soluble paper, but he ignored it. There was no time to print a fourth version... Blowing gently on the paper to dry it, he held it in the air and folded it very carefully once, twice, again and again, until it was as narrow as a cardboard match and hardly any thicker.

Tahmina was surprised, later that morning, when he offered to go marketing with her and help carry back the groceries. It was not men's work. But he was known to be foolishly uxorious with his young wife, and he hoped that the inevitable observers would only laugh at him rather than becoming suspicious.

They went to a market somewhat more distant than the one where Tahmina usually shopped. She was well trained; she did not question his statement that they would buy their food at the Sherozi Market today. The advantage of the Sherozi was that it was only one block from the blue-painted apartment building where the American lived.

He left Tahmina bargaining for a shoulder of lamb, with some loud comments about women and the time they wasted shopping, and announced that he would be back after he got a cup of tea. Hopefully that would be enough to confuse any watchers. He walked slowly out of the alley of the butchers' stalls, then more quickly around the back of the market and down Kalot Rushan Street. Halfway down the long second block he spotted the American's car. He slowed just for a moment as he passed it, just long enough to push the note into the crack between the door and the frame on the driver's side. Done!...

On the way back to the market, of course, he second-guessed himself. Should he have stuck his note under the windshield wiper, where it would have been sure to be seen? No, that was too obvious. If anybody had followed him, they could have collected the note before the American even knew it was there. He would just have to hope that the man had been decently trained by his agency – well enough trained to recognize the significance of a tiny folded paper falling out of the car when he opened the door.

On the outskirts of the market, before rejoining Tahmina, he purchased flowers. She would be inordinately pleased by the trivial gift, and the action would reinforce his image as a loyal member of the RLP who just happened to be soft in the head about his pretty little wife.

*** 

I didn't have to go back to Hormuz Rakhim's apartment immediately; as I've mentioned, the CIA presence in Taklanistan was so slight that they didn't even have a technical officer who could go with me to place a bug. Someone would be flown in, Gary told me. But he didn't know who, so it was a pleasant surprise when we picked up an old friend at the airport the next evening.

"Sheng! I thought they were going to keep you stuck in a basement somewhere, doing polygraphs!"

"I wish they had," Sheng grumbled. "You know the nice thing about basements in Langley? No bombs, no floods, no earthquakes, no civil wars. This isn't an upgrade from my previous punishment, Thalia. It is a downgrade."

"Oh, don't be so gloomy. Taklanistan isn't in a civil war."

"Not yet. They did brief me. Martial law? Street riots being put down with massive government force? I know what the run-up to civil war smells like."

"Well, it hasn't got there yet. There haven't been any earthquakes, either. Look on the bright side, Sheng. The fruit is great: apricots, big black grapes, thirty-one flavors of melons. And I've discovered a tea house where they make the most amazing selection of pastries. Kind of a Central Asian version of dim sum. And you'll get to stay with us, in this romantic old apartment building with blue walls and yellow woodwork."

Sheng indicated that staying close to me wasn't one of his dreams, given that I'd been intimately involved in the debacle that got him into trouble in the first place. He was even less thrilled when he discovered that he was going to have to share a room with Ben.

"*Two* topologists they sent here? To this wide place in a camel track?"

"It'll be a short assignment," Lensky said. "We're just here to shepherd the country through a slightly tricky turning point."

"Oh, is that what they're calling a civil war these days?"

"Stop griping," I said, "or I won't tell you the best snacks to order at the Moskva Chaikhana."

For a change, we weren't going to hit Hormuz Rakhim's apartment at two in the morning. It wasn't large enough for us to count on bumbling around in the living-dining area without waking him up in the bedroom. Too, my Paris experience suggested that the man was a very light sleeper. And beyond all that, Brad was dead set against even the suggestion that I might teleport into the apartment when Rakhim was there.

"But if we don't bug it, how will we know when he goes out and it's safe to bug it?"

"You can teleport back to the street outside the apartment tonight. With me, not Sheng. I'll figure out what the street address would be if they hadn't torn down all the signs and numbers. Then Gary and I can take turns driving over there, parking outside and watching the building until Rakhim exits. Once he's well clear of the building, I'll call you. Then you and Sheng can place the bugs."

Okay, he'd worked it all out while I was telling Sheng about pastry. And it sounded reasonable... except for the part where Brad was staking out the apartment building for hours, all by himself.

"My *job*, Thalia!"

I grumbled but slowly subsided.

In the event, we didn't have that long to wait; two days after Sheng's arrival, Rakhim left the building and got on a crowded minibus headed towards the southern suburbs. Brad phoned me, then pulled out and followed the bus, hoping to learn more about Rakhim's activities as long as he had eyes on him.

Thanks to Brouwer teleportation, Sheng and I were able to get into Rakhim's apartment without trudging up twelve flights of stairs. Even that didn't make him happy; he griped that the usual approach to a target gave them the chance of checking the surrounding area for traps. What would we do if we were caught here? How did we know Rakhim hadn't given keys to this apartment to half a dozen trusted lieutenants?

"We don't," I admitted, "but seeing the man's life is in danger here, I have to think he's too paranoid to hand out keys at random."

Sheng, lying on his back under a low table, heaved a great sigh. "And I suppose if we are caught, we'll just have to use the standard emergency line."

"What would that be? 'The landlord told me this apartment had a plumbing problem?'"

"No. I prefer, 'I want to speak to someone at the American embassy.'"

I wasn't sure I did. I was tired of getting yelled at and shipped out of countries I'd barely seen.

"Only problem is," Sheng went on, squirming to get his elbow out of a tight corner, "given Rakhim's reputation, that line just might get our heads delivered to the embassy in plastic bags. Bodies to arrive later. So let's get this done and…"

"Shh!"

Oh, it was just my phone buzzing. Sheng was making me nervous. I turned the phone off; I'd catch up with Ben, or whoever it was, after we got out of the apartment.

A few minutes later he scooted out from under the table, stood up and groaned. "My *back*!" He put one hand on the small of his back and massaged it tenderly.

"Are we done here?"

"Almost. I just want to—"

There was the sound of a key in the lock. I grabbed Sheng's free hand and said, "*Brouwer.*"

"—test a couple of things," Sheng finished, standing in the living room of our apartment on the other side of town.

"Too late. Sit down. I'll be back in a minute."

I turned sideways and vanished, but only very briefly. A moment later I was back in our apartment for good, a bit dizzy from all the teleporting. I asked Sheng to get the sack of chocolate-covered *pilita* I'd brought back from the Moskva Tea House for emergency snacking. While he was rummaging around the pantry, I turned my phone back on and glanced at the history.

A call from Lensky.

Hmm.

*Five* calls from Lensky, beginning while we were still in Hormuz Rakhim's apartment.

Double hmm.

The phone rang. With a sense of foreboding, I answered.

"*Thalia!* Get out now!"

"We are out," I reassured him.

"Ahhh...."

Heavy breathing.

"Brad, it's all right, we didn't get caught, we're back at our own apartment. What's the panic?"

"When Rakhim finally got off the minibus... it wasn't him. It was somebody else with a fuzzy blond beard and round specs. He must have suspected something and set this up to shake me. I thought he was doubling back to the apartment. I thought he'd catch you! Why haven't you been answering your phone?"

Confessing that I'd ignored his calls wouldn't be a great idea, not while he was so excitable. I don't like to lie to Brad, but that doesn't mean one has to tell all the truth when doing so would cause unnecessary pain to one's fellow creatures. I settled for a truth that sounded like an explanation. "You warned me cell phone service was unreliable here."

"Oh, is that it? Well, thank god you didn't have to face Rakhim. You dodged a bullet there, Thalia. *We* dodged a bullet. Okay, I'll be back as soon as I can, something's holding up traffic here."

Minutes after he hung up, we heard dull booming noises and a threatening rattle from the general direction of downtown.

Ben surfaced from his bedroom, holding the Kindle he'd been reading on. "What was *that?*"

"Uh—bombs? Machine guns?" The noises reminded me of London during the Blitz, but they weren't precisely like anything I'd heard on that one night in the past. Which I couldn't very well discuss in front of Sheng. Teleportation made him skittish enough; add time travel, and he'd probably run away screaming.

"It sounded like tanks firing," Sheng said. "I told you this place was a civil war waiting to happen."

If Lensky had followed that minibus to the southern part of the city, this civil war was happening between him and the apartment. I nibbled my fingernails and tried not to scream at Ben and Sheng as they launched into a cheerful and ill-informed argument about precisely what weapons were being deployed out there. At least the boys were happy.

"Thalia, leave your fingernails alone, that's not going to do your blood sugar any good!" Ben interrupted his own argument to nag me. "Eat the *pilita*, that's what we got them for!"

I took an unthusiastic bite off the chocolate-covered end of one braid. It exploded into tiny crumbs that all but choked me. "They're stale."

"No, they aren't." Ben went into the kitchen, took a bottle of water out of the refrigerator and shoved it at me. "Wash the pastry down with this. You need to recover in case we have to do more teleporting in a hurry."

He was right. In an emergency, I had once found Lensky when he was across Austin in a location I'd never seen. More recently, with the help of a World War II buff, I'd found him in a foreign country and a different century. Given enough chocolate-covered *pilita*, maybe I could find him here in Merzadeh if he couldn't make it back to us. I dug in to the pastries with renewed interest.

Before I'd consumed even a third of the bag of pastry, though, I heard somebody coming up the stairs two at a time. I dropped the *pilita* I was holding and flew to the door.

It was Brad, unscathed as far as I could tell and practically ebullient. He reacted that way to being shot at and missed. And Gary followed him, taking the stairs one at a time like a normal human being.

After Brad wrapped his arms around me and spun me around a few times, we all settled in the living room for our refreshments of choice; beer for the guys, more *pilita* for me, and a wide-ranging if ill-informed discussion of what the outbreak of violence downtown portended. Gary downplayed it as a minor glitch on the way to the elections the State Department hoped to see; Sheng prognosticated that within the week Merzadeh would be a smoking ruin. Brad and Ben took intermediate positions.

In the short term, Gary appeared to be right; after that first day of fighting, a sullen peace ruled over the city and there were rumors that there really would be elections in a few weeks. There were no more clashes between demonstrators for the Religious Liberation Party and troops supporting the Ergashi dynasty. In the absence of more little chores for the CIA, Ben and I even resumed going out to the Moskva Chaikhana in the mornings.

# 14. Excuses for the devil

On a crisp blue and gold fall morning a couple of days after that little unpleasantness, Ben and I were about to head out for our regular midmorning pastry-and-tea stop when Gary Shields, lugging a bag full of equipment, stopped us on the landing. Sheng, similarly burdened, trudged up the steps behind him.

"I'm interviewing a Mr. Walker here today," Gary said, "and I'd like one of you to sit in on the interview."

"How come?" Ben wanted to know.

"Walker? Is he an American?" I asked.

Gary informed me that "Mr. Walker" was CIA code for a "walk-in" – somebody who, rather than having been recruited, turned up out of the blue asking to act as a CIA informant – and told Ben that checking the bona fides of such a would-be agent was always tricky and he felt he could use all the help he could get. They were meeting him at this apartment because the potential agent was afraid to come to the office, but as long as we were here, we might as well make ourselves useful.

"We aren't telepaths, you know," Ben warned him.

Gary shrugged. "All the same. Just watch and listen. Perhaps you'll think of some ways of checking his story that wouldn't be open to me."

It wasn't an unreasonable request; at least Gary showed a refreshing open-mindedness about the potential of applied topology. After I assured Ben that Merzadeh had been so quiet that I felt no nervousness at all about traversing the few blocks to the Moskva Chaikhana on my own, we agreed that he would stay to assist with the interview and I would bring back pastry for everybody.

That morning, Kalot Rushan Street was quieter than usual. The cheerful hubbub of the Sherozi Market seemed muted, there weren't quite as many boom boxes as usual making the air of nearby Akbaital Street hideous, and the few drivers on the street were demonstrating an attitude of peaceable accommodation that was downright un-Central Asian. I won't say I exactly missed the blare of horns, the screech of brakes, and the mid-street explosions of Taklan and Russian cursing. But I did note their absence.

For such a pretty day, the Moskva Chaikhana didn't seem to be doing the kind of business I would have expected. The pastries stacked on big brass plates behind the counter looked as if they'd been out since dawn. By ten o'clock the plates had usually been emptied and refilled at least twice. I dug in my pocket and fished out the tiny plastic-bound English-Taklan phrasebook that had been all the bookstore downtown could offer. It had its shortcomings, not least the fact that the Taklan phrases were printed in the Cyrillic alphabet, but at least I could look up "fresh" and point to the Cyrillic characters opposite that word while placing my order.

For once, though, I was in luck. The matriarch of the family, an old lady whose wrinkled cheeks and gray hair disguised a spirit of adventure that had seen her through the Russian occupation, the civil war, and the establishment of the current regime, was serving behind the counter herself. I'd discovered on an earlier visit that she spoke English, French, and Russian as well as Taklan.

"Madame Firozi, good morning!" I greeted her brightly. Ben would have been more polite, coming up with a Taklan greeting phrase. Aware of my limitations with foreign languages, I figured the politest thing *I* could do was to spare her my fumbling and mispronunciations.

"Thalia." She did not seem pleased to see me. I was slightly dashed; we'd been *very* good customers.

"I need to buy pastries to take back to my friends – *all* my friends," I emphasized, hoping to remind her that I might be small, but I represented a big order in take-out. I started mentally counting. Brad was off doing CIA stuff at their office, but at the apartment we had Ben, Gary, Sheng, and… should I count "Mr. Walker?" Oh well, why not? If he didn't want to stick around for coffee and *piliti*, the other guys would probably be happy to eat his share. Or Brad might come back.

"Come back here," Madame Firozi said, raising the hinged counter top and beckoning me back into the family's side of the restaurant.

"Oh, well, I don't want to…"

*Crash.*

My head whipped around and I saw a cloud of smoke in the street. The few customers who had been lounging near the front of the chai house had made themselves scarce, and two of Firozi's grandsons were lowering the flexible metal shades that went down when they locked up the place at night.

"… impose on you," I gasped, and whisked myself past the counter and into the corner chair she pointed at.

"Stupid American," she said. "Do you not know what it means when the streets are so quiet?"

"I am beginning to work it out," I told her. "I'm sorry, we don't have a lot of practice with this in America."

She sniffed and called out to her grandsons to hurry up. Her tone suggested to me that she was calling them a lot worse than 'stupid.' If I'd had my phone set to record, I'd probably have been able to come home with a copious library of Taklan insults.

Ah, that was assuming I was going to come home at all. At the moment, cowering as I was in a small, dark room that was protected by iron barriers, the chances of that didn't seem quite as good as I'd have liked. I couldn't figure out any way of departing inconspicuously. I could claim I needed to use the bathroom, which would certainly get me out of sight long enough to teleport home. Problem was, they were bound to notice when I didn't come back from a windowless room in a locked building. That kind of thing was strongly discouraged. The CIA didn't want us to inspire any speculation about our special abilities.

Once the place was locked down, Madame Firozi pulled out a second kitchen chair and sat down beside me, gently patting my hand. "Do not be afraid," she said. "I have seen armies marching through the streets and executions outside my front door. I lived through the shelling of Merzadeh in '91. This is nothing."

"I'm not –" Oh well, why pretend? Madame could see right through me. "It's pretty scary to me," I admitted.

"Lack of experience." She sniffed, and I got the feeling she thought the peacefulness of America was a bad thing, breeding soft people. She might have a point; I was feeling pretty damned soft right then.

Her grandsons went off to the kitchen, where they tuned an antique radio set to pick up broadcasts from who knew where. I thought I heard one announcer giving a play-by-play account of the battle – if that was what it was – in Russian, another one in Taklan, and yet a third station where I thought the guy was speaking some language I'd never heard until he broke off with, "Oh la la la la la la la!" just as if he were commenting on the World Cup finals from Paris.

French, then.

Very *rapid* French.

Not at all like Aunt Alesia's gentle flow of perfectly accented words.

Madame Firozi started telling me about all the times it had been worse in Taklanistan, beginning well before she herself was born in 1938. "Things get better," she told me. "No matter how black it seems, things always get better. You think this is bad, this little puff of a fight? When my grandmother was a young woman, the Bolsheviks conquered all of Taklanistan!"

"That must have been terrible."

She cackled. "It was, and it was not… Our *men* thought it was the end of the world. It was different for some of us women. Before the Russian revolution… My great-grandmother went blind at forty and her husband said it did not matter, because a decent woman never left the house anyway. My grandmother's older sister had already had a dozen children when the Bolsheviks took over. She was twenty-six and she looked like an old woman in the pictures I have seen. But my grandmother? She threw away her veil, went to the university, and met her husband before she married him. People say terrible things about the Bolsheviks, but Russia brought the women of this country into the modern world." She spat into the crumpled newspapers on the floor. "Now this RLP wants to bring back the old ways!"

"But – aren't *you* Muslim, Madame Firozi?" Or had I been getting the wrong message from her head scarf?

"Yes, but I am Ismaili," she said crisply. I would have to look that up when I got back; it was a flavor of Islam I hadn't heard of before. "*They* are Sunnis, and their leaders want to drag us back into the bad old times, and I hope Jamal Ergashi kills them all!"

"I don't think they're quite that bad," I protested.

She gave me a bright, amused glance. "No? Little American girl, do you even know evil when you see it?"

I didn't want to get into a political fight with my hostess. But I had to say something. "I have met Hormuz Rakhim. I think he wants the best for Taklanistan. I hope all people who truly want the good of Taklanistan can agree. *Without* trying to kill each other."

"Americans, Americans," Madame muttered, sounding disgusted. "They would make excuses for the devil himself."

We sat in a silence broken only by the sounds of war.

After those sounds diminished, then stopped altogether, Madame Firozi's grandsons rushed back into the room, talking a mile a minute. One of them ducked under the counter and went to the cranks that raised and lowered the shutters.

"They say the fighting is over… for today." Madame patted me on the shoulder. "Go home, little foreigner. Go home… to America!"

But she loaded me down with twice what I'd asked for in pastry, saying that I might as well take it for free as leave it to go stale. Only halfwits and Americans, she said caustically, would go out to a tea shop on a day like today!

She told one of the boys to walk me home. "You don't need to do that," I protested, but she was immovable. Oh, well; if I couldn't teleport, at least I'd get some exercise. Halfway there we met Brad, who ran to greet us, thanked Madame Firozi's grandson in Taklan, then switched to English to upbraid me. He had not been able to get back from the office until the fighting died down, and he'd suffered a nasty shock when he did reach the apartment only to discover that Ben and Gary had let me go out.

"It looked safe enough when I left the apartment," I said. I may have sounded just a bit sulky; I was tired of being told that I was a naïve fool who didn't understand the country. Who wanted to understand this country full of maniacs, anyway? "How did the interview with 'Mr. Walker' go?"

*\*\**

The interesting part, Ben told me when we got back, had been over while Lensky was still trapped downtown by the sporadic fighting.

Shortly after my departure, a haggard-looking, middle-aged Taklan man had tapped on the apartment door. Sheng had already taken over the dining table with his polygraph equipment; now he suggested that Ben and Gary make themselves scarce so as not to distract the subject.

"We went into my room, because it's the one with twin beds," Ben told me.

That was where we were seated now; Brad and Gary were in the living room having a serious, low-voiced conversation about the new sort-of agent.

"Gary was just explaining to me that the guy's beard meant he was probably telling the truth about belonging to the Religious Liberation Party. It was a serious chin fungus, must have taken well over a year to grow out to that length. I mean, he hadn't just stopped shaving yesterday in order to pass as a devout RLP member; that beard suggested he was the real thing."

"Why would he be so afraid of being seen talking to Americans?" I asked. "Hormuz met with us the other day, and he was all for having Americans understand his party platform better. I should think he'd be delighted to have 'Mr. Walker' visit us."

"*Kambiz yuldashev.*"

"Huh? Ben, I don't speak Taklan." And neither did he.

"That's his name," Ben repeated patiently, "Kambiz Yuldashev."

"Walker was easier to remember," I groused.

"Whatever. Don't you want to know about the polygraph?"

"I thought you had been shooed off to a back bedroom for that part."

"Doesn't matter," Ben said with a grin, "because it didn't happen."

He and Gary had barely finished their discussion of beards, Islam, Amish farmers, and responses to Western technology when the shooting started. The first explosion hadn't been all that close to the apartment—"

"I know *that*," I interrupted. "It was in the street right outside the Moskva Chaikhana. I saw the smoke!"

Ben waved a dismissive hand and talked right over my attempts to describe my own experiences. The second boom, he said, had shaken the windows of the apartment house. When it was succeeded by a rattle of machine-gun fire, Sheng abandoned his polygraphing and burst into the bedroom.

"That's it!" he shouted. "I'm through!"

Gary tried to calm him down. "Sheng, they're not using anything heavy enough to attack buildings. All this noise is aimed at discouraging people from gathering in the street. You're perfectly safe here."

"You don't get it," Sheng snapped. "I already had that guy hooked up when the shooting started. And he didn't react! I've seen more interesting squiggles generated by a corpse. How the fuck am I supposed to test somebody whose reactions say he's already clinically dead?"

He stomped back out to pack up his equipment, and Gary shrugged. "I dunno. I guess there've been enough minor skirmishes by now that the locals take a bit of street shooting in stride. Or maybe Yuldashev is more afraid of his friends in the RLP than he is of being shot. Not unreasonable," he allowed with another shrug.

"After that—"

"Ben, this doesn't make sense," I interrupted. "There's just nothing about the RLP to make anybody that nervous. This must be some kind of double or triple bluff."

Now it was Ben's turn to shrug. "Look, Thalia, you've met with Hormuz Rakhim—"

"Twice," I interjected.

"Twice," he allowed, "that still doesn't make you the CIA expert on the whole party. Hormuz may be the ineffectual charmer you've made him out to be, but we *know* some of his associates aren't all sweetness and light. You told me yourself that the guys who took you and Lensky to that second meeting were in two minds whether to kill you and toss you in the river instead of driving you to see Hormuz."

"That's what Brad told me later. They were speaking Taklan; I don't know what they really said."

"You think Lensky would lie to you?"

"No-o… but it was a tense situation. He could have missed some nuances. Anyway, Ergashi's people had just tried to kill all of us at the pickup place. It's understandable if they were a little rattled."

Ben sat up and fumbled under his bed.

"What are you looking for?"

"Something Lensky didn't want you to see, a couple of days ago. He thought it would upset you."

The crumbly, pale pink pages of the only newspaper still operating in Taklanistan were covered with screaming black headlines… in Taklan, naturally. In the Cyrillic alphabet, to boot. "Why? I can't read that… and neither can you."

"A picture," Ben said grimly, "is worth a thousand words… Here!"

He had folded the paper into quarters. A grainy photograph dominated the section he pushed at me.

I glanced down and looked away quickly, fighting the urge to throw up.

"Lensky translated the caption for me. Those are the bodies of Taklan soldiers who served at one of the outposts the Russians maintain to protect the Afghan border. They were captured and executed by the RLP for betraying Taklanistan by serving under Russians."

Even with my eyes closed, the image of headless bodies, hands bound behind their backs, was all too clear. I swallowed – hard. "I don't think I like Taklan press standards. At least in America that kind of picture wouldn't be front page material."

"No," Ben said, "you'd have to go looking for it on the Internet, wouldn't you? Thalia, you're missing the point. These are the kind of people your buddy Hormuz hangs out with. The ones that frighten Kambiz Yuldashev more than tanks firing in the street."

I sat down on the end of his bed. "I need to think."

But all the thinking in the world didn't help me to find conclusions in this array of conflicting evidence. It was like trying to prove a theorem without benefit of all the relevant axioms; I could go around in circles forever.

Had the picture been faked? I doubted that the *Taklan Inquirer*, or whatever the paper's name was, had a lot of employees who were experts in Photoshop. Anyway, those twisted, crumpled, pathetic bodies had looked incontrovertibly real.

*Someone* had done that.

"Ergashi isn't a savage," Brad's voice said in my memory, "he doesn't have his enemies beheaded."

But how could he know that for sure?

"I prefer my head attached to my shoulders," Hormuz Rakhim took over my memories, "and my heart beating within my chest."

I didn't believe Brad would have lied about the newspaper story. But the story itself could have been a lie.

At the end, I had to go with what I knew of my own personal experience.

I *knew,* as certainly as I knew that I could teleport into the next room, that Brad would not lie to me. And probably not to Ben either.

I *thought* that Hormuz Rakhim was a good man. Certainly I'd received only good treatment from him – even when I turned up in his hotel suite, trying to steal the rubies back. I owed it to him to keep an open mind.

And I *knew* – didn't I? – that the Ergashi regime lied about their dealings with the RLP.

I sighed and leaned back against Ben's shoulder. "Ben, it's too complicated here. Ferozi was right; we simple Americans aren't equipped to deal with this place. I want to go *home.*"

# 15. When in doubt, throw something

It turned out that Brad and Gary hadn't just been discussing Kambiz Yuldashev. Gary had persuaded Yuldashev to continue pretending to work with the RLP for the time being, gathering information about the party's plans which he could relay to them via dead drops. Yuldashev hadn't even wanted money; all he asked for, Gary said, was an assurance that the CIA would exfiltrate his wife Tahmina if he was caught.

"What about yourself?"

"By the time you know that I have been caught," Yuldashev said gloomily, "it will be too late for me." He added that he had wanted to disassociate himself from these murdering savages for some time; only his fears that their vengeance would fall on Tahmina had kept him in line. If the CIA could assure her safety, he would give them whatever aid he could.

"*Can* you assure her safety?" I asked.

Gary sighed. "We can try. Yuldashev is going to try to bring her to the embassy if he feels himself in imminent danger. Naturally, we'd prefer he doesn't do that too soon; he won't be much good as a source of information after that. We'll probably wind up exfiltrating both of them. I just hope we get enough good stuff from him, first, to make it worthwhile."

Once again, I wanted to go home. This cold balancing act between human lives and national interests was alien to me. Maybe I could bring up a textbook on my Kindle and lose myself for the rest of the day in the world of mathematics, where everything made sense and nothing was spattered with blood.

That plan was short-circuited by Brad. As I said – that intense discussion between him and Gary hadn't just been about the new agent. They had also been wondering why they weren't getting anything useful from the bug in Hormuz Rakhim's apartment.

"Oh, isn't it working?" I tried to keep my voice completely neutral. "Sheng, I'm surprised! I thought you were more competent than that."

"It's working," Gary growled. "I download the recordings to my phone twice a day. Would you like to know the contents of Rakhim's last grocery order? I've got it. Also some lively discussions with his cleaning woman about dust bunnies in the bedroom, and the entire broadcast of a Russian-dubbed version of *Star Wars: The Last Jedi*."

"I guess he doesn't have a very interesting life." But I couldn't keep the corners of my mouth from twitching. And Brad is extremely good at reading me.

"Come clean, Thalia. He's been warned not to discuss politics and strategy in that apartment, hasn't he? *What did you do?*"

Sheng's eyes narrowed. "When we teleported out of his apartment and back here, that day… You disappeared again, right after we got here safely. Oh, it was just for a second, I didn't see how it could matter…"

"You didn't want us to bug him, did you?" Brad pressed me. "You thought we should treat the bastard as an ally."

"I don't know what difference that makes," I said, sensing a loophole, "you people spy on our allies all the time. Remember, I'm the one who bugged the Israeli political officer's apartment in Paris for you. I'm the one who almost got my leg eaten off by that damned dog in the Egyptian cultural attaché's place."

"No, that was me," Sheng said. "I was between you and that monster. It would have gone for me first."

"Sheng, stay out of this!" Brad snapped. He advanced towards me, blue eyes flashing, and I took a step back. I just happened to notice that there was an empty vase cluttering the dining room table.

"I swear to God, I did not say one word to Hormuz Rakhim about you bugging his apartment!" I appealed to Sheng. "I wasn't gone long enough to have a conversation with him, was I?"

Sheng shook his head. Brad ignored him. "Not good enough, Thalia. You forget, I know you topologists. You can lie without ever saying an untrue word!"

"Just because I can outthink you doesn't make me a liar, dammit!" I grabbed the vase and threw it at his head. As long as I could throw things, I wouldn't have to lie to him.

Ben dodged; the vase bounced off the wall behind him and broke into three pieces. "Thalia, cut it out! *I* didn't do anything to you!"

"I'm not aiming at you," I said, "I'm aiming at *him*." For emphasis I sent a serving spoon spinning through the air at Lensky. It missed.

"I know, I know," Ben said. "And like always, the people you aren't aiming at are the ones in danger. I'd feel a lot safer if you'd just let me teach you how to throw properly."

"Your safety is not my major concern at the moment!" A water bottle just missed Lensky's ear before smashing against a wall and dousing the plaster.

"If you two could possibly cease this fascinating discussion of pitching and catching," Lensky said, quite mildly now, "Thalia and I still have something to settle here." His direct blue gaze transfixed me. "Let me guess. You didn't *say* a word, you weren't mysteriously absent long enough for a *conversation*... You wrote him a letter, didn't you, Thalia? You probably had it already written, but of course you couldn't leave it while Sheng was there with you."

My cheek itched; I scrubbed at it with one hand. "Why would I be writing letters to Hormuz?"

"To warn him," Brad said very softly, "that his apartment had been bugged by the CIA, and that he shouldn't say anything there that he wouldn't want half a dozen American officials to hear."

"What if I did?" I grasped the serving platter that dominated the center of the table. "You knew I didn't approve of spying on the one reasonable man we've talked to in this medieval hellhole, but you made me help you anyway! You can hardly blame me if I stood up for my own standards after you twisted my arm into betraying Hormuz!" The damn platter was too heavy to throw. I could barely lift it. Oh well, I was finding it hard to maintain my pose of righteous anger. Brad did have a point, after all. Maybe several points.

Brad fell into a chair on the far side of the table and put his head in his hands. "Thalia. That 'reasonable man' is a barbarian whose followers are terrified that their families will suffer if they defect, who orders his opposition beheaded. Ben, I think you need to show her that picture we didn't want her to see."

"I already did," Ben said. "It didn't help."

Having run out of things to throw, I took my own seat at the table. "It was a terrible picture," I said. "It proves that an atrocity was committed. But why should I believe that Hormuz Rakhim ordered it done?"

"Because that's what it said in the accompanying newspaper article?" Brad rubbed his own face. "I can translate it for you if you don't believe me."

"I believe that's what the newspaper said, sure. Would that be before or after they mentioned the Founder of Peace and National Unity, Leader of the Nation, President of the Republic of Taklanistan, His Excellency Jamal Ergashi?"

"It's state-run media," Gary said. "They were legally required to refer to the president that way."

"My point exactly. They were also, no doubt, required to slander the opposition party."

"And Jamal Ergashi hasn't assumed all his father's titles yet, so no, those phrases don't appear in that particular article." That was Brad.

"Irrelevant. I believe we've established that you can't believe the newspaper: it's in the business of repeating whatever propaganda the regime is pushing."

Gary sighed. "I wish you'd stayed here to talk to Kambiz Yuldashev. He doesn't share your roseate view of that murdering bastard."

"Ah, precisely which murdering bastard would that be? Ergashi or Rakhim?"

I thought it was a fair question under the circumstances, but the guys all rolled their eyes at me.

"Thalia," Brad said quietly, "we need to have a serious talk."

Sheng, Ben and Gary announced their intention of going out to get food, and offered to bring some back for Brad and me. The cowards practically trampled one another, each trying not to be the last one out of the apartment. That really wasn't necessary. Brad and I had got past the part of the argument where things tended to go flying through the air. It wasn't his anger that worried me now; it was the sadness in his face.

"I hate that I'm always making you unhappy with me," I said after the sound of the guys' exodus had died away. It was the closest I could bring myself to an apology.

"Yeah. Me too." Brad ran a hand through his hair. "Thalia, would it kill you to just do what the Company requests once in a while, without injecting your personal beliefs into the job? I know you think Hormuz Rakhim is a great liberal reformer, practically the second coming of Kemal Atatürk."

"Who?"

"Oh… never mind. I also know you're wrong about Rakhim, but I'd just as soon not have that fight now. I want you to think seriously about why we are here – why *you* are here – and why we should both keep our personal opinions out of the job."

That sounded much more reasonable than it really was. "The problem is," I said, "the job and your personal opinions are perfectly aligned. You really believe the best thing for Taklanistan is for the Ergashi dynasty to continue running the country, trampling on human rights, killing opposition leaders, creating a personality cult. Or else you believe it's so important to stop the flow of drugs coming over the Afghan border that whatever damage the regime does to its own citizens is… what? Collateral damage? Unimportant?"

"Thalia, that's a very harsh way of saying it."

"Show me what I got wrong?"

He got up and walked around the table, slowly, until he stood behind me and could rest his hands on my shoulders. "You're all tense and knotted up. Doesn't it hurt to keep your hands twisted together like that?"

It did, but I hadn't been aware of it until the gentle, warm pressure of his fingers encouraged the tense muscles to relax.

"We don't always have the luxury of supporting a perfect liberal-democratic regime," he said while his palms made warm, relaxing circles against my back. "I know you think Hormuz Rakhim represents that kind of future for Taklanistan, Thalia, but… well. I did say I wouldn't get back into that fight. But look, nobody in the CIA, nobody in the State Department, is thrilled about having Jamal Ergashi automatically succeed his father. The kind of truly fair elections we have in the West aren't even an option here, though."

"I suppose you're going to say Taklanistan isn't ready for democracy? That's the excuse you people usually dredge up for supporting dictators, isn't it?"

"Thalia. I'm not 'you people.' I'm your husband. And yes, I would say that Taklanistan is nowhere near ready for a true democracy. Both the major political parties regard ballot boxes as things to be stuffed or destroyed, not as tools to discover the will of the voters. These people have achieved amazing things in a very short period, they've recovered from years of Soviet domination followed by a devastating war and they are on their way to building a strong civil society. But they need time – time to develop the social structures that support democracy. An educated citizenry, an independent judiciary, a police force that doesn't take bribes, political representatives who aren't corrupt… Chaos won't help anything. They need *not* to have to fight a war over their border with Afghanistan, they need *not* to be plunged back into a civil war between the two principal parties. And for now, a peaceful transition of power from Jahandar Ergashi to his son is the best way to buy them time to build a stronger society."

"Unless Jamal Ergashi completes what his father started, and turns Taklanistan into a totalitarian dictatorship."

Brad began running his fingers through my hair. "Thalia, if you're willing to learn more, I'll bring you all the recent CIA reports on Taklanistan. I think they will convince you that if Rakhim's party seizes power, the country is in for a civil war that will make the last one look like a walk in the park, a war that will leave them completely vulnerable to Chinese aggression, Russian aggression, hell, *Afghan* aggression… Taklanistan doesn't exactly have the luxury of being in a good neighborhood. But for now, I just wish you would agree not to go off on your own trying to negate whatever the Company achieves here."

That sounded reasonable... perhaps deceptively reasonable. Brad's impromptu neck and scalp massage was releasing all the tension I'd collected throughout the day, and his calm words were reminding me that there were usually two or more sides to every question.

"People say terrible things about the Bolsheviks, but Russia brought this country into the modern world," Madame Ferozi's voice sounded in my memory.

"What?"

I realized that I'd spoken aloud. "Something the old lady at the chai house said today. Even she isn't old enough to remember Taklanistan before the Soviet Union, but there were family stories. She thought the Bolsheviks had been good for women's rights here. Two sides to every question."

"Progress comes slowly," Brad mused, "three steps forward, two back... Not unlike our relationship, Thalia. Do you think... maybe we could try doing things differently? Talking before acting?"

"Does that work both ways?"

"What do you mean?"

"One reason I don't tell you what I'm thinking of doing is that you don't discuss it with me. You're just all, 'No! I forbid it! You can't do that!' Why would I talk to somebody who never listens?"

"Am I really that bad?"

He sounded hurt.

"I didn't say you were bad... just... disinclined to listen to different opinions?"

He chuckled. "Pot calling the kettle black?" He slipped a finger under my chin, tilted my face up and leaned down to kiss me. "Perhaps we can both try to do more talking and less shouting past each other."

I leaned back against him. "It's a radical idea, but it just might work. OK, if you'll listen when we have differences, and don't just shout me down, I won't do anything without consulting you. But can I keep trying to persuade you to give Hormuz Rakhim a fair hearing?"

"You can try."

That was all I asked, for now. And it was enough for us to cease hostilities with another kiss, and maybe a bit more than that.

When the guys came tramping back upstairs with their boxes of food, Brad shouted at them through the bedroom door to put whatever they didn't eat in the refrigerator. We'd investigate it later.

# 16. The Lake Shaimak Threat

I spent much of the next day lounging on our bed, dipping into the stack of printouts Brad had brought over from the office first thing in the morning. There weren't any sounds of tanks or machine guns outside today, but I was in placate-Brad mode. If we were actually going to achieve adult conversation about serious topics, I didn't want to tease him by going out to places he thought dangerous. And after the previous day's fighting, he seemed to feel that way about every part of Merzadeh outside our apartment door.

That couldn't go on, of course. I might argue with him about it after a couple more peaceful days had passed, because I had no intention of letting him put me under house arrest for the duration of our time here. But yesterday had been quite draining, what with one thing and another. As long as our tiny refrigerator kept the bottles of water cool, and Ben or somebody else brought in fruit and pastry and those little balls of ground meat with almonds, I could handle being a lady of leisure for a day or two.

Well, one day, anyway.

Probably.

The stuff he most wanted me to read, about all the awful things Hormuz Rakhim and the RLP had supposedly done, was too depressing to spend much time on. Particularly when Brad wasn't around to be asked exactly what sources the CIA had for these stories and why I should believe that they weren't just propaganda put out by the Ergashi regime.

He wasn't around to grumble that I was cheating by avoiding the information I didn't want, either. I flipped through the printouts until a familiar name caught my eye. I looked at the title: *CIA Technical Paper R-312: The Lake Shaimak Threat*. Would that be as in, the Shaimak Rubies? Below the title was a picture of a beautiful, calm mountain lake that didn't look threatening at all. On the next few pages aerial photos and topographical maps showed the long, complex outline of the lake, like a long blue dragon lying among the high mountains in the eastern part of the country.

As I read, though, the lake's resemblance to a dragon grew sharper and clearer. And not a nice, friendly, sexy dragon like the one in the last fantasy novel I read – which had come perilously close to dragon porn – but a traditional dragon. The kind with claws and teeth and a bad habit of sweeping down the valley with flame breath, destroying all before it.

"That's not a bad description of Lake Shaimak's potential for disaster," Gary said when I brought up the subject over dinner. He confirmed that the studies I'd been reading were serious stuff, not newspaper scaremongering. Lake Shaimak had been created over a hundred years ago when a 7.0 earthquake sent a massive landslide into what had been a mountain pass, creating a natural dam sixty meters high. Not only the village of Shaimak but the entire valley in which it lay were flooded, creating the present dragon-shaped lake with a volume of nearly twenty cubic kilometers. At the same time – probably because of the same earthquake, though geologists' reports were ambiguous – the only entrances to the Shaimak ruby mines had collapsed.

Topology, my mathematical specialty, doesn't use a lot of numbers apart from zero, one, and infinity. I blinked and registered these numbers as "Dam is too high," and "Lake is *way* too big."

The problem was not just that another earthquake could destroy the dam and release a catastrophic flash flood (see: sweeping down the valley with flame breath, above.) The first earthquake had left a very large rock mass in not very stable equilibrium towering over the edge of the lake. Three cubic kilometers of rock, Gary said. In my measuring system, that was, "Rock is also way too big."

Even a minor earthquake in the wrong place could tip that rock mass into the lake, creating a displacement wave that would spill over the top of the dam. And since the dam was basically just a big chunk of dirt (okay, a very *big* chunk of dirt) civil engineers feared that the spillover would proceed to erode the dam and send all twenty cubic kilometers of the lake crashing downstream, taking out a large part of central Taklanistan and killing millions of people.

"Why doesn't somebody do something about it?" I asked after the guys got through wallowing in their visions of death and destruction.

Gary gave me a sour look. "So what would *you* do? They can't blow up the rock mass; that might start the very sequence they're afraid of. This government is doing the exact same thing every other government of Taklanistan has done since the original earthquake: hoping nothing changes. Even the Soviets didn't have the nerve to try and destroy the Dragon of Shaimak."

"That's what they call the rock pile?"

"Appropriate, don't you think?"

Brad patted my hand. "Don't worry, Thalia. It's been stable for over a century, you know. And even if the dam did collapse, the flooding wouldn't reach as far as Merzadeh. I think."

After dinner, Brad grabbed one of the empty beer bottles Gary was collecting. "Hold on, I might have a use for this one... and this one too... oh, why don't you just leave all the empties? I'll take out the ones I don't use later." He rinsed the bottles in the sink and lined them up along the dining table, then started pulling little packages wrapped in twists of newspaper out of his pockets.

"Phew!" Ben complained as Brad opened the first one. "Take the stink pots to your own room, can't you?"

"Now, Ben," Brad said. "We agreed this was the best way to handle the problem."

"To handle what problem?"

They ignored me. Ben had overcome his first objections and was helping Brad open packets and crumble the contents into empty beer bottles. After they'd loaded four bottles with bits from the four packages, they started mixing and matching and cackling to themselves.

"Mink in Heat mixed with Honey Jasmine!" Ben said of one combination with a sickeningly sweet smell and a musky undertone.

They were mixing Pineapple Essence with Tomcat Supreme, or so they said, when the object of this exercise undulated into the room and I suddenly got what they were up to. TheSila swayed over to the table and bent over the loaded beer bottles, taking deep breaths. "This one!" she announced, sticking her nose into the third special mix the guys had prepared. "You may give me more of this perfume, little pets; it pleases me."

"Sadly, we have no more," Brad said. "I dropped it all inside the bottle, and my clumsy fingers can't reach in to retrieve it."

TheSila might be an extremely powerful supernatural being, but nobody ever said she was *smart*. Sneering at Brad for his human limitations, she became an attenuated shape of dark flame and poured herself into the bottle. Brad whipped a cork out of his pocket and jammed it into the neck of the bottle. "Gotcha!" he gloated. "Ben, where's the sealing wax?"

Ben produced a stick of dark red wax and a cigarette lighter. Holding it over the cork, he coated the entire neck of the bottle and the protruding cork with melted wax. He would have left wax spots all over the table, too, if I hadn't caught them with *CIA Technical Paper R-312: The Lake Shaimak Threat*.

Brad took the wax-covered bottle and set it on top of a kitchen cabinet. "One nuisance out of the way!" he said, dusting his hands.

"How long were you two planning this little trap?" I asked.

"We only thought of it last night," Ben told me. "We spent an hour in the Sherozi Market this morning, collecting the stinkiest perfumes they had."

Brad eyed me warily. "You're not mad, are you, Thalia? I thought that oversexed djinn irritated you almost as much as she did me!"

I laughed. "Possibly more. No, I'm not mad. Except…"

"Except?"

"You're not thinking of trying anything like that on Mr. M., are you? He can be annoying too, but he's my *friend*."

Brad assured me that he had far too much respect for Mr. M., my friendship with him, Mr. M.'s brains and his capacity for revenging himself on people who tried to trick him, to contemplate anything of the sort. I relaxed. "There's just one thing, then…"

"What?"

I pointed up to where he'd stashed the bottle. "In an earthquake-prone city, do you really want to store TheSila's bottle on a high shelf?"

Brad colored, retrieved the bottle, and took it off to our bedroom to find a safer spot.

***

Three days later, when Merzadeh was almost calm enough for Brad to be okay with my taking a walk around the block, Gary Shields plunged into the apartment in mid-morning. "Where's Lensky?"

He grabbed Brad's arm. "I need you. *Right away.*"

"What's the rush?" Brad said equably. We'd been enjoying a late breakfast. There wasn't any shooting outside. Ben had even gone down to the Moskva Chaikhana to Skype with his girlfriend.

"It's Republic of Taklanistan Freedom from Russian Occupation Day."

"They do like long names, don't they?" I observed.

Gary gave me a frantic glance. "That's irrelevant, Thalia. The important thing is, everybody in Merzadeh has the day off and half of them want to use it to make trouble. Yuldashev told me that Hormuz Rakhim is leading a huge protest rally towards Independence Square, demanding a date be set for elections. And my agent inside the Presidential Palace just sent me a warning that Jamal Ergashi plans to have the Presidential Guard arrest Hormuz and the other ringleaders."

"On what pretext?" Brad asked.

"Inciting to violence. Leading a banned political party. Breathing while opposed to the Ergashi regime. Pick one. The point is, the remaining embassy staff – including the ambassador – are too chicken to go to Independence Square. It's on you and me to make Ergashi see reason. We can tell him that international observers will never certify the elections if he arrests the opposition's leader. Or kills him."

Still seated at the massive dining table, I crumbled a bit of pastry between my fingers. "Wouldn't it be simpler to warn Hormuz Rakhim to stay away from the rally?"

"Wouldn't work," Gary said impatiently. "According to Yuldashev, this whole thing was his idea. I think the man's bent on becoming the latest martyr to his cause."

Actually, Rakhim's intentions were quite different, but of course we didn't find that out until later.

"Besides," Gary added, "he's already left his apartment. He'll be surrounded by a crowd of supporters. No, our best chance of stopping this thing is to go directly to Ergashi."

Lensky looked at my frown and at the growing mound of pastry crumbs beneath my hands. "Okay, Gary, go wait in the car. I'll be down in a minute."

"I still think—" I began after we heard Gary on the stairs.

"I know," Lensky interrupted. "You think that Hormuz Rakhim is a reasonable man, you think he likes you, you think you can persuade him to call off this rally. Thalia, even if all that were true, it's too late to stop this thing! By now, Akbaital Street will be filled with protestors marching on Independence Square – and believe me, no matter what you may think of Rakhim personally, his supporters are not nice people. You can't reason with a crowd of riled-up fanatics."

"It still seems wrong to let him march to his death." Because I didn't think Jamal Ergashi would stop at arresting Hormuz. Even if he wasn't killed at the rally, after being arrested he would disappear like the previous leader of the RLP, Suhrob Abdulin. And if there were fanatics among his supporters, wasn't that all the more reason to preserve the life of a reasonable man who would discourage the extremists?

None of those arguments moved Brad, and he was in too much of a hurry for the kind of calm, logical discussion he'd promised the other day.

"Thalia, you're thinking of teleporting right into this disaster-in-the-making to warn the man, aren't you?"

I had promised not to lie to him or to go off without telling him, and *I* keep my promises. "It's the logical thing to do."

"Well, I can't let you." He took my arm in a firm grip.

"You *promised*—"

"Yes, but this is an emergency. My first priority has to be keeping you safe. We can talk all you want after I get back." He reached into his pocket and pulled out something metallic.

"Where did you get those?" I stared at the handcuffs.

"Technical supplies from the office."

Silly me, I'd always assumed that 'technical supplies' meant bugs and disguises and fake papers.

With quick, deft movements, Brad clapped one of the handcuffs on my wrist, slid the short chain joining them behind a table leg, and cuffed my other wrist. I couldn't believe it.

"You rat! You *bastard*! All the time you were talking about reasonable discussions, you were planning this!"

"Only," Brad said, with that extreme calm that descends upon him in emergencies, "if you insisted on being unreasonable. You can call me all the names you want when I get back. At least I can go into this with peace of mind, knowing you'll be safe in spite of your reckless notions."

And he was gone, galloping downstairs while I stared alternately at the closing door and at the handcuffs.

Could I overturn the table and slip the cuffs under the leg, to be free even if still cuffed?

No way. I couldn't even begin to lift it. The thing was a massive slab of wood that had been in the way ever since we moved into the apartment. Despite bruises and frequent curses, even the guys hadn't attempted moving it out of the way. And I certainly didn't have the strength to teleport something that heavy along with me – not to mention that I did not really wish to materialize in Independence Square attached to a dining room table. I drooped in my chair, considered my options, and deeply regretted not having spent more time studying Ben's way with locks.

Maybe I could still free myself topologically, even if I had been concentrating on playing cards and coin tosses while Ben systematically studied the structures of various kinds of locks. The locks on a pair of handcuffs couldn't be very complicated, could they? I closed my eyes and visualized a bar holding – something or other – in place. Mentally moved the whole contraption into a non-metric space and pushed on the bar.

And pushed.

And reminded the bar that topologically it was *not* part of a closed curve. It was just jammed up against something else such that the two pieces together had a superficial resemblance to a closed curve.

If only I could reach my stars! Brad had moved too quickly for me to reach into my jeans pocket, even if I'd realized what his traitorous, promise-breaking, rat-fink intentions had been.

A surge of angry energy accompanied that thought. I felt something shift inside the lock. Sweat beaded my forehead, and—

No, I couldn't wipe it away. The cuffs were still locked.

I couldn't even get at a pastry to give myself a little extra energy.

I heard feet on the stairs; had Brad realized his mistake and returned?

No such luck. It was only Ben, returning from the Moskva Chaikhana with a paper bag that, judging from the smell, held some of those fried dumplings filled with spiced ground mutton.

"Ben! Give me one of those! No, never mind that." Why waste time refueling? He could do this much better than I could. "Get me out of these things!" I jingled the handcuffs against the table leg.

"How did you get in such a fix?"

"Brad and I had a small disagreement. Can you open the cuffs? My shoulders are hurting," I added, trying to look little and pathetic. Well, the 'little' part wasn't hard.

"Let me have a look." Ben dropped the sack of dumplings on the table and slid down to the floor. There were a few minutes of uncomfortable closeness, with his head on my lap, and then there was a sharp metallic click and I could move my left hand.

"Bring your hands up to the table so I can do the other one without being a contortionist," Ben suggested. I laid my handcuffed right wrist, decorated with a short chain and a dangling open cuff, on the table top while he squeezed and wriggled his way out from underneath.

This one took longer. Ben swore under his breath, reached into a pocket for his own stars and set them to dancing around the lock.

"What's the problem?" I asked. I was beginning to think of teleporting without waiting for him to get the thing off my wrist. But I'd really prefer not to do that; this wasn't the kind of bracelet I felt like sporting in public.

"Oh, some idiot bent the—" and he used a technical term I didn't recognize. It didn't matter; I was pretty sure I knew who the idiot had been. I flushed, Ben squeezed his eyes shut, and the right-hand cuff opened with a screech of protest.

"Mind telling me *why* Lensky cuffed you to the table?" Ben asked before cramming a mutton dumpling into his mouth to recoup his energy.

"I told you. Minor difference of opinion."

"Yeah, right. Come clean. Where did you want to teleport yourself to this time?"

I quickly filled him in on the emergency of the day.

"Sounds to me like he was right," Ben said. "Independence Square isn't going to be a healthy neighborhood today."

"I don't care, I have to try. I can't just lounge here eating dumplings while the only reasonable man in Taklanistan gets 'disappeared' into one of the president's dungeons!"

"He's not that reasonable," Ben said. "Kambiz Yuldashev said—"

"You sound just like Brad, that traitorous rat fink son of a bitch. I don't have time to have this argument again!"

Ben looked mournfully at the twisted opening of the right-hand cuff. "If these things weren't broken, I'd consider cuffing you myself. Okay, let's go."

His sudden about-face confused me. "Huh?"

"I can't talk you out of this," he said impatiently, "and I certainly can't let you go alone." He took my hand. "What's our destination? How about the steps in front of the Culture of Taklanistan museum? At least there we'll be above the crowd and able to see what's happening."

It would have been a good idea if we hadn't landed ourselves on the bottom step.

# 17. Hostages

While I had been stuck in the apartment, the protestors had had time to reach and fill Independence Square. I couldn't see over the heads of the men surging angrily in front of me, shouting slogans in Taklan interspersed cries of with "Allahu akbar! Allahu akbar!" At first, all I could take in were isolated details. There were posters waving above the crowd here and there, but I couldn't read what they said. The crowd surged and eddied, as though those in front weren't nearly as interested in moving forward as were those behind them. And that made sense, because there were also people moving on the steps of the Presidential Palace: soldiers whose red caps and crisp green uniforms contrasted sharply with the everyday tunics and trousers of the shouting men in the square. Most of these men in the square, I did notice, sported serious, full beards. Evidently Jahandar Ergashi's shave-the-fundamentalists program hadn't been quite as far-reaching as Hormuz had led me to believe.

"C'mon!" Ben tugged my arm and I backed up, getting a couple of steps higher where I could see a little more. There was Hormuz Rakhim's curly blond beard, right out in the forefront of the protestors. There was the Presidential Guard, lining up at the top of the steps into the Presidential Palace, carrying arms that looked like cannon from my perspective. There was Jamal Ergashi himself, standing on a balcony facing the square, dressed in a scarlet and green uniform like his guards. Only his uniform glittered with gold braid and medals.

And there was my husband, standing beside Ergashi and saying something, I couldn't make out what over the roar of the crowd; I could only see his lips moving. Gary was on Brad's other side. As I watched, he grabbed Brad's arm and pointed downwards at the soldiers on the steps.

The Presidential Guard were raising their weapons.

Brad fell silent.

So did the crowd.

"Ben, we have to stop this!"

"Shut up!"

He still had a firm hold of my arm.

I could see Hormuz Rakhim clearly. He wasn't more than thirty paces away from us, but the space between us was solidly filled with protestors.

That didn't matter, of course; not when I could actually see where I was going.

"*Brouwer!*"

Ben, taken by surprise, didn't let go in time. He teleported with me.

There was, I realized tardily, one little problem with the clear patch of pavement I'd teleported to.

It was between Hormuz Rakhim and the Presidential Guard.

I wanted to save Rakhim, but not by throwing my body between him and the bullets.

Fortunately, there was an alternative.

"You can't stay here," I panted at Rakhim, "they'll kill you!" And I grabbed his arm.

At the same time, Ben yelped in surprise and I felt somebody behind me wrapping an arm around my waist.

"Ben – just don't fight me, okay? *Brouwer*," I said again, and I made a picture of the pavement outside Merzadeh Airport against my closed eyelids.

We arrived at the airport in a staggering, untidy heap: me, Ben, Hormuz Rakhim and no less than three of his buddies. These guys sure were grabby. No wonder I was dizzy; the effort of teleporting all these people had sucked out my energy. I reached for Ben, wanting to lean on him, but hands behind me pulled me away from him and somebody twisted my arm up behind my back. I saw Ben struggling in the grasp of two bearded men.

"Hormuz, we're trying to help you!" I gasped. "You can get a plane, get out of the country from here."

"Oh, yes. You will certainly help me," Rakhim said quietly, and his voice no longer had that warm aura of decency and good will that had always reassured me before.

"You can leave Ben and me here," I said, "we're not in danger."

"Oh, yes, you are." The jerk who was twisting my arm pushed me forward, and from the corner of my eye I saw Ben being manhandled in the same direction. I felt the hard, cold pressure of a gun against my neck.

There was a small plane on the runway, just beginning to move. At first I thought Hormuz had gone totally crazy and meant to throw all of us – and himself – under its wheels. But then one of the men who'd been holding Ben ran towards the plane shouting something in Taklan and pointing a gun, and the wheels stopped moving. A moment later a door near the back of the plane opened, and metal stairs descended.

Flimsy-looking ones.

"Let the girl come up first," a man shouted from the open door of the plane. In English.

Hormuz laughed and answered him. "She comes last! You take us all, or she dies – and her friend too."

I twisted against the hands gripping me, and achieved nothing more than a stabbing pain up my arm that made me sick and even more dizzy than the effort of teleporting had done. By the time my vision cleared, I was being pushed up the steps and into the plane. I could just see Ben ahead of me.

And Hormuz Rakhim.

And two white-faced tourists in trekking gear, pressed back into their seats.

Rakhim was talking, angry, and there was a gun in his hand. "You take off now!"

The man in the pilot's seat shook his head. "What are you going to do if I don't cooperate? Shoot me?"

"No," said Rakhim, "I will shoot *him*." He jerked his head at the man sitting beside the pilot. One of Rakhim's buddies moved forward, resting his hands on that man's shoulder.

"You can't do this! We are a civilized country now, the police will arrest you!"

Hormuz Rakhim laughed, sounding relaxed and genuinely amused. "Oh, they have tried that already." Without changing expression, he raised his pistol and fired at the co-pilot's head. There was a sickening spray of red and white stuff suddenly covering the side of the plane up there, and the co-pilot's body – and what remained of his head – slumped sideways in the chair.

Somewhere behind me, a woman screamed briefly.

"Messy," said Rakhim. "I should prefer not to have to do this again. It makes the interior of the plane so unpleasant." He said something in Taklan to the man who'd been holding the co-pilot down. His buddy grasped the body by the upper arms and dragged it back down the aisle past us, then tossed it through the open door at the rear.

Another barked command, and the door slowly closed.

"I recommend that our new passengers take their seats," Rakhim said, still in that light, gently amused tone. "It would be a shame if anyone were to be hurt... accidentally."

Ben pushed me into an empty seat, then sat beside me. His hands worked busily over our seat belts. I sat, useless, staring at the monster whom I'd risked our lives to save. One of Rakhim's buddies took the seat that had been occupied by the co-pilot; he did not seem troubled by the spatter of blood and brains slowly drying on the panel beside him.

"My friend here does not speak English," Rakhim said, "but he can read an instrument panel. If you attempt to warn the controllers, or make any deviation from my instructions, he will tell me and I will shoot..." He studied the pilot carefully. "No, you need all your limbs, do you not? But I believe you could still fly this airplane without a few of your fingers, and it will be less untidy to have Jalil here simply cut them off. It will be better for both of us, don't you think, if you fly very carefully and I am not required to take such drastic measures? Let us all be reasonable men, here, and no one need be hurt." He turned his head to survey the white-faced passengers, including Ben and me. "Do not be afraid," he advised us. "Your lives guarantee my departure in safety, that is all. Afterwards you will be freed – if you are sensible, and make no trouble now."

With Rakhim's other two buddies smiling and fingering their pistols, none of us were inclined to move or speak. We sat in frozen silence while the plane took off and whisked us away. We were heading towards mountains, I could tell that much, but it wasn't much use: in these parts, there were mountains in almost any direction you pointed. I knew, because of the pilot's complaints, that Rakhim was insisting he fly much lower than he considered safe.

"Under the radar," Ben murmured in my ear, the sound of his words covered by the noise of the plane.

So much for the hope that the air controllers would track and rescue us. My only hope now was that Rakhim had been telling the truth about releasing everybody as soon as he was safely away.

No. There was another, and better hope. I wondered if Ben had seen anything. "Did you see what happened to Brad and Gary?" I murmured, scarcely moving my lips.

"They should be all right. They were right up there with the President."

"I know, but—"

"And the President was protected by his guard." Ben grinned at me. It clearly wasn't easy for him to do, but I appreciated the effort. "What's the matter, Thalia? Are you *worried* about the 'traitorous rat fink son of a bitch'?"

"Not in the least," I lied firmly. "He always comes out on top." I rubbed my cheek with one hand. "I just want to be sure he's in condition to rescue us, that's all."

One of the guys with pistols objected to our conversation then, and we lapsed back into unhappy silence.

*** 

"*No,*" Lensky said, leaning over the Defense Minister's desk. "You are *not* going to shoot that plane down. What part of 'There are hostages on board,'" did you not understand?"

The Defense Minister made some statements about Taklanistan, sovereignty, and air space.

"*American* hostages," Lensky growled.

"Speaking for the American ambassador," Gary put in, "it would be most distressing should the amity between the United States and Taklanistan be shattered by an unwise response to the present crisis."

"Shattered?"

"Smashed into tinkling smithereens," Lensky amplified. "Not to mention the distinct possibility of war."

The Defense Minister threw up his hands. "To tell the truth," he said, "our tracking systems are having some difficulty following that plane. It keeps appearing and disappearing on the radar. Probably flying low to the ground wherever possible, they tell me… I do not think that shooting it down would be technically possible."

"Good," said Lensky. His shoulders relaxed imperceptibly. "Good that you understand that you aren't going to shoot it down, that is. Not so great about the radar. I need you to track it as closely as possible."

The Defense Minister shrugged again. "Maybe America would like to give us a better radar system?"

He heaved a sigh of relief, and wiped his forehead, when the two crazy Americans left the building to go harass the trackers at the airport.

"Do you think they were really speaking for the ambassador?" one of his aides asked.

He spread his hands. "Who knows? If I have just failed to capture Rakhim when I could have done so, Jamal Ergashi will have me shot – but Rakhim couldn't have been on that plane, he didn't have time to get there from Independence Square, so maybe I will live. If I'm responsible for a diplomatic breach with America, he will have me shot. And if shooting that plane down causes the Americans to go to war with us, they will flatten Taklanistan and we will all be dead." With so many possibilities for disaster, he felt that the safest thing to do was nothing. He looked at the aide. "Start writing a memorandum about the inability of our air tracking systems to follow small planes flying at low altitudes. Put it in terms of the difficulty of stopping the drug trade. And date it… oh, some time last spring."

He wondered exactly what a smithereen was.

"Do we even know that our people are on that plane?" Gary asked after they were out of the building and well away from any possible bugs.

"It's the only thing that makes sense," Lensky said.

The news that a pilot had been killed execution-style and his body dumped from a small plane had focused their attention away from the protests and toward the airport. What little they'd learned certainly suggested that Thalia and Ben were among the hostages on the plane.

"I saw the two of them in Independence Square," Lensky said, enumerating their data points on his fingers. "Idiots. What were they trying to do, get shot by the Presidential Guard? Then they disappeared, and so did Hormuz Rakhim and two, maybe three men standing beside him. The Taklans have no explanation for that, but *we* know that either Thalia or Ben could have pulled off that disappearing act.

"Minutes later at the airport, a small plane that was preparing to take off stopped, opened its door, and took on a number of passengers; the people at the airport weren't clear about how many people there were or what they looked like. Then the copilot's body was thrown out onto the airstrip and the plane took off, but it didn't follow the flight plan that had been filed. The Taklans say it couldn't have been carrying Hormuz Rakhim because there was no way he could have gotten from Independence Square that quickly, practically instantaneously – but again, *we* know how that could have been done. The speed and the cold-blooded style are typical of Rakhim.

"Finally, the pilot's one communication with Air Control confirmed that he was carrying armed men and hostages." Lensky relaxed imperceptibly at that point. "I have to say one thing for the Taklans, they have codes for both contingencies." Although it might be a black mark against the country that they needed codes like that.

"It's too bad they didn't have enough of a code to tell us how many of each were on board," Gary said. "Then we'd know for sure—"

"There is nowhere else they could be," Lensky interrupted. He blinked and tried to put out of his head a nightmare vision of Thalia and Ben lying dead in a ditch somewhere between Merzadeh and the airport, executed like the copilot. That was logically impossible; Thalia had to have been alive to teleport all of them to the airport, and since she wasn't at the airport now, she had to be on the small plane that Rakhim had commandeered.

The back of his head was not amenable to logic.

"Well, in any case," Gary said, "when the pilot filed his flight plan, he said he was ferrying two American trekkers and a guide to Darvoza to meet up with one of those tourist treks into the mountains, and taking an American woman and her child to join her husband at the border crossing post in Lairon. So we know for sure the hostages include one Taklan and four Americans."

"Six Americans," Lensky said. "Thalia and Ben are on that plane. And we are going to find it."

When they arrived back at the airport, the controllers were waving their hands and shouting at each other in Russian. Lensky ground his teeth. He could pick out just enough Russian words to gather that they were exchanging blame for some disaster.

"What are they saying?" he practically begged Gary.

Shields shook his head. "I'm no good with languages."

"Russian damn well ought to be a requirement for anybody who's stationed here," Lensky snarled.

Gary decided not to ask whether the requirement should have applied to Lensky as well as to himself.

Within a few minutes, the airport authorities produced a balding middle-aged man who spoke authoritatively to the controllers in Taklan and stopped the screamfest. Moments later, a young man with curly hair hurried up, introduced himself as an interpreter, and summarized the substance of the controllers' information. Before they lost track of the plane – and started blaming each other – it had been observed to slow down and level off somewhere approximately fifty miles east of the capital. They could not pinpoint an exact location, but some more bullying from the controllers' boss and an intense session over a topographical map of Taklanistan resulted in a wobbly, ill-defined circle drawn over an area that included part of the road from the capital to a town called Jirgatal.

"Good, get us a car," Lensky said.

Then the ground began to shake under their feet.

# 18. Playing tag with the mountains

After less than fifteen minutes, maybe ten, the plane began to descend and, sooner than I'd expected, made a bumpy landing. I thought the pilot had taken more time to take off and land than he'd spent flying. That was a relief, and not only because the short flight had involved a series of sudden turns and changes in altitude that had inspired one of the trekkers sitting across the aisle to vomit into his hat. (Paper air sickness bags were not among the amenities of this plane.)

No, better than that, we couldn't be that far from the capital. And Rakhim was unruffled, so this had to be his destination. If we were to be released here, I could call Brad and reassure him before he got crazy. Too crazy. I didn't think he would be exactly calm even now.

To everybody's intense disappointment, Rakhim ordered us to stay on board with our seat belts fastened. He didn't trouble to inform us that the plane was going to take off again with us still captive, but I deduced that from his order. One of his goons took the trekker's hat and threw it outside with a remark that had to mean, "I'm not flying any farther with that stench."

That guy then trained his pistol on us, while Rakhim still held the pilot at gunpoint. Not the best circumstances to attempt an escape; Ben and I would have to unfasten our seat belts to teleport back to Merzadeh, and that would give this bastard plenty of time to shoot at least one of us. And what would they do to the other hostages?

The woman who'd screamed was sobbing quietly behind me. While our captors were busy loading something onto the plane and refueling it, I took the opportunity to twist around in my seat and get a look at her.

It was another *oh shit* moment: there was a toddler on her lap. I remembered the cavalier attitude Omar al-Zanji had taken towards his child hostages – particularly the threat of executing them if we didn't call off the rescue attempt – and felt almost sick enough to throw up, myself. Between fear and the picture of the co-pilot's shattered head, which would probably remain etched on my brain for the rest of my life, I had a hard time restraining that urge.

The fact that, unlike the trekker, I didn't have a hat to vomit into probably helped even more than the knowledge that it would make me miserable, show weakness in front of these bastards, and help nobody.

Sitting beside the young mother was a beardless Taklan man. Probably not allied with the others, since he wasn't wearing a face fungus to show off his piety. *Good.* (I was having a really hard time finding good things about our present situation, especially now that it appeared we weren't to be released here. Wherever 'here' was.) The man was patting the baby's back and crooning a little song in some foreign language, probably Taklan or Russian.

I stuck a hand between Ben's seat and mine. "Hi," I said. "I'm Thalia Lensky." Lame. Couldn't I come up with anything more encouraging? The mother was probably going to cry even harder once she realized how useless Ben and I were.

"Are they going to kill us next?"

"I don't think so. They could have done that at Merzadeh Airport if they'd wanted to." Oh, great, Thalia. Reassure the woman by telling her our captors could be even worse. "I think we're hostages. They'll keep us alive and probably take pretty good care of us; we are their best chance of getting away." I rubbed my cheek. I didn't completely believe that myself. But at least she stopped sobbing.

"Do you really think so? – Oh," she said, before I had to answer that question with more reassuring half-truths, "I'm Penny Nicholson. And this is my son Ryan. We're going – we were going to join my husband at the border post in Lairon."

"I am Koshan Idrisov," said the young man beside her. In English, thank God. "I was supposed to guide these two –" he jerked his chin towards the trekkers seated across the aisle "—to meet up with the Lakes of the Pamirs trek. We were going to disembark at Darvoza. That is the only other real airport in Taklanistan, you know?"

Penny nodded. "I was supposed to get a ride in a jeep from there to Lairon. Oh, *Jim*—" She sniffed and her eyes filled with tears.

Koshan patted her hand. "Now, now. We may still be freed at Darvoza. These small airplanes do not have very much fuel, I think. Our captors will have to go far to be out of reach of the army, and they may not wish to use up fuel to carry our weight past Darvoza." And even more weight was being loaded now, in the form of smallish boxes that the terrorists lifted and set down with grunts of effort suggesting that the boxes were indeed filled with something heavy. Like books. I didn't think.

"Oh, do you really think so?" Penny Nicholson said again.

"It seems very likely," said the trekking guide. His eyes met mine, and I could tell that he was thinking the same thing I was. They could as easily dispose of the extra weight, and at less risk, by killing us and throwing our bodies out of the plane.

The plane's engines roared to life again, and the two goons sat down quickly at the back. The takeoff was so short that I gripped the armrests of my seat. It felt like we were rising at a forty-five degree angle. Was this plane, with all its extra cargo, able to take off so sharply?

A glance out the window explained it, sort of. The so-called runway where we had landed and taken off was a frighteningly short strip of asphalt. The tall, pale grasses at the end of the asphalt strip were bowed to the ground; the pilot must have taken off at the last possible moment. I breathed a short prayer of thanks for the skill of the pilot.

I don't remember exactly how long we were in the airplane for this second trip; I was too busy, alternately distracting little Ryan (who was *through* sitting on his mother's lap, and made his displeasure so clear that I was afraid one of the goons would be irritated enough to shut him up) and trying to control my stomach and the urge to scream as the plane zigzagged through those barren mountains that I'd admired – when looking at pictures of them. When the window showed those mountains so close that I was afraid the wings of the plane would brush against them, they didn't look nearly so beautiful.

At least we were allowed to talk now; the goons had stretched their legs out and were trying to sleep, although hands still resting on their guns were a warning against attempting anything. In any case, I don't think any of us thought that starting a fight in a small plane that was playing tag with mountains would be a good idea.

As we got farther into the mountains, the plane rose higher and we became unhappily aware that the cabin was unpressurized. Ben and one of the trekkers complained of headaches, and the trekker said he felt nauseated.

"Try not to throw up," his companion and I said simultaneously.

"Think of something else," Koshan advised. "And do you happen to have any energy bars in your packs? It might help to nibble on one."

The trekker – really, it was absurd that we hadn't even exchanged names yet – rummaged in the pack at his feet and came up with a colorfully wrapped fruit bar. Without the wrapper it looked much less attractive, a brownish stick with a rough texture, but he broke off half of it and nibbled a minuscule bite at a time and started to look much better. He offered the other half to Penny, who encouraged Ryan to gnaw on it. This had a wonderful effect in calming the kid and led to a sociable exchange of names. I learned that our companions were George and Tommy. They had chartered the plane because they'd been too late for the start of the trek they'd signed up for. They had hoped to get to Darvoza ahead of the others and wait for the group there. As for Koshan, he was being flown out to meet the same party, to replace a guide who had fallen ill and returned to the capital.

"How long do you think until we reach Darvoza?" I asked Koshan.

He looked unhappy. "Darvoza… is not in the high mountains. Also it is north-east of Merzadeh, and we are traveling east only." He glanced behind him, at the mystery boxes that had been loaded at our previous stop, and looked even more unhappy. For fear of upsetting Penny again, I decided not to press him. He might, after all, simply have been bummed out by the prospect of losing the paying job he would have picked up in Darvoza.

Tommy, the trekker who'd thrown up on the first flight, provided a distraction by going through his own pack and pulling out a wool shirt which he offered to Penny. She wrapped up Ryan and Koshan took the toddler on his lap for a bit of a change. Now warm, and chewing (and dribbling) on the piece of fruit bar, he was cheerful again and I think we all felt happier for looking at him.

I wouldn't have minded having that warm, wriggling little body on my own lap for comfort, but it would have been foolish to disturb him when he was so happy with Koshan. Besides, I reminded myself, the dribbling was reaching epic proportions, and I really didn't need to get my shirt soaked with baby drool. I had a feeling it might be some time before I got a change of clothes.

When the plane started to descend again, I made the mistake of looking down. All I could see was snow and rocks. We got closer to the ground, and now all I could see was rocks. This wasn't airplane territory! It wasn't even *helicopter* territory.

I heard a sharp click behind me and twisted around to find that Koshan had unfastened his seat belt. I started to ask if he'd lost his mind and then saw what he was doing: pulling out the belt so that he could put it around Ryan as well. "These little ones are so light, they can bounce around the cabin in a rough landing," he said quietly.

*That* rough it was going to be?

Oh, yes. I didn't even have time to dial up the panic a notch when we slammed into rocks, bounced into the air again, hit more rocks and came to a shuddering halt approximately eighteen inches from the mountain cliff that reared up in front of us. A door flew open; the sound of metal twisting filled the cabin, and there was a stink of burning rubber.

Ryan began to wail. He also contributed a stink of his own to the air inside the cabin.

"You *bastard*," our pilot said bitterly to Rakhim. "I had a half share in this airplane."

Rakhim shrugged. "Now your partner will have a full share of the wreck," he said, smiling, and shot the pilot.

# 19. A broken city

First the ground shook, then it seemed to swoop in a sickening curve, and then things began falling.

Large, heavy things.

Like walls.

Like ceiling tiles.

Like pieces of the roof.

Lensky shook his head, half blinded by the dust that the collapsing roof had raised. Where was Gary? He'd been standing right there…

Where there was, now, a jagged piece of roof and a spreading red stain.

*No.*

He plunged forward, got his hands on the roof fragment and heaved. Nothing moved. He put his head back and bellowed, "*Help!* I need some help here! There's a man trapped!"

A moment later he remembered how to say it in Farsi.

Then he tried Polish. It should be close enough to Russian…

Something worked. A pair of gloved hands slid under the fragment, next to his. On his other side, a man in a sweaty blue shirt hissed with effort. Slowly, slowly they levered up the fragment…

"Can you hold it?" Lensky demanded, first in English, then in Farsi; then, as his mind started working again, in the local dialect.

"*Taklan. It's a language, not a dialect,*" Gary's voice said in his memory as he dove under the trembling fragment, found Gary's arms and pulled him out. There was blood, too much blood.

"Where?" he demanded as his helpers let the roof fragment crash down again.

"Just my head," Gary said with a twisted grin. "Too hard to damage. You know how scalp wounds bleed."

His face was half white with plaster dust. The other half was nearly as white. And when he tried to stand up, his right leg buckled under him and he collapsed. Lensky felt along the leg; just below the knee there was an unnatural swelling, and when he pushed on it ever so lightly Gary screamed.

"Ambulance! I need an ambulance!"

So did far too many others, many of them hurt worse than Gary.

They made the jolting ride to the hospital in a rusted-out sedan belonging to the man in the blue shirt. Lensky never did find out his name.

In a hallway filled with gurneys, a white-coated man cut off Gary's pants leg to reveal what looked like a very bad break, took Gary's pulse, and said, "Not an emergency. He can have some pain medication. A doctor will set that when he has time. It may be some time; do not let him move that leg."

The man who drove them to the hospital had scooped up his sport coat and thrown it over Gary when he started to shiver. Now, when someone brought blankets for Gary, Lensky retrieved his coat, slipped it on and buttoned it up so that he looked at least halfway respectable. Looked like someone that doctors would listen to. At least it covered up the Glock on his hip.

It didn't help. Everybody was working desperately on more serious cases, people who wouldn't make it if they didn't get treatment right now.

Time crawled. Gary made lame jokes, then fell silent. Suddenly his eyes flew open. "*Yuldashev,*" he said.

"Huh?"

"Kambiz Yuldashev. I was to meet him this afternoon. You'll have to go."

"I don't have time. Thalia—"

"The radar guys don't know where the plane landed. Yuldashev might know where Rakhim would flee to. *You have to go.*" Gary gave a street address and an apartment number, and Lensky jotted the information down on his arm.

At last they wheeled his gurney away, and Lensky fell onto a wooden chair and started thinking again. Would Gary be kept at the hospital? He couldn't wait. He would miss the appointment.

He buttonholed a woman in a white uniform and demanded to know what would be done with the patients after emergency treatment. He extracted a promise that yes, if he was discharged after treatment the American could stay at the hospital until someone from the embassy came for him. "Though he will have to go back out to the hall again," she warned him. "He is not hurt badly enough to be given a room."

"How do you know?" She hadn't even been there when the doctor did his one-minute appraisal.

She gave him a pitying look. "If he was not taken for treatment until now, he is not one of the really bad cases. *They* get the rooms… those who live."

There were more people piling in through the emergency entrance now, injured people from the other side of the city and their families screaming for help. Just how bad had this earthquake been, anyway?

Never mind – it was over now. But the delay had been almost too long; he glanced at the clock on the wall, realized that he would have to hustle to meet Gary's informant. Lensky pulled the coat sleeve back over his arm and walked outside.

To his surprise, he was able to get a taxi almost at once. Every driver had been taking wounded people to the hospital; the one he waved down was happy to get a paying fare back to downtown. He was somewhat less happy when it transpired that Lensky actually meant downtown, where there was some serious earthquake damage, rather than the fringe of the commercial district. But he kept his bargain, and even agreed when Lensky asked him to wait outside the apartment building for a few minutes.

A splash of water to rinse the worst of the dust off his face and hands, a clean shirt, an extra clip for the Glock, and he put the dusty sport coat back over his holstered weapon. Time to get on with it.

"6122 Street of January 14," he told the driver.

The man looked surprised. "You are sure? Is not nice neighborhood for Americans."

"I'm sure, and twenty ergashis on top of your fee if you get me there before…"

His watch was smashed. When had that happened? "In twenty minutes," he substituted.

Too many streets were blocked with wreckage. The driver took him on a wild ride, tires squealing in protest against the sudden turns required by impromptu detours. There were fallen masonry everywhere, and half the buildings were obviously damaged.

And once, at a traffic light where armed guards were enforcing the traffic laws, he felt the taxi quiver for no apparent reason. An aftershock?

Street of January 14 was in a district of Soviet-era apartment buildings that stood way too tall for an earthquake zone. None of the shoddily constructed towers seemed to have fallen down yet; the earthquake must not have been as bad here as at the airport. But it seemed like the entire population of the neighborhood was out in the street. The cab crept through the milling people until Lensky dug in his pocket, tossed the cab fare and the promised twenty-ergashi tip into the front seat, and said, "I'll walk from here." It would be faster.

Would Yuldashev even attempt to make this meeting, or was he dealing with earthquake-related emergencies of his own? As Lensky drew closer to the address he'd been given, he saw an anomalous movement: someone was going *into* the tower that others were fleeing. He thought it was a man wearing a gray cloth coat. Yuldashev had been wearing gray on the day of the polygraph. But he wasn't close enough to make a positive ID.

Five pushing, swearing minutes later, Lensky reached the front door of the tower. Inside he was greeted by darkness. Of course. There was no electricity. And even if there had been, would he have wanted to trust himself to a poorly maintained, Soviet-era elevator?

"Stupid question," he muttered to himself. "If I had a sense of self-preservation, I wouldn't be here to begin with."

At least the apartment was only on the fifth floor. Sweating with nerves as much as exertion, Lensky worked his way up the stairwell by the light of the one narrow window set in the wall at each landing. Twice he felt light aftershocks shaking the building. With the first one he paused to ride it out. With the second he paused, crossed himself, and remembered a prayer from his boyhood.

The apartment door was ajar, a slightly lighter shadow in the darkness of the narrow hall. Lensky slipped inside and saw that Kambiz Yuldashev was standing there, as quietly as if he was waiting to buy a box of cigarettes.

He pulled together enough Taklan to thank the man for his sense of responsibility in coming to the appointment under such difficult conditions.

"They suspect me," Yuldashev said. "You promised to take care of Tahmina if that happened."

Lensky thought of pointing out that they hadn't actually had any information from Yuldashev yet, but he thought it would be useless. If the man believed he was under suspicion, it was unlikely that he'd be able to persuade him to resume his role as one of Rakhim's loyal lieutenants. Besides, he couldn't see abandoning an agent at risk just because little things like an earthquake and the start of a civil war got in the way.

"Take her to the embassy," he said. "I'll make some calls. Give them my name if they give you any trouble. Perhaps you had better stay there too."

In his first show of emotion, Yuldashev began expressing his eternal gratitude to his benefactor, the savior of his family, the –"

"Later," Lensky cut him off. "I need to know something. Hormuz Rakhim has fled in a small plane. It landed less than thirty minutes after takeoff. *Where did he go?*"

There was a country house, Yuldashev said, that was used as a gathering place for leaders and as a storage center for arms and other things. He himself had been there only once, blindfolded, but he had recognized certain things. They had driven out of town on the Merzadeh-Jirgatal highway, but had turned off after an hour to take a road that climbed steeply and was very poorly paved. Then there had been a sharp turn, a few yards of well-paved road, and a stop where guards interrogated them and his driver made a joke about wasting so much barbed wire to guard a place that was out in the middle of nowhere.

Lensky pressed the man for other details, but learned very little more. He couldn't even say how many people were usually at the house, how they were armed, or what was in the boxes they were guarding so carefully.

Then the floor began to shake. Another aftershock, and a bad one! The building was shaking all over as he and Yuldashev ran for the stairs. At the bottom Yuldashev grabbed his wrist before they could exit to safety. "You will make that telephone call to the embassy?"

Lensky promised again.

"Because if you 'forget,'" Yuldashev said, "and I take Tahmina there, and we are turned away, our deaths will be on your head."

"I *will* call," Lensky said, "but I'm not going to do it from inside a shaking apartment tower! Go out. I'll give you a couple of minutes so we won't be seen together, then I'm leaving."

It wasn't so easy to get a taxi from this neighborhood back to the embassy. He had plenty of time to call the embassy, to tell them about Gary and to find the right man to talk to about Kambiz and Tahmina Yuldashev. He slightly exaggerated the time Kambiz had been reporting to Gary and the value of the information he hadn't actually given them, to make sure that the embassy personnel fulfilled his promises to the couple.

If Yuldashev's hints about the opposition hideout helped him find it – and Thalia – his own obligation would be boundless.

Just getting to the embassy seemed to take forever, with endless detours and holdups. Sometimes the reason was obvious – large pieces of buildings lying across the street – and sometimes, as when they were greeted by Taklan soldiers holding rifles, it seemed to be at the whim of the administration. Once they had an interminable wait while a line of armored personnel carriers rumbled by.

"Our nation has tanks!" his driver said proudly.

"Those—" Lensky cut short what he'd meant to say and congratulated the driver on Taklanistan's military preparedness. There really wasn't any reason to explain to the man that not every armored vehicle was a tank. It was the kind of mistake Thalia would have made.

*Thalia…*

He called the embassy again and, without having to drop more than four or five mentions of important people at Langley or in Washington whom he knew personally, arranged for a jeep and a guide to be waiting for him when he got there. When he hung up this time, the taxi driver slewed round and congratulated him on knowing so many prominent people. Could Lensky introduce him to the President of the United States?

"That... might be difficult to arrange," Lensky said, feeling the back of his neck getting red. It really was not necessary to confess to a taxi driver that he'd been lying about his influential contacts in D.C.... was it?

There was a Russian-made jeep parked outside the embassy, with a slim, thirtyish woman sitting in it. She beckoned to Lensky; he jumped in and registered the two 9-mm pistols lying on the seat between them. So far, so good. But –

"Ah, I was expecting a local guide," he said. A *man*, was what he meant. He didn't hold with dragging women into danger.

"You might have to wait a while," the woman said, pulling into the passing traffic with a quick jink that almost dislodged the pistols before Lensky could grab them. She had short brown hair in a cut that made it lie in smooth dark wings against either side of her sharp-featured face. "Besides, I'm the best guide you could ask for. I've been intercepting communications from the opposition headquarters for some time, triangulating the information from signal intercepts."

Well, that was suitable work for a woman, something she could do while sitting safely in some basement office. Personally invading a rebel center, on the other hand— "I can't locate the HQ on a map yet," she interrupted his thoughts, "but I've got a better shot at finding it than some local guy you only pick up because he wants a job working for the Americans." She zipped across two lanes of traffic, yanked the steering wheel to avoid a construction beam in the far lane, and yanked it back before they veered into some other vehicle. "Oh, by the way, I'm Jennifer McAusland." She turned as if to shake his hand and Lensky cringed.

"For God's sake, watch the damn road!"

"Oh, I am. Relax, CIA. I can actually drive and chew gum at the same time, you know." She slammed one hand on the horn and passed a startled driver with inches to spare.

"I don't doubt it," Lensky said, swallowing his views on women in danger. This one clearly didn't value human life, including her own.

Before they'd even left the city, they had to stop for a roadblock – a serious one, backed up by armed police. The police searched the vehicle ahead of them, pulled out two AK-47s – then gave them back to the occupants and waved them through.

They pulled up to be searched and the woman said in better Taklan than Lensky's, "How come you gave those people back their guns?"

"We are only searching for grenades. Three of them exploded in the market earlier today."

"Oh! Well, we don't have any grenades." She stepped on the gas and drove around the barrier. The back of Lensky's neck itched, but he didn't hear any shots.

Once out of the city on the Jirgatal road, their progress was faster. Ms. McAusland had chosen that road without prompting from Lensky, which increased his hope that her signal interception project would prove useful. He told her what little else he'd learned from Yuldashev: an hour's drive towards Jirgatal, the turnoff onto a steep and poorly paved road, another sharp turn onto pavement and the probability of encountering guards and barbed wire shortly thereafter. She nodded and said, "That's consistent with my results. We should probably turn off at Deha."

They took only forty-five minutes to reach the cluster of houses nestling between hills that was Deha village. Just past the village, something that could charitably be called a road climbed up a hill. Jennifer McAusland swung the wheel violently to the right and took the "road" at a bone-rattling pace.

"Isn't it a bit too soon to turn off?" Lensky asked. "My agent said it took an hour to get to the turn."

Ms. Macfarland gave him a quelling glance. "When people are blindfolded, they typically overestimate the time they spend in that condition. Furthermore, your agent's people probably didn't drive as fast as I do."

That second statement was undeniably true; nobody with any sense of self-preservation would drive like this woman. Lensky shut up and fingered the 9mm. He preferred his Glock, but this would do for a backup piece. He could stick it into the back of his pants when they stopped.

The jeep must have been better constructed than he had thought at first; a few pieces fell off on the last and rockiest part of the climb, but at least none of them were vital to its functioning. They certainly didn't manage a quiet approach, though. The smooth pavement that Yuldashev had promised, when it appeared, turned out to be about long enough for an average driveway in an American suburb. McAusland shot the jeep over the crest of the hill (rattle, ping, clank), yanked the wheel to the left to turn onto the pavement (screech) and stamped on the brake not five feet in front of a barbed-wire-festooned gate (unnatural silence). The gate itself was a solid wooden construction, but on either side there were merely five-strand barbed wire fences. Beyond the wire they could see a concrete house, dark against the skyline.

"Want to go in?" McAusland said after they had stared at the gate and fences for a full minute.

"I'll go. You stay here." Lensky stepped out of the car and stashed one of the 9-mm pistols in his waistband.

"Hell, no." Macfarland took the other pistol and joined him. "Why should you have all the fun?"

"Uh – because we need to have the jeep ready for a quick departure?"

"Fine, *you* turn it around and sit in the driver's seat. I'm the one best suited to go in anyway, at least I speak fluent Taklan."

"I'm getting pretty good at Taklan myself."

"*And* Russian."

"Oh, shut up."

After that bickering, and after they cut the barbed wire to one side of the gate to make a quiet entrance, it was a distinct let-down to find the place occupied only by three guards, one of whom Lensky knocked out before he even noticed them coming. The second one appeared to be half-witted and smelled strongly of goat, and the third guard, though perfectly willing to tell the menacing strangers anything they wanted to know, really did not know much of value. All three were local men who'd been hired by the people who used to stay in that house.

"What people?"

Guard Three shrugged. "Rich people. They paid five ergashis a day. For each of us! Do you think they're coming back? I was saving to get married."

"*Where did they go?*" Lensky entered the interrogation with a ferocity that must have made Guard Three fear that lack of savings wouldn't be the only thing interfering with his chances of marriage. His eyes started showing a lot of white and he began babbling.

"I, I don't, they didn't, don't shoot me, I'm just the hired help, *please* don't shoot me!"

"Back off, CIA," said McAusland. "You're scaring him."

She interrogated the guard more gently and elicited the information that yes, a small plane had landed on the strip behind the house just that afternoon. There might or might not have been some people on board besides the two men who disembarked and proceeded to load those boxes from the basement into the plane. Well, obviously there were more people than that, because they had to have a pilot and co-pilot, didn't they, and Georghi and Bozghast couldn't fly, could they?"

"Tell me *exactly* what you saw," Lensky said. "And who are Georghi and Bozghast?" He thought Guard Three was getting a bit too relaxed here.

Georghi was an Uzbek who'd shown up a few weeks earlier, in a truck. He had been warmly welcomed by Bozghast, who was also a foreigner – meaning, in this case, not somebody from another country, just someone from another *oblast.*

"Oblast?"

"Administrative district," McAusland said. "The term is a leftover from the Soviet period; Ergashi had been trying to de-Russianize the Taklan language, but he had not had much success before he was assassinated."

What had Georghi brought in the truck? Why, those boxes he just told them about, that he and Stinky, there (a jerk of his chin towards the goat-smelling guard) had to carry down to the basement. What boxes? He didn't know, did he? It wasn't like they were *labeled.*

There had been as many as twenty people at the house, off and on, but there were only six or seven regulars. Of those, only five had been there when the plane landed, and after it took off again they had taken off too. And they'd taken the only truck, leaving the three of them stuck up here!

"Let's go," he said to McAusland.

"Wait a minute," he said, minutes later, when she reached to start the jeep. "I have to make a call first. I need to find out if the airport radar trackers picked up that plane again after it left here."

Jennifer McAusland said, "Are you nuts? After the earthquake almost destroyed the airport, you think those guys were sitting in the control room worrying about some small plane that was already miles away? They would have been too busy canceling and diverting incoming flights."

She was right.

And now Lensky had no idea where to look for Thalia and Ben.

# 20. The continuous perception of reality

They hustled us out of the plane and into the back of a truck so fast that Ben and I didn't even have a chance to think about escaping.

Then they unloaded the heavy boxes from the back seats, slowly and with a bit of acrimonious shouting and waving of hands, and attention was off us for a couple of minutes. By then, unfortunately, I'd had time to think of the problems associated with simply teleporting to the safety of Merzadeh.

It didn't seem like we were going to be in this particular location for as much as half an hour, maybe less if the guys doing the unloading and loading quit yelling at each other and got a move on. So if Ben and I teleported back to, say, the apartment in Merzadeh, what was the chance we could get a rescue effort organized in time to get back here before the truck took off with the rest of the other hostages? Not good. Even if we lucked out and found Lensky in the apartment, his quick reactions would be neutralized by the need to get other people on board.

And there was another thing that worried me. I leaned up against Ben's shoulder as if exhausted by the trip. Didn't have to work too hard on that bit of acting. "I'm going to disappear for a minute," I murmured into his ear. "See what happens." I actually had a kind of good reason for doing this, apart from researching our guards' reactions.

There had been someone standing over us with a gun ever since we scrambled into the back of the truck, but the guards kept changing: with only three people to do the manual labor, they were all determined not to let any one person duck out of the work by standing guard the entire time. I waited until the oldest guard, a tired-looking man with the beginnings of a paunch, had his turn at duty. He looked like somebody who might have a daughter my age. Somebody who might think I was cute and harmless.

I smiled sweetly at him and said, "I know you can't understand this, but Penny and I really need to *go* before we start again."

I kept babbling and making gestures, and Koshan, bless him, added a few words in Taklan. Our guard got the idea quickly enough. He nodded and almost smiled. *Damned women, if it's not one thing it's another.* He gestured for Penny and me to get out, and shouted something at the other two. One of them set down the box he was holding, very gently and slowly, and ambled towards us sporting a gun and a nasty, leering smile. He prodded us to one side of the truck and down into a ditch with a little very cold water at the bottom. Then he stood watching.

The creep.

I had been working on a topological visualization all the way from the truck, building an image in my head of a surface disguised by open covers from the background. I thought, "*Camouflage,*" and the image merged with reality. And we, if I'd done it right, now looked like a blurred section of the far side of the ditch.

"He can't see us," I told Penny. "But hurry."

She gave me a wide-eyed, disbelieving look, then raised her hand and gave our guard the finger. Not a totally bad test. When he failed to react, she unzipped her jeans and hauled them up again faster than any woman in the Western world. Except, of course, me.

And even with that, we hadn't been quite fast enough; I heard shouts and thuds coming from the truck even as I dropped the visualization.

"Hey! What are you doing?" I shouted as I scrambled up the side of the ditch. "You're not going to *leave* us here, are you?"

Ben and one of the trekkers were sprawled on the floor of the truck now. But at least they were moving, and the jerk who'd been swinging his rifle butt at them stopped on Rakhim's command.

Rakhim himself was looking at me with narrowed eyes. "Mrs. Lensky. You never did tell me how you infiltrated my room at the Hotel-Spa Eiffel… or how you flickered in and out of the apartment where I received you in Merzadeh."

I shrugged. "*I* haven't done anything special. Maybe you're having brain problems? I hear certain kinds of lesions can interfere with the continuous perception of reality." My face tingled: I'd never heard anything of the sort. It just seemed like a good thing for this bastard to be worried about. *Much* better than having him try to figure out how I'd done a few little impossible things.

He gave me a long, measuring look but finally turned away with a few low-voiced words to the guards.

When we finally left this stopping point, I was tied to Penny Nicholson, and Ben was tied to Tommy, the trekker who had felt nauseated on the plane. The other trekker, George, held Ryan on his knees. They told me that when I'd vanished, the guards stopped stacking boxes to berate them. George had gotten a rifle butt to the head, Ben to the back. "I think they would have killed us if you hadn't reappeared. How did you *do* that, anyway?" George asked.

"We just stepped behind some bushes for privacy," I said, scratching my ear. "They're awfully edgy. I didn't realize they'd get so bent out of shape."

Ben gave me a *look* but had the sense not to say anything.

That confirmed what I'd feared. If Ben and I teleported ourselves to safety, Rakhim's goons would take out their frustration on the other hostages.

Could I teleport everyone out at once? Not now, when we were all crowded into half of the truck bed and the guards sat among us, holding on to the ropes that bound us. I wasn't even sure I could do it if we were all able to move freely. Three adult men, a woman, a kid… and how far to Merzadeh? If it was only a hundred miles or so, Ben and I might be able to do it with the help of the "stars" in our pockets. But Koshan Idrisov had timed our second flight, which I hadn't had the wits to do, and his numbers were not encouraging. He estimated that we were a solid three hundred miles or more from the capital, and moving farther away every minute. There was a limit to how much the stars could amplify our results; even with Ben's help, a mass escape was an iffy proposition.

And the farther we went in among the mountains, the less likely it seemed that Ben would be able to help. At first he just complained that his head hurt and that he'd probably be peeing blood after that blow to his back. But as the truck labored up a dirt road, he quit grumbling about his kidneys and fell silent. "Are you okay?" I whispered.

"Yeah, I just feel like shit. Dizzy." He had started breathing fast and shallowly. "They don't keep enough oxygen in the air here, y'know?" He swallowed convulsively, leaned away from Tommy and vomited on a guard's boots.

The man shouted angrily but didn't hit Ben, just moved away when Koshan said something to him.

"How did you do *that*?" I asked, impressed.

"Do what?"

"Persuade him not to beat Ben up." I'd have been pretty ticked off if those had been my shoes.

"Oh. I just told him that the American has altitude sickness and that hitting him would probably make him throw up again."

"Oh." Altitude sickness? That sounded a lot better than concussion, which was what I'd been worrying about; he might have been hit on the head back when I vanished briefly. "That's not so bad, then. I mean, he'll get better as soon as we go down into a valley, right?"

Koshan sniffed the air. "I would guess that we are about twenty-five hundred feet above sea level, here. And in this part of the country," he said, "the *valleys* are at least two thousand feet above sea level."

"I'm guessing that would be a no."

"And if we keep going this direction, we will have to go over the Gundiz pass. And on the far side of that are the high valleys at four thousand feet."

"That high… You're sure?"

He gave me a pitying look. "I grew up there. Why do you think somebody with a degree from the University of Merzadeh is working as a guide to high country trekkers? Being a native Pamiri turns out to be a better job qualification than a degree in psychology."

"But… he'll acclimatize, right?" Ben's breathing was beginning to scare me.

"Maybe." Koshan put an arm around my shoulders, then apologized to Penny for the fact that his hand had brushed her neck. Our present arrangement didn't allow for a lot of privacy. "Thalia, I will try to persuade them to leave Ben at the next village. I will tell them that it's simple murder to force a man who's this sick into the high Pamirs."

He didn't sound too confident, and I didn't feel optimistic myself. We had, after all, been treated to a graphic demonstration of the fact that Hormuz Rakhim had no objections to murder. All I could hope was that if he still wanted American support, he must realize that killing an American wouldn't help.

But then, taking five Americans hostage – six if you counted Ryan, which I certainly did – indicated a certain lack of interest in State Department opinion.

I listened to Ben gasping for breath.

After a while, Ryan Nicholson began crying again. It was a thin, miserable wail in comparison to his earlier cries, and he kept stopping to cough. George did what he could, including contorting himself so that Ryan could at least lean on Penny, even if her bound hands kept her from comforting him. Koshan crooned the Taklan song he'd been singing to Ryan on the plane, but nothing settled the baby for more than a few moments.

"Does he have any heart valve problems?" he asked Penny.

She gasped. "How did you know? The doctor said it probably wouldn't give him any real difficulty, he might have trouble with some sports but it wasn't bad enough to put him through an operation at his age."

Koshan waited until she was fully occupied with Ryan before speaking again. "People with heart complications," he said, very quietly, "are more likely to suffer from altitude sickness, and it is more likely to cause them… grave consequences."

I didn't have to ask for clarification. He meant, more likely to kill them.

I listened to Ben's rapid, shallow gasping and wondered if he had a "minor" heart problem that he'd never mentioned.

It was almost dark when the truck finally pulled up in front of a cluster of flat-roofed houses. Two young women came out, smiling. One of them held a basket of bread.

"My people," Koshan said proudly, "we Pamiris, we hold hospitality sacred. All visitors we welcome with bread and salt – even *these*." His tone expressed utter contempt for Rakhim and his accomplices.

He listened to Rakhim's demands. The tone was calm, even polite, but even I could tell that he was issuing orders, not making requests. "We stay here tonight," he said. "He demands the villagers vacate one house for him and the rest of us. They are not happy about it, but it is not a fighting matter; they simply feel that he is rude and uncultured."

By the time we had been untied and shoved into a hastily vacated house on the outskirts of the village, Ben's every breath ended in a hacking cough. Ryan had cried himself into exhaustion after vomiting the fruit bar all over George's shirt, but he kept waking himself up with coughing and gasping. All of us looked exhausted in the flickering light of the single petroleum lamp we'd been given, but Ben looked like a corpse.

"Koshan," I asked, "do you know the name of this village?"

He looked slightly offended. "Of course I do. This is Tireza."

I borrowed a pen from George and scribbled the name on the cuff of Ben's shirtsleeve. I was getting terribly worried about him.

"Ben, can you take yourself and Ryan to Merzadeh?" I asked, as quietly as I could.

He looked blank. "Wha'?"

"Brouwer teleport?"

"Uh…"

"Cerebral edema," said Koshan behind me. "His brain is swelling." That cut my options down to exactly one.

"Not a good sign," I said, "he already had too much brain for his own good." I could crack a joke about it because suddenly I wasn't conflicted. There was only one thing to do, and I was going to do it. I turned to Penny. "Let me take Ryan for a moment."

With the baby's head against my shoulder, I wrapped my free arm around Ben's waist and pictured the apartment in Merzadeh.

The smoky darkness of the mountain hut changed into the clear, clean darkness of the in-between. My stars spiraled us along bright lines and sharp turns and impossibly convoluted surfaces, all the long dark way to Merzadeh. The three of us slid from a crumpled, mountainous surface to the smooth flatness of an apartment floor, from cold moonlight to the warm light of electric lamps.

Brad was there, asleep with his head on the dining room table. I didn't see Gary or Sheng. I pushed Ben into a chair.

Brad startled awake with our arrival. "Thalia? How—"

If I gave myself time to think before returning, it was going to break my heart. I set Ryan down on the table. "These two need a clinic. Immediately." I pulled Ben's cuff down so the writing was obvious. "This is where we are tonight."

I didn't even dare wait to kiss him good-bye; he might have tried to keep me with him. The stars swirled from my empty hand and carried me back into the in-between.

It seemed possible that my heart was going to break anyway.

# 21. All the help he could get

It had been a hellish day. Lensky hadn't been able to think of anything to do but hang around the embassy waiting to get word and making a nuisance of himself. Couldn't our own radar systems track one small plane? Ok, not from America, but hadn't we given the Pakistanis some excellent radar equipment to sweeten the latest deal with India? Well, yes, there *were* some rather high mountains in the way... What about satellite imagery?

At this point the Deputy Chief of Mission drafted him to help a driver who was being sent over to the Taklanistan Royale to collect random Americans stranded by the earthquake and the renewed hostilities. He was not entirely surprised to find Jennifer McAusland at the wheel of the minibus.

"What's my role in this mission?" he asked. "Prayer?"

"If you like. But I'd prefer you stayed ready to shoot anybody who tries to stop us."

Based on his previous experience being driven by McAusland, Lensky felt only sympathy for anyone who actually got in her way. But the situation had already deteriorated. Instead of policemen at barricades, now they had to deal with rioters who, whenever they recognized the driver of the minibus as a foreign woman, threw rocks and bottles at them. Lensky emptied one clip from the Glock at a knot of such protestors who had turned their bottles into Molotov cocktails. That was at the corner of Akbaital Street. After McAusland made the turn onto the commercial street with her usual lack of regard for Newtonian physics, he steadied himself with one elbow on the window while he reloaded.

"We really should have taken automatics," she said regretfully as she pulled up in front of the luxury hotel. "Oh well, at least we got here."

The people huddled in the lobby sported expensive suits, equally expensive tans, and terrified faces. McAusland and Lensky had a difficult time persuading some of them that yes, their best option really was to run across the few feet of sidewalk between the hotel and the minibus and scramble aboard.

"Can't he lay down covering fire?" one businessman demanded, pointing at Lensky.

"No," McAusland snapped. "You watch too much television." Bullets spraying from the front of the hotel would only focus rioters' attention on it. And they needed to conserve ammunition for what was clearly going to be a wild ride back.

After they delivered a dozen wild-eyed Americans (who had probably, a day earlier, been patting themselves on the back for their courage in refusing evacuation with their compatriots) they found the remaining embassy personnel busy with preparations for immediate shutdown. They were busy stuffing documents into shredders and burn bags while trying to ignore the anti-American slogans blaring from megaphones outside the building.

"What did *we* ever do to piss them off?" the Community Liaison Officer asked plaintively.

"Supported Ergashi," said the junior Political Officer. "Those outside, they're the opposition making their sentiments known. Don't shove that whole binder into the shredder! You'll jam it." He looked up at Lensky. "Can you take the burn bags to the roof?"

"Sure. Have we got an incinerator there?"

"No, but we've got a 50-gallon drum, and you should be able to burn this stuff while you're getting rid of the thermite."

McAusland sputtered. "I forgot about the thermite!"

She gave Lensky the background while they were hauling everything up to the roof. The box of thermite grenades had been discovered in the basement of the embassy some time previously. They thought the grenades represented war materials that had been intercepted on the way to Afghanistan, but had no idea who'd decided to store them there. When the embassy's security officer asked the State Department where to send the things, he was told that there could not possibly be any thermite grenades in the embassy at Merzadeh, because there was no record of them ever having been put there.

"The ambassador told us to be inventive," McAusland said cheerfully, "and I guess it's time to be just that."

They tossed one grenade in the drum and topped it off with the bags of documents. Smoke and heat covered the roof; for some time they couldn't see to move. When the smoke thinned, they saw that the grenade had handily eaten a hole through the bags.

"Hurry up," said McAusland, "we need to get rid of the rest of the grenades before they finish on the documents and burn through the drum." She pitched grenades into the drum one after another, igniting a fire that roared up from the roof like a furious dragon.

"If the wind conditions are just right," she said, admiring the flames, "that could start a fire tornado. Ever seen one of those?"

"No," said Lensky, "nor do I wish to see one. Hey, that thing is trying to burn through the roof now!" He pointed at the flaming drum.

McAusland handed him a pair of asbestos gloves. "That's why I brought these. We'll have to push it off the roof."

Lensky stared at her.

"Well, come on! This ought to discourage some of those bastards in the street, don't you think?"

After the thermite disposal, things did get a bit quieter on the street. By dusk, Lensky felt it was safe to slip back to the apartment on Kalot Rushan Street. The embassy was clearly worthless as a source of information on that damned plane, and he wanted to get away from panicky people who asked every five minutes why the US hadn't sent a plane to evacuate them yet.

A call to the hospital reassured him that Gary was doing all right. Sheng wasn't in the apartment, and that should have worried him more than it did. He was running out of capacity to worry. A brief sit-down, something to eat, and he'd pull up some maps of Taklanistan and start figuring out how to find a twelve-seater Russian charter plane in a country with more mountains than farmers. There had to be a way...

He didn't know what had awakened him, but he raised his head with a start and saw Thalia on the far side of the table, glowing pale gold in the lamplight, with a sleeping child in her arms. A dream? No. *Teleportation.* She set the baby on the table between them, and the smell convinced him this was entirely real.

And there was Ben, slumped into a chair and looking like death warmed over. The slight scrape of pulling the chair out must have been what woke him.

They were safe.

They were both safe.

"Thalia," he breathed, reaching across the table towards her. "How—"

"These two need a clinic," she interrupted him. "Immediately."

She pulled on the cuff of Ben's sleeve, pointing out some writing on it. "This is where we are tonight." And she stepped back into the colorless chaos the topologists called "the in-between."

The last thing he saw was the glitter of tears on her eyelashes.

"Ben?"

Ben was incoherent and close to unconscious.

He already knew that the hospital was overwhelmed. And there were no taxis in the street. A call to the embassy got him the promise of a car that would take Ben and this nameless kid to the Firdausi Ismaili Clinic, on the far side of Akbaital Street.

The driver was – hardly to his surprise – Jennifer McAusland, who helped him load Ben into the back of the car and plopped the wet, smelly baby into his arms before taking off like a kamikaze ambulance driver. "Looks like altitude sickness to me," she yelled over the cacophony of horns and megaphones on Akbaital. "Nothing serious, the clinic can treat it."

The Iranian doctor at the clinic agreed with her on both counts. "Both patients should make a full recovery," he told Lensky after Ben and the baby had been whisked out of sight. "You did well to get them immediate treatment. There is just one thing I do not understand."

"What?"

He frowned slightly. "The young man is suffering from HACE – High

Altitude Cerebral Edema. The baby may be similarly affected, but pulmonary edema is more pronounced. These ailments commonly affect travelers who ascend too quickly from sea level to altitudes well above one thousand meters."

A possible clue to Thalia's whereabouts? The memory of a topographical map of Taklanistan dashed that momentary hope. Half the damned country was more than three thousand feet above sea level, some of it twice that. There was a reason why explorers had called their mountains "The Roof of the World."

"So?"

A more pronounced frown. "Merzadeh's elevation is less than six hundred meters, and the surrounding countryside is even lower-lying. How did two people suffering acute altitude sickness turn up here?"

Lensky shrugged. "I don't know, I was only asked to get them across town. I believe there might have been an emergency helicopter evacuation involved." *If only.*

McAusland was still with him when Ben was pronounced well enough to talk. Even if he could have edged her out, Lensky thought he wouldn't. She'd been around enough of today's desperate search to have earned a share in whatever information Ben could give them. And a woman who drove like that probably wouldn't pass out over the mention of a little thing like teleportation.

After hearing Ben's story, Lensky noticed that for no reason, unforgivably, his hands were shaking so hard he was afraid to touch his weapon.

"CIA?"

McAusland looked worried.

"I'm fine." He had to be fine. There was nobody else to help Thalia.

"Good. Drink this anyway."

There was so much sugar in the tea, it reminded him of the stuff Thalia's mom poured over baklava. But it did help. He stopped shaking.

But he couldn't *think.*

Or rather, all he could think was, "How could she do this? How could she leave me like this?"

"Stop thinking of yourself," Ben said brutally when he voiced those thoughts. "She went back because she was afraid Rakhim's goons would take it out on the other hostages that we'd disappeared."

"Oh, and offering herself to be beaten up instead was so much better?"

Ben looked as miserable as Lensky felt, but he insisted, "I don't think they will beat her up. Rakhim's got a soft spot for her."

"Huh. She told me all his oily flattery was faked."

"Not as a woman," Ben said impatiently, "more as a… a mascot or something. She must be the only person on the face of the earth who ever believed that Hormuz Rakhim really was a liberal democratic reformer. I think he'll be trying to regain some of his halo in her eyes."

"And another thing," he said after resting for a moment to catch his breath.

"What?"

"They were moving us so fast."

"So?"

"Well, look. I could teleport you back to where we *were*… at least, I could probably do that in a few hours…"

Lensky remembered the word scribbled on Ben's cuff. "Tireza?"

"Yeah… but I can't do it yet, and tomorrow they won't be there any more. But they're going somewhere, and when they get there, they'll stop."

Lensky wondered how mathematicians could consider themselves so brilliant when they made such staggeringly obvious statements. "So?"

"Don't you see? I bet she's planning to stay with the other hostages until Rakhim reaches his destination. Then she can teleport back here and tell us *exactly* where they are, and we can stage a rescue. All we have to do is wait."

That was the one thing Lensky felt he couldn't do.

Outside Ben's room, he had a brief colloquy with Jennifer McAusland.

"You want to follow them? Of course you do," she answered herself. "We can keep in touch with the embassy by phone. Let's see, we know they were heading east, and you think they're in a village called Tireza and judging from your friend's condition, it's probably at three thousand feet or higher. Fastest way to catch up, start with the Merzadeh-Darvoza flight. If there is one. I understand the airport is not in great shape after that earthquake."

It wasn't. Half the main building had collapsed, and both runways were damaged; the only functioning parts were the control tower and the helipad. The daily flight to Darvoza was canceled until further notice.

Lensky mentally brushed off his list of contacts in Washington and elsewhere and got to work with his own phone. Within two hours they had the promised loan of a helicopter that would take off from the helipad at the airport at daylight, weather permitting.

For the first time in their brief acquaintance, McAusland looked impressed. "How did you do that?"

Lensky's lips twitched. It hadn't exactly been the first string he'd tried to pull... "I didn't. My wife has an aunt in Paris. Slightly insane, but she has a good heart... and she happens to be a very close friend of Taklanistan's ambassador to France, who just happens to be a cousin of Jamal Ergashi's."

McAusland whistled. "You could hardly come up with better credentials than that!"

"Oh, I don't know." Was he finally going to be able to tell this woman something she didn't already know? "The family tries to keep it quiet, but Hormuz Rakhim is also a cousin of the ambassador's."

"You mean this whole war is a *family quarrel?*"

"Those are generally the worst kind," Lensky said.

Dropped off back at the apartment, with McAusland's promise to pick him up before dawn, Lensky was too worried and too twitchy to go to sleep. Sheng Williams had come in and was sleeping on the spare bed in Ben's room. He tried to pace quietly, without waking the man, but he kept bumping into the monster dining table. Going into the bedroom he'd shared with Thalia hurt too much; the sheets still carried a memory of her scent, and there were a few black hairs on one of the pillowcases.

But there was also some potential aid in there, and he needed all the help he could get. Thalia's snakebot mage was snoozing on the dresser. Lensky grabbed Mr. M. with one hand, pulled a bottle out of the top drawer with the other, and set both down on the dining table. He cut across Mr. M.'s drowsy complaints about having his hibernation interrupted with a promise of infinite cups of black coffee for the rest of his life if the mage would just apply himself to the problem of finding Thalia.

"She should have taken me with her to Independence Square," Mr. M. groused.

Maybe she would have thought to do that, if he hadn't distracted her by playing that stupid trick with the handcuffs.

"I can sense her presence… very faintly." Mr. M. undulated over the spread-out map and came to rest over a series of valleys leading to a long, dragon-shaped blue area in the High Pamirs.

"Lake Shaimak?"

"Within a hundred miles to the west of the lake."

Lensky couldn't find a village called Tireza within the area Mr. M. had indicated. Possibly the place was too small to show up on any but the most detailed maps.

And the size of the area was impossible for any kind of search, especially given that most of it was vertical. Lensky broke the wax seal and uncorked the beer bottle. A shape of flickering lights eddied within.

"TheSila, Thalia is in danger. I need your help to find her!"

Darkness poured forth from the neck of the bottle and took shape. "And I," TheSila said, "need my freedom."

Lensky looked at Mr. M. "Excuse me, did I not understand the rules here? Doesn't she have to obey me, as long as the bottle I trapped her in is intact?"

"Technically, yes," said the turtle head at the end of the silvery snake body. "But all the Djnoun are known for their love of trickery and misleading humans, and this kind of Djinn is one of the worst."

"I made Omar al-Zanji think that his enemies were drowned," TheSila reminisced, "I told him I had forced them into the ocean, but I did not tell him that they had a boat." Her shape swelled forth, attaining human size, and she slipped an arm around Lensky's neck. "*You* were one of those enemies, you whom I did not drown; are you not grateful to me?"

"I am, I am," Lensky said hurriedly. "But TheSila, we have a new problem now."

"And what should I care for that?"

"I believe," Mr. M. advised, "that you would be wise to earn her gratitude by freeing her. Break the bottle!"

The beer bottle exploded in a shower of amber fragments, and TheSila danced through the air in delight. "Now let us go to my little pet!"

Mr. M. and TheSila disappeared.

"Who the *fuck?*" asked Sheng Williams, standing in the doorway of Ben's room and rubbing his eyes. "Sounded like you were having a *party* out here."

# 22. I dislike hurting women

The central room in the house was full of people yelling at each other, their shadows dancing crazily on the walls in the light of that one petroleum lamp. For a moment I hoped that I'd been able to make my return unnoticed in the confusion. Then the "nice" middle-aged guard who had agreed to give Penny and me a pee break caught sight of my face, did a double take, and slapped me so hard I almost lost my footing. I was already shaky enough from that long jump to Merzadeh and back.

I could make a pretty good guess at what he was yelling. It had to be Taklan for, "Where did you go and what did you do with the other two?"

By the time he'd said that, the other two goons were crowding around me. I took a couple more slaps and then one of them had the bright idea of twisting my arm. Same arm they'd twisted when forcing me onto the plane, to make matters worse. I yelped in pain.

Hormuz Rakhim shouldered his way to the front. "You will bring back the other two hostages," he said in a voice that was all the more frightening for being so calm and quiet.

"Can't," I panted between the waves of pain rolling up my arm. "Didn't let them go, can't get them back." Ignorance was a poor card to play, but my hand was essentially empty.

Rakhim started to say something else, but he was interrupted by a shrieking fury. "*What did you do with my baby?*" Penny Nicholson threw herself on me with such force that the guy behind me let go of my arm, startled, leaving Penny and me rolling on the floor.

"Ryan is all right," I gasped, but I don't think anybody heard me. The men were talking among themselves and Penny was screaming and trying to bang my head on the floor. Koshan tried to separate us. It worked better when Tommy got behind Penny and lifted her bodily off me. I sat up, leaning on a wooden chest, and rubbed my cheek. I did have some excuse this time; Penny's nails had left their mark.

I looked up at Rakhim. "See? I didn't do anything. If I were trying to rescue my friend, do you think I'd be stupid enough to kidnap somebody else's baby at the same time? And then come back here so the mother could try to kill me?"

Penny was sobbing now, twisting in Tommy's grip and all too clearly still bent on ripping me to shreds.

"Come with me," Rakhim said. He gave me a hand to get up and motioned towards the door of the house.

Outside, we sat on a low wall enclosing a vegetable garden that was cultivated right up to the walls of the house. It was quite dark now, and the bowl of sky above us seemed massive and intimidating, a vast blackness filled with more and brighter stars than I'd ever seen before. A sliver of moonlight fell across distant, snow-capped peaks. I felt as if I had been brought to the end of the world.

"Now," Rakhim said, "you will tell me *exactly* what you have been doing."

Time to lie.

But maybe I could sow a little confusion and discouragement first.

"Sure. Right after you tell *me* what part of your ideal liberal democratic state requires murder and kidnapping. You almost had me convinced that you were a decent human being, you know that, Hormuz?"

"I never said that I desired a democracy," he said calmly. "You Americans are very prone to hearing what you wish. What I desire is a nation that bows to the will of Allah, as all nations will in time. As for murder... you are weakened, as a people, by your fear of death. Here, life – and death – are very simple. All is in the hands of Allah, and all will be as it was written."

"Oh, yeah? Seems to me you did a little free-lance editing of Allah's will, today. Or were those two pilots already on his little list?"

"They were only infidels," Hormuz said. "One was Ismaili, the other Christian."

Huh. Madame Firozi had said she was Ismaili.

"Ismailis aren't Muslim?"

"A Shiite heresy," Hormuz said, "regrettably popular in these desolate parts. But all that will change now."

"Really? You are running away in a battered truck to hide out in the mountains. I gotta tell you, Hormuz, this does not look like victory to me."

"The prudent man," Hormuz said, "adapts his plans to the will of Allah as it is made manifest. This is not precisely the path by which I planned to achieve my victory, yet the prize is still within my gasp."

"I'd like to know how you expect to achieve that."

"In time, you will."

We looked at the stars in silence for a few minutes. Farther up the hill, a sheep – or maybe it was a goat – let out a plaintive cry. In a nearby house, the flicker of the lamp went out and the glow of light from the skylight vanished. Apart from the bitter cold that ached right down to my bones, it could have been a peaceful moment … had I not been sitting next to someone who had executed two men in cold blood today.

At length I heard him stirring beside me. "Mrs. Lensky, in our brief acquaintance you have shown a remarkable ability to appear where you should not be, and to disappear when you should not be able to. And please, do not insult me by babbling of lesions and brain damage. My men have also observed you in action. Now you will tell me exactly what that action has been."

"Why should I tell anything to a murderer?"

"A stubborn woman," Rakhim sighed, "is a very great nuisance. Mrs. Lensky, let us both acknowledge reality. You know something that you do not wish to tell me, but you must also know that if I inflict enough pain, you will give up your little secret. I dislike hurting women almost as much as I dislike unnecessary killing—"

Oh, *great*. He'd already made it perfectly clear that he killed as casually as I would swat a mosquito.

"—but I will not and cannot tolerate having a 'hostage' who laughs at my control and goes here and there as she wishes!"

He grasped my wrist and showed a gun in his free hand.

What, were we going to skip the whole "hurting women" bit and go straight to "unnecessary killing" for the win?

How was I going to get out of this? Even apart from the fact that I was still feeling extremely shaky after taking Ben and Ryan all the way to Merzadeh, I couldn't teleport or fly to safety with him hanging onto me. Was there anything else I could do? A shield wouldn't work for the same reason; it would automatically include Rakhim. Lighting something up with Riemann fire would be gratifying but unwise; it might startle him into shooting.

Small object manipulation as applied to the workings of a handgun was *definitely* something worth pursuing, but it was a little late to begin studying that now.

That left only camouflage in my little bag of tricks.

And… perhaps I could persuade him that camouflage was my only trick? That would, I supposed, be better than nothing. Certainly better than being shot.

"All right, I'll tell you." I didn't have to work at sounding sullen and defeated; I *felt* defeated. "I have this one little thing I can do. I can make people not notice me."

"You make yourself invisible?"

"Not exactly. It's more like, well, all they see is a kind of blurred image of whatever is right behind me." I was building the open covers visualization as I spoke; now I implemented it.

Rakhim drew in one long breath, but he did not let go of my wrist.

"I know you are there," he said, "I can feel your arm. But…"

I dropped the visualization and had the small satisfaction of seeing him jump. "How did you do that? Where did you learn this sorcery?"

"It's not sorcery," I said, "just… mathematics. See, first you visualize a simple closed surface around yourself, then a set of open covers…"

He wasn't listening. People frequently don't listen when I try to explain how applied topology works, and then they get all testy when they can't make it work without turning on their brains. One good thing about the CIA's non-disclosure agreements is that I don't have to go through this too often.

"You will teach me how to do this."

"That will take time," I demurred. "Do you think I began my own studies by doing something this difficult?" Actually it wasn't terribly sophisticated mathematics, but there was absolutely nothing to be gained by making this sound too easy to him. "You will need to understand Boolean logic and elementary set theory, the properties of three-manifolds, open and closed sets, countably and uncountably infinite sets…"

This got a resigned sigh from Rakhim. "All sorcerers claim esoteric learning, but in your case it may actually be true. Oh well, at least I can keep you by me and use you to invoke this magic when I need it."

I had no intention of being that accommodating, but we could discuss that some time when he wasn't holding a gun on me.

We sat for a few minutes longer outside the house he'd commandeered: long enough for him to explain to me how everything odd he'd noticed could be explained in terms of what he insisted on calling "invisibility." Clearly I had made myself invisible in the house just to arouse the clamor and confusion that would cause, giving Ben a chance to create his own invisibility cloak around himself and the baby, and to slip out into the dark unfollowed. He would either return or die; he could not have gone far in his condition, and unfamiliar with the mountains as he was. What on earth had possessed him to saddle himself with the baby?

I shrugged. "He didn't talk to me about that part of it."

Absolutely true. He hadn't talked to me at all – he'd been in no condition to do so – but if Hormuz wanted to edit his own memory and convince himself Ben hadn't been too sick to stage an escape, that was fine by me.

People. They'll generally tell you what they want to believe and convince themselves of it at the same time, if you just give them a chance.

I felt half frozen by the time we went back inside. To judge from the way my companions were sleeping all huddled up together, they too were feeling the cold. I found a niche beside Tommy and Koshan, burrowed my way into the heap of exhausted bodies and fell asleep.

Some time later, well before morning, I was awakened by Penny Nicholson. I jumped and took a deep breath, ready to yell and wake up everybody else if she tried to kill me again.

"*Is it true?*" she whispered.

I blinked and rubbed my eyes. "Huh?"

"Before," she muttered impatiently. "You said Ryan was all right."

"I didn't think you heard me."

"I didn't believe you," she said. "But Koshan seems to think you're not a baby-stealing monster. Convince me."

I wriggled out of the people pile, reluctantly leaving the body heat behind. It seemed even colder now than when I'd been talking to Hormuz. But I couldn't risk having what I meant to tell Penny become general knowledge.

Sitting on that low wall outside, we shivered and wrapped our arms around ourselves while I tried to convince her that I really had transported her baby to a clinic in Merzadeh – or as good as; I didn't know where the best clinics were, and I'd trusted Lensky to take care of that end of things.

"It all sounds kind of like the Arabian Nights," she said when I got through with the short form. "You really expect me to believe that story?"

Well, no, I hadn't expected her to buy it without a demonstration, but it had been worth a try.

"You have to promise not to scream," I told her.

She nodded and put one hand over her mouth. I was still much too shaky to try anything impressive; I simply gazed at a spot some fifteen feet away from us and relocated myself there. I gave her a cheery wave, then teleported back to the wall and resumed my seat.

I wouldn't have blamed her for freaking out, but I underestimated a mother's single-mindedness. All she said was, "Merzadeh is a lot farther away than that."

"Yeah, and it takes a lot more energy to get there," I told her. "I wasn't faking being dizzy when I got back here. I can't do a jump anywhere near that long again until I rest and get something to eat; even if you wanted me to take you to Ryan right now, I couldn't. Not to mention that I don't know exactly where he is. My husband was going to take him to a clinic, but we didn't discuss which one."

She blinked hard for a moment or two. "I'm going to believe you," she said, "because it's either believe that Ryan is safe in Merzadeh right now, or fall apart thinking of him being dragged around this godforsaken place by your crazy friend. Also, you did come back. I can't think why you would have done that if you really had stolen him – for yourself, I mean." She grabbed my chin and stared into my eyes. Her own eyes were shining in a distinctly unnerving way. "But if you are lying to me, Thalia Lensky, I – will – *kill* you."

She dropped her hand. "I guess we better get some sleep. God only knows what tomorrow will be like. I suppose it would be too optimistic to hope that the day starts with a big breakfast that gives you the strength to teleport the rest of us back to civilization? It doesn't have to be Merzadeh. Darvoza is closer. Or Lairon – my Jim is in Lairon. If he isn't out looking for us."

I explained that I couldn't take us to Darvoza or Lairon because I had never been to either town. Our choices of destination were very few and not very good. The mountaintop where the plane had been wrecked. Clearly in the hands of the RLP, so not a good choice. The safe house where Hormuz had stopped to collect his mystery boxes. Same problem. Or the long jump to Merzadeh, which had half killed me when I had only Ben and the baby to carry. I couldn't say when, if ever, I'd be up to teleporting all the remaining hostages to safety at once. And we couldn't exactly try sequential jumps with a chance to rest and refuel in between, because by now it was clear that the hostages left behind would pay the price for those who got away.

"Our best chance really is that we get to some kind of stopping point where we can expect to stay for at least a couple of days," I summed up. "Then – if it's not too far — I can teleport to Merzadeh."

"How far is too far?"

A good question. I was worrying about that myself. "The most I've done was about three hundred miles," I admitted. "But I bet I can manage more in this emergency."

"I still think we should go to Lairon."

I'd already explained once why that wouldn't work. I settled for, "Once I tell my husband where we are, he can organize a rescue."

"He can do that?"

"He's CIA," I explained, "and very…" How to describe Brad? I settled for, "Very *intense*. People generally do what he wants. And the Company owes him for a hostage rescue he pulled off single-handed this summer." Actually my hands had been involved too, but that was an unimportant detail right now.

This time, when we went back inside, I was too cold to get back to sleep easily. Oh, all right, admit it; even talking about Lensky and the possibility of rescue had got my hopes up. Every rustle of dry grass, every rattle of shutters in the wind sounded to me like the rotors of a distant helicopter. I knew nobody was going to land a helicopter by moonlight in these mountains just for us, but I kept listening just the same.

# 23. The Bronx is up

Lensky strapped himself down next to McAusland in the helicopter. She had clearly taken her own advice to wrap up warmly; she was half buried in layers of sweaters under a windproof jacket. Her head and neck were protected by a knitted hat and a long knitted scarf, both in a very loud red-and-green checked pattern.

"What's that, your clan tartan?" he asked, indicating the flapping end of the scarf.

"Don't be stupid, tartans are woven, not knitted. I picked these up at a handicrafts stall at the Sherozi Market. I don't know if you've noticed, but the Taklans like bright colors and plenty of them."

"I've noticed," Lensky nodded. Actually, Jennifer was wearing the same color scheme sported by the Presidential Guard. But that was probably accidental.

Once the helicopter took off, there was too much noise for casual conversation. Lensky had nothing to do but review the decisions they'd already made.

McAusland had wanted the helicopter to take them only as far as Darvoza, where she knew for sure that they could get a jeep or a four-wheel-drive of some sort to take them into the mountains. Lensky had argued for the village whose name Thalia had scrawled on Ben's cuff, but had to agree with McAusland that they might have trouble getting any kind of transport from such a remote area. If the hostages had been moved again, they would need a vehicle to follow them. If by a miracle they had been abandoned at Tireza, they would still need a vehicle to bring them back.

They had settled on a border outpost in the Gundiz valley, the closest such place to the village where the hostages had been last night. They would get a vehicle there and follow the track to Tireza. After that… things might get complicated. At least Ben's report that the fugitives had a sizeable truck and a load of boxes meant that they would be restricted to actual roads; the valleys that were only reachable by footpaths would not be available to them.

Flying over the high pass into the Gundiz valley was a strain on the helicopter. Lensky heard bolts popping in the clear, dry air as the machine labored up to clear the pass. He was so cold and his head hurt so much that he thought he wouldn't care if the pilot flew a little lower and took more chances of hitting something. Then an ice-covered slope shot by him, so close that the scrubby trees clinging to the thin layer of dirt shook in the breeze of the rotors, and he revised that opinion.

"Greatest helicopter ever made for this territory!" Jennifer McAusland shouted cheerfully over the noise. "Specially designed for high altitude performance!"

If they actually landed – alive – he would have to ask her about those popping noises.

Once over the pass, the helicopter descended to a more reasonable altitude and the pilot guided it through rocky canyons to the stone-built fort at Gundiz, a relic of wars long before the Russian occupation. He hovered low over a dry riverbed and shouted at them to jump out; he wasn't going to attempt landing and taking off again.

They climbed a rocky excuse for a road up to the fort, only to discover that the vehicle McAusland had tried to arrange was not there and that nobody in charge would admit to any memory of the promise. They might even have been telling the truth; it was evident that the Russians stationed here to command a handful of Taklan soldiers had just one amusement to get them through the bitter, high-altitude winters.

The colonel's office was in a basement. Safest place in the fort, Lensky thought – if it weren't for the supplies they had to thread through to get to him. Sandbags were stacked next to crates of grenades and ammunition, and he distinctly saw a rack of antitank rockets in a corner.

It was eight in the morning but to judge from the sounds emanating from the colonel's office, he was already up. Or perhaps that should be, *still* up. He was rendering a Russian folk song in a light, pleasant tenor that was no match for the vodka-fueled swoops and embellishments he was attempting. The private who'd brought them knocked on the door and the song stopped abruptly. A moment later, a surprisingly young man with a luxuriant crop of curly blond hair knocked the improvised door aside. "Amerikanski!" he shouted. "I love America! New York, New York, it's a hell of a town… Iosif, why is there no vodka for our guests! Tell me, why the bronx is up if the battery is down? What *is* a bronx?"

"Tell him that's okay, we don't need a drink, we're in a hurry," Lensky muttered to Jennifer.

McAusland gave him the you-unbelievable-idiot look she'd been perfecting since their first meeting. "Tell him yourself, he's speaking English."

Colonel Grisha ("Grigori Timofeyevich, but Grisha to my friends") wanted to enjoy this break in the monotony to the fullest before letting his surprise visitors go. Lensky waded into the battle and won some, lost some. On the "Loss" side he counted being forced to down three shots of ice-cold vodka: one as a greeting to Grisha, another as a thank-you for an officer who produced more bottles of vodka, a third shot to celebrate international amity. On the "Won" side, he was actually in the promised jeep and on the way to the village before ten o'clock. And back on the "Loss" side…. He had passengers. Colonel Grisha and his aide had decided that it was their duty to help rescue the hostages, and in support of the project they had filled the back of the jeep with machine guns, ammunition, and vodka.

And that maniac McAusland was driving. He wasn't sure whether that counted as a win or a loss.

*** 

It was barely light when the guards kicked us awake. Stumbling outside, I glanced at the sky in spite of the fact that I'd heard nothing. It was blue and blank.

And the truck was warming up.

Rakhim moved among us; I shrank aside. "You, you, you and you," he said, pointing at the trekkers, Penny and Koshan. "You will stay here. If anybody has followed us, you will explain exactly why they will not continue."

"You keep just one hostage?" Koshan demanded. "Is that not foolish? Let me go with her."

I had hoped that Rakhim's failure to point at me had been a simple oversight. Now he took my arm in a tight grasp and I lost that hope. "This one may be useful to me. You are more useful here. You can explain to the others – and to anyone who comes looking for us – why they will not follow farther, but will instead return and convey my demands to the so-called president in Merzadeh." He pointed at the truck. "The Semtex in here will win the nation for me."

"The Dragon of Shaimak," Koshan said quietly. "That is what I feared. But you cannot get to Shaimak, you know. No one is allowed to enter the restricted zone without a permit."

Rakhim laughed and said something to his men, who raised their machine guns. "This is all the permit I need."

"If anybody has actually followed us this far, you will tell them that they will stop here. They need not call in air support, either. At the least sign of aggression, I will blow up the Dragon of Shaimak and topple it into the lake. Then we will all learn if the engineers' prognostications are correct, will we not?"

"If they are," Koshan said tightly, "you will be a mass murderer!"

"Precisely," Rakhim said. "Now, please, you will make this clear to your companions." He started to turn towards the truck.

"At least give the woman some warm clothes," Koshan pleaded. "If you think she can be useful, you need to keep her alive. Look at her! She is half frozen already."

All four of our captors were now wearing fur hats and down coats. Bastards.

With no expectation of traveling out of Merzadeh yesterday, I was the least practically dressed of all the hostages, in jeans and a short-sleeved T-shirt.

Thanks to George's generosity, I was wearing a long, loose wool shirt over my own clothes, but that wasn't enough to keep out the biting cold. And I had nothing to cover my head.

The trekkers looked at each other and shuffled unhappily. They were already wearing all the clothes they had, except for what they'd loaned to Penny and me and the shirt that had been wrapped around Ryan. Koshan himself was shivering in a sweater over a long-sleeved shirt.

"Trade her clothes for local garments, you idiots!" Koshan snapped. "We Pamiris know how to dress for winter."

One of the goons slapped him and said something angry in Taklan. I could guess. Something like "Don't take that tone with the boss!" only phrased more as Meadow Melendez would have said it.

Hormuz shook his head at Koshan but gestured at me to go back inside the house. "Do not waste time."

Ha! The more time I could 'waste,' the better the chance of rescue. But... now I knew what was in the truck. If that longed-for helicopter came for us now, would Rakhim choose to detonate the explosives and kill us all rather than live and lose his evil game? I decided, unhappily, that I had better not try to drag this out.

Moments later a young girl came in. "Rukshana," she said, pointing at herself. "I... I learn English at the school." She opened a carved wooden chest and riffled through the contents with familiar ease. I supposed it was her family's house that we'd taken over.

First she brought out thick cotton boxer shorts and a matching undershirt. "Ter-mal," she said proudly. "From market at Lairon." I skinned out of my jeans and T-shirt, put on the underwear and stood there shivering.

Next came some knitted purple tubes, wide at the top and tapering to a point at the bottom. "For the legs," Rukshana said.

I toed off my Nikes and pulled on the thigh-high stockings. With no heel, and a seam under my foot, they were not exactly comfortable after I put on the thick socks she handed me next. But they were warm!

Over all that, I put on a pair of loose pants (bright red) and a knee-length blue wool tunic decorated with embroidered yellow flowers. As a final touch, she gave me an outsize, very thick shawl that smelled faintly of goat, and showed me how to wrap it to protect my head and neck. "Protect against evil spirits of cold," she said.

I felt bad about taking so much from people who seemed so poor, but I did want to survive. I did my best, emptying my jeans pockets, but I had only a few ergashis on me. Rukshana shook her head. "We *give* to guest," she said firmly.

I noticed that she was stroking my jeans, dirty though they were by now, paying special attention to the machine stitching and the zipper. "Then I give to my host," I said, and pressed the jeans and T-shirt into her hands. Her look of astonished delight showed me that I'd made the right choice.

That was when TheSila and Mr. M. showed up, complaining that I'd made myself difficult to find, what with being inside a house and wearing the wrong outfit.

I looked over at Rukshana. Her eyes had widened, but at least she wasn't screaming.

"Guys, I can't tell you how glad I am to see you! But it's not nice to frighten our hostess."

Rukshana nodded, then shook her head. "Spirit people," she said. "Like dragon?"

"Uh – yes, like dragon," I said. Like anything at all that would reassure her.

"Dragon of the Lake," she said, and the capital letters were obvious. "Friend. Say Rukshana send… how-do-you-do?" she finished, clearly unsure of the last words.

"Greetings?" I suggested.

She nodded vigorously. "Greetings."

I had been under the impression that the Dragon of the Lake was that huge mass of rock that Rakhim planned to blast into the lake. I wasn't sure how I would establish friendly relations with a rock. But with any luck I wouldn't have to try. I turned back to Mr. M. and TheSila. "Can you take us all to Merzadeh?"

"Yes," said TheSila, "but it is not safe there."

Like it was safe here?

"Lensky is not there," said Mr. M. with a sniff. "Not that *he* can do more for you than we can."

I would still rather be with him and away from Hormuz Rakhim. "Then take the others to safety and me to him, wherever he is."

They informed me that he was traveling too fast for even TheSila to teleport me to him. "Following you," said Mr. M., "for what that is worth. In a jeep."

Mr. M. and Brad have never really appreciated each other. It was worth the world to *me* to know that he was coming.

If I wasn't getting out of the mountains, I would need the felted wool boots Rukshana was pressing on me. I sat down to pull them on and added my good walking shoes to the pitiful little stack of clothing I was giving her.

TheSila was a much stronger teleporter than I was, although I surmised she drew her power from other sources; she was much too stupid to master applied topology. I considered asking her again to teleport the other trekkers to Merzadeh after they took me away, but decided against it. The threat Rakhim had made was too serious. I wanted Lensky and whatever army he was bringing with him to hear it from human beings. He had a tendency to discount Mr. M., and I couldn't trust TheSila not to get distracted and forget the warning altogether.

"We will come with you," Mr. M. announced. "You may need some help dealing with the dragon."

I was more likely to need help dealing with Hormuz Rakhim than with a hunk of rock, no matter what the local superstitions claimed about it. But I didn't argue with them; I wanted their company. When I'd asked if they could take the other hostages back to Merzadeh, I'd become aware of a queer hollow feeling under my breastbone.

About then Rakhim stamped into the house, demanding angrily how long it took a woman to change clothes. TheSila and Mr. M. became invisible, and I meekly followed Rakhim to the truck.

# 24. The dragon of the lake

We had another long, cold trip broken only by one small bit of excitement. Rakhim's dedication to keeping me alive didn't extend so far as giving me a seat in the cab of the truck. Goons 1, 2, and 3 rotated in enjoying that honor. The oldest of them, the one who'd allowed me a pee break, sometimes looked guilty when we stopped to let him scramble into the warmth of the cab. But evidently his guilt didn't extend to letting me have his turn inside. Every so often I looked up at the snow-capped mountains around us and tried to be grateful that the *really* cold season hadn't started yet.

There was no pee break today. I was glad I had missed out on the butter tea everybody else at Tireza had drunk while I was being costumed as a Taklan mountain girl. I had nothing to do all day but huddle in the niche I'd made between stacked boxes of Semtex, reminding myself that it was very stable and wouldn't go off without a detonator. I thought.

Well… that's not quite true. I had plenty to do, but it was all in my head.

This summer, in East Africa, I'd neutralized a Semtex bomb using a modification of Riemann fire. The modification was crucial: not being sure whether actual fire would act as a detonator, I didn't want to set this stuff on fire. Besides, the two guys who were currently in the back of the truck would probably notice. However, the changed algorithm didn't actually create fire, just a lot of warmth. As in, enough warmth to make the Semtex crumbly and inactive. It was a good thing terrorists were so unimaginative; I wouldn't have known what to do with a different flavor of explosive.

There was a *lot* of Semtex in that truck: eight heavy boxes. Personally, I thought Rakhim had gone overboard with the stuff, but that didn't matter. It just meant I had to neutralize all of it. On the other hand, the fact that it was right there beside me made it easier. And the one experience in East Africa had given me some idea how much heat would ruin the stuff without setting it on fire.

On the *other* other hand, I was starting from a much lower temperature than in East Africa. It took a lot longer to bring it up to crumbling heat.

And on the fourth hand (Yes, I'm keeping count. Just think of me as an Indian goddess, okay?) visualizing a Riemann surface was a lot harder when I was shaking with cold.

It got easier when I figured out how to extend the warmth effect to myself. In order to do that, I needed to be right next to the box I was working on. That meant I shifted around a lot. The goons, fortunately, thought I was moving around in search of a spot where I wouldn't be extra-chilled by the wind. They also thought it was funny. Bastards.

Once I figured out how to warm up myself as well as the explosive, the work was a bit easier. It was still slow, though, because I was afraid to hit the stuff with a blast of high heat; I worked upwards slowly, gradually raising the temperature. When it got high enough to be uncomfortable, I narrowed the effect to take in only the inside of the box I was working on, and just lived with the cold and the wind-chill factor. This kept me cold and shaking enough to convince my guards I was suffering, which in turn kept them amused. Did I mention they were real bastards?

I was about halfway done when things started to go sour. The two guards on duty looked worried and started fingering their machine guns. That worried *me*.

The truck slowed even more – it hadn't been going all that fast on the bumpy excuse for a road – and I abandoned the box that was my current project to peek ahead. The back of the truck was somewhat wider than the cab, so I got a reasonably good view of the wooden bar set across the road and the two men standing in front of it.

One of them shouted something in Taklan, then repeated himself in

Russian. Then, as the truck didn't slow any more, he tried English. "No passage from here without a permit. Show me your papers!"

The guards in back grinned and took positions facing out, one on each side of the truck. One of them said something. I could guess what he'd said: "These are our papers!"

Rakhim gunned the engine and the truck picked up speed. As it approached the barrier, the two men jumped aside and the guards opened fire. They didn't bother aiming, just sprayed bullets across the general area of their targets. That worked just fine. I stared at the bloody corpse on my side of the truck and swallowed hard. How long had it taken Rakhim to become so casual about killing? I didn't think I would ever get used to it.

It probably hadn't taken him any time at all. The man had ice water in his veins.

As the truck crashed through the barrier, I looked back and saw two more men running out of the little hut to one side of the roadblock. They were armed. They aimed at the truck and I cringed. Would a bullet detonate the live Semtex? I'd only neutralized about half the stuff so far.

If I got out of this, I really needed to spend some time figuring out how to use my small object manipulation skills on things like bombs and guns.

The bullets never reached us; we were already out of range.

And the speed at which Rakhim was driving gave new meaning to the word "bumpy". I was bounced around so much that I couldn't concentrate on my application of topology. It was hard enough staying in the truck. The leather-gloved guards could hold onto the sides of the truck without freezing their hands. I didn't dare try that.

At the time we crashed through the barrier, one of the guys in the truck was the older man. Keeping a hold of the side with one hand, he reached the other to me. I grabbed it gratefully, though I suspected his motives were less humanitarian than fear of what Rakhim would do if they lost me.

After too long, the truck slowed to a semi-reasonable pace over an uphill "road" that consisted mainly of rocks and ruts. That meant my butt was bruised black and blue from the jouncing, but at least I was no longer afraid of being pitched out of the truck bed. I scrambled back to lean against the boxes of Semtex and resumed my work. Every so often I took a break to peer over the side and look for the famous lake, but it remained hidden. We must be taking a long way around it. That made sense: probably the sides of the lake were as steep as the mountains on this side that hid it from view.

While I finished neutralizing the Semtex, the truck went up a steep slope, curved around to the left, and stopped briefly at a high pass between two barren mountains. I knew it was high because I felt like Ben at the start of his altitude sickness; headachy and not getting quite enough oxygen. I was relieved to see that the two guards in back looked almost as unhappy as I was. One of them was holding his head and the other was panting in short breaths. Rakhim wouldn't force us high enough to incapacitate his goons, would he? I hoped viciously that he too was suffering from the altitude.

When the truck started again, we were moving ever so slightly downhill. I took a look out the other side of the truck and realized that the high valley ahead of us, and the mountain at its end, weren't exactly barren. That final mountain's slope was less steep than that of the two guarding the pass, and starting above a rock mass at the bottom there were mud-brick houses tucked into the side of the hill. They were much the same color as their surroundings, but I was able to pick them out because their sides were rectangular. After a bit of looking I saw that not only was the valley a patchwork of fields, but there was a bit of terraced land around each house. I couldn't begin to imagine the amount of work it had taken to achieve that.

The track we were bumping down came to an end where the village began. Rakhim jumped out of the truck and the lucky guard whose turn it had been to ride in the cab got out on the other side, somewhat more slowly. He shouted at the guys in the back and, groaning, they too climbed out. Rakhim pointed at the Semtex boxes and shouted something else. They groaned and griped some more, but eventually each of them took one box and plodded away along a narrow path that led down and away from the village. Thank goodness I'd neutralized all the boxes! The crumbling remains of explosives in the boxes were completely inert.

Now that it was just us, Rakhim condescended to speak English. "Shaimak," he said, pointing at the houses.

"I thought that was a lake."

"Lake Shaimak is around that way," he said, pointing the way the guards had gone. "This is Shaimak village."

I thought that over. My head was all fuzzy with cold and altitude and fatigue. "We stay there? Aren't you afraid of being drowned if you bomb the lake?"

"We are at the head of the lake, and well above it," he explained. "The villagers of Shaimak rebuilt here after the earthquake made a dam; the lake did not fill overnight."

"Oh."

"As long as you are here, you may as well make yourself useful." He pointed at the remaining boxes.

"Um, I don't think I can lift –"

"With the proper motivation, I believe you will find that you can."

I knew what that meant, even before he patted the gun stuck into his pants. Evidently he had decided that I was more use as a porter than as a sorcerer, now that we were well past any opposing forces.

I staggered under the weight of the box I slid out of the truck. It wasn't really that heavy, but it was compact and I was feeling weak. Then I felt an invisible force under the box, buoying it up until it weighed no more than I could handle. TheSila was still with us! I followed Rakhim's directions and went the way the others had gone. Being careful to stagger.

Around the curve of this mountain, I was briefly out of sight and earshot. A cliff fell off to my left, and the path narrowed. I considered throwing my box over the cliff and regretfully discarded the notion. There were four more boxes in the truck; the guards would be coming back. If I wasn't carrying a box, they would tell Rakhim. If I camouflaged myself, Rakhim would know what I'd done.

But could he do anything about it? While pondering this question, I staggered around a sharp turn and saw it.

Lake Shaimak.

The water was a milky blue and rocky mountains rose on either side, just like the pictures I'd admired. Between the mountains, the lake seemed to go on forever.

There was one thing that looked much more menacing in real life than in the photos from the CIA report: an enormous pile of massive rocks blocking the path ahead and towering over the lake. It was even sort of dragon-shaped, with a mass on top sticking out like a head, jagged rocks going down the back, a pile of rubble tailing off at the bottom.

The three guards were leaning against the largest bits of that rubble, but when they saw me they scrambled to their feet. One of them pointed to a crevice between two rocks, then all three headed back on the path I'd taken. Excellent. I didn't know what I'd do with my time alone, but there had to be *something*.

The first thing I thought of was more a gesture than anything else, but it would be satisfying in its way. "TheSila, can you help me throw this box into the lake?"

Mr. M. made himself visible on top of the box. I'd given him a free ride all this way! Oh well, he wasn't that heavy, and TheSila had done most of the work.

"I would advise against that," he said. "It might annoy my cousin."

"Your… cousin?" Surely this was too cold for turtles.

"My cousin many times removed," said Mr. M., which hardly clarified the matter, "but we still have a family relationship upon which I daresay I may call at need. The Dragon of the Lake."

I stared at the huge mass of rocks and wondered if Mr. M. was delusional. "Um, I don't think…"

"You seldom do," Mr. M. snapped, and began singing a wordless tune I'd never heard before. I tensed, but the rocks did not fall. Instead, a narrow gray and green shape slithered out of a minuscule crevice in the pile. At first it looked like a snake, but then it expanded; grew a head and neck, broad silver wings, legs.

It spoke: grating words completely unlike any Taklan I'd heard so far. Or Russian either.

Mr. M. replied with similar sounds, then turned to me. "He might have asked, 'Who might disturb my peace?' And I may have told him, 'Those who have done you a favor, and now might request your help.'"

"How about, 'Who desperately need your help?'" I suggested.

"You do not understand his language," Mr. M. said.

Well, that was true enough. And if the dragon liked to put everything in the subjunctive, that was his privilege. I just hoped his help wasn't subjunctive.

"I will explain the plot of the evil ones, and how you have foiled it," Mr. M. told me before launching into a lengthy speech in some language that sounded as if he'd loaded a machine gun with consonants and sprayed the area like the guards had doused the border crossing.

The dragon nodded thoughtfully and replied in the same language."

"He wants to know if the evil ones would steal his rubies."

"What rubies? Oh, never mind. If that'll make him side with us, then tell him they're international ruby thieves. Oh, and tell him that Rukshana sends her greetings."

"Who?"

"That girl in Tireza, remember? She seems to have a good relationship with him."

There were another couple of rock-crushing exchanges, and then the dragon advanced and picked me up in its claws.

I closed my eyes against the dizzying swoop upwards. When I got the courage to look, I half wished I hadn't. Part of me was dangling over the path, part over the milky blue water. If the dragon dropped me, it was not going to go well for me. "Mr. M.," I said, sounding squeakier than I'd have liked, "did you explain to it that I'm not – not exactly qualified to be a sacrifice?"

"Do not be silly," Mr. M. said, flying up to hover by my head. "Adjdaak's people would not require virgin sacrifices."

Oh, how reassuring.

"Or any other human sacrifices," he added.

He could have said that first!

"He might merely be moving you to a place of safety."

The dragon's – Adjdaak's – wings unfurled and flapped once, twice, three times. We rose into the air and I saw more of Lake Shaimak's incredible extent; then I looked down at the sharp rocks below us and had just time to panic again before Adjdaak furled his wings, one section at a time, and dropped me on a ledge behind a large triangle of rock. A lancing pain shot through my ankle and I crumpled onto the ledge. He settled himself above me, looked down and said something that sounded like stones grinding together. From his expression, I guessed it was something like, "Sorry, I misjudged the distance."

I gritted my teeth, sort of smiled, and gave him what I hoped was a cheery wave. Safe from the terrorists with a sprained ankle still beat the hell out of not-safe.

His color changed to match the rocks.

Chameleon dragons?

I really wanted to see what was happening. If I could stand up, I'd probably be able to peer between two triangular flat rocks.

Getting to my feet was not much fun. I had fallen on the same ankle I'd injured in May, and it never had fully healed. Now I was paying for ignoring all those recommendations about physical therapy and strengthening the muscles around the damaged ligament. But I managed, with the help of some oddly jutting bits of rock, to stand without putting much weight on the bad ankle. I was able to lean on the rock with my weight on my left foot and my right knee. The knee had also taken some damage in May, but at least it hadn't been re-injured just now.

I could just see the path from here.

After a wait just long enough for me to start panicking again, four men came around that last sharp turn. Oh – right. Eight boxes. The guards and I had carried four boxes. Four boxes left. Evidently Rakhim had grown tired of waiting for me and had decided to compromise his dignity in order to get his bomb set up at once. He may have thought I had camouflaged myself and hidden from him, which would have been a good idea once I was left alone – if I'd thought of it. I blame altitude sickness.

It was still a good idea, if I wanted to see what happened next. I managed the chameleon visualization with some effort; I *really* wanted more oxygen.

A group of men in some kind of military-cut coats came running around the turn. They were carrying rifles and… I squinted. Two of them had oddly bulging coat pockets. The guards turned, dropped their boxes and raised their machine guns.

In the front of the new group was a broad, blond man I'd have known anywhere, even disguised in an army coat that was too tight across the shoulders. I screamed a warning and the new arrivals backed up until they were hidden behind the shoulder of mountain at the turn. One of them raised his head just enough to spray the area with bullets, while Lensky popped up and took aim at the guards. Two of them fell and the third yelled and charged forward. Behind him, Hormuz Rakhim waved a small black box and shouted something. The detonator? They mustn't let him get away with that threat. But I hadn't had time to tell them that the explosives were harmless now.

I was all but hopping up and down on my good foot by now. "Shoot Rakhim! Shoot Rakhim!" I shouted. Then I remembered to drop camouflage so that they could see that the person yelling at them was one of the good guys. I hoped.

One of the men with Lensky aimed at Rakhim, then his hands jerked and he dropped the machine gun. Wounded? No, he was fine. The gun must have jammed. He reached into his bulging coat pockets and threw an oval thing at the rocks. It exploded in mid-air, too far from Rakhim to kill him. I filled my hands with stars and threw Riemann fire at Rakhim's back. Even that drained what little energy I still had, but I had the satisfaction of seeing half a dozen spots on his shoulders and back bursting into flame. Rakhim dropped the detonator and slapped madly at his back, stumbled forward and then pitched headlong onto another grenade that was rolling quietly towards him.

The sound of the second explosion was muffled.

Immediately after, I was nearly deafened by six or seven grenades going off all over the space in front of the rocks. Rakhim had disappeared, and a pinkish mist...

Oh.

While I tried to control my gagging, the grenade-thrower began a victory dance. "Amerika, Amerika!" he shouted. "I love beisbol! What you say, I have an *arm*, no?"

There was a low grumbling noise in the distance, but I had no attention to spare for it. Adjdaak had unfurled his wings again.

I clung to my own rock in the wind of his wings.

The rescue party, intelligently, ran for cover.

Adjdaak swept down on the bodies of the guards and I learned the true meaning of dragon breath. A flame so hot that it burned blue wrapped around the guards. One of them screamed. He must not have been quite dead yet. I had once pulled a screaming man out of a burning building...

But the building hadn't been consciously bent on killing anybody. Adjdaak sent out another spurt of flame and the screams stopped; then he landed beside the bodies and...

I am not going to describe what happened next, except to say that topologists generally need to eat after performing major applications like Brouwer teleportation. Apparently flambéing people had a similar effect on dragons, except that after burning them to death the dragon had a nice meal of roasted human waiting for him.

Mr. M. was still buzzing around Adjdaak's head, but the dragon merely shook his head and pushed him away, saying something that was decidedly irritable in any language. I hardly had the energy to worry about that. I was too busy trying to ignore the smell of roasted meat and the sound of crunching bones. Dragons might not require human sacrifices, but they certainly enjoyed them when they came their way.

It didn't take Adjdaak long to finish his meal. I hoped he was full now.

It certainly seemed like it. His stomach was bulging and instead of flying to the top of the rocks, he ambled that way on his four legs and said something that sounded like a question. Mr. M. flew up to me and translated.

"You might have neutralized the explosives as you did in Africa, have you not?"

I nodded.

"Good. He may thank you for the excellent meal. Would you like him to repay you by splitting and fragmenting the rocks? He had always felt before that it was too much trouble, but one good turn might deserve another."

"Not into the lake!"

Mr. M.'s turtle face looked offended. "Of course not. It would be wasteful to drown all those people and their herds."

I hoped Adjdaak was more interested in the herds than in the people, but I was doubtful. After all, animals were wrapped in leather and hair, whereas people came conveniently unwrapped except in clothes, which were easy to burn away. Well, that was a worry for another day. I had a more pressing concern right now. I dropped my camouflage to concentrate on teleporting.

It was like before we had the stars; I moved up an inch or so and fell back against the rocks in practically the same position. Even the mild efforts of raising camouflage and attacking Hormuz with Riemann fire seemed to have exhausted me. Well, I *had* spent several hours earlier destroying that Semtex with Riemann heat. And the air *was* awfully thin.

Before I had time to worry, a cold, blue funnel swept me up into its whirling and deposited me, dizzied, beside the rescue party. I shook with cold. It had been bad enough before TheSila added her own magical chill.

I had only a moment to feel cold before a warm body was wrapped around me. The man hugged me so tight I thought a couple of ribs would go the way of my ankle. I hoped Adjdaak would recognize him as a friend. I tried to get enough breath to remind him of the danger, but all I could manage was, "Uh, *dragon.*"

He turned with me so that I could see that the dragon wasn't attacking people any more. He was more interested in the huge rock mass teetering dangerously over the lake.

Adjdaak began flaming the rocks farthest from the lake, the ones at the end of the "tail." As they shattered and crumbled into piles of gravel, he worked towards the lake, making sure to destroy the rocks in a pattern that ensured the remaining ones always fell backward over the destruction rather than forwards over the water.

Someone shouted in Russian and Lensky let me go for a moment. Surprised, I let some weight fall on my right ankle. I yelped and grabbed his shoulder for balance.

"You're hurt! Are you hurt? Where? What's wrong?"

"Later," I breathed between clenched teeth. That grumbling noise from the distant mountains turned into a thundering roar. Adjdaak's head jerked and he shattered the rocks directly under the "head".

That last enormous boulder fell into the lake and we all – even Adjdaak – held our breath for a moment. Splashes of water rose around where the boulder had fallen, and beyond them, ripples spread out. But they faded away before going far enough to be out of sight.

"Not large enough," Mr. M. said with a sigh of relief.

But now there was another crisis. The snow-topped mountains flanking the pass seemed to quiver as they roared at us. Then a flood-tide of white poured down the sides of both mountains.

We decided – all of us except Adjdaak – to get back to the village and find out what was happening. He wanted to sprawl out on his new gravel pile and talk about his plans to let the villagers build him a suitable residence. Mr. M. stayed to chat with him.

TheSila, cooperative for once, whisked the rest of us back to Shaimak village.

# 25. A divided *khngl*

Shaimak pulled out all the stops for our triumphant return.

The avalanche we'd seen had closed the only pass by which the village communicated with the outside world. I would have thought the prospect of being snowed in for months might dampen their exuberant hospitality, but Rukshana explained to me that they were usually snowed in from mid-November until May in any case. (Yes, she had joined the party in the jeep when they stopped at Tireza. She thought they might need an interpreter, and besides she wanted to come home. Her aunt in Tireza expected her to work even harder than her parents in Shaimak did, she said.)

For the feast, most of the adult population of the village crowded into the largest of the houses.

I learned that they managed their food supplies with a view to surviving the long, isolated winter; we'd just missed the last desperate weeks of the end of harvest, when every able-bodied person was busy threshing and winnowing grain or bringing in the herds from the pastures beyond the pass or piling winter fodder on the roofs or… well, you get the idea. Now, with the work done, it was time to hunker down, tell stories, and make music. And they loved the idea of kicking off winter season with a party that included three Americans, two Russians, and the vodka Colonel Grisha kept pulling out of his jeep.

One of the little surprises I encountered at the feast was that one member of the rescue party was a woman. I think I can be excused for not having noticed that in the heat of the fight, considering that she was muffled up in a Russian Army greatcoat and a red and green Taklan knitted cap. Unwrapped, she came across as slim, competent and definitely female.

"She drove us," Brad said, to my surprise. "Your Taklan friend – Koshan, right? He told us about Rakhim's bomb threat. He also told us the explosives were Semtex. Well, I trusted you to deal with the Semtex, but that meant we had to catch up with you before Hormuz discovered that he no longer had a bomb. McAusland got us here faster than any sane person could have."

"I'm surprised she believed you about my being able to disable the Semtex."

"Oh, she didn't. She just thought that the simplest thing would be to kill Rakhim before he had time to set up the bomb and detonator. The woman is certifiably insane."

While describing previous events such as the earthquake, the outbreak of civil war and the evacuation of the embassy, Lensky happened to mention that Jennifer McAusland had already been his driver through some of the worst of the fighting in the capital. Not to mention hustling Ben and Ryan to the clinic, and taking him to the opposition hideout where our plane had stopped to load the Semtex, and going with him by helicopter to the border post where they had, somewhat inadvertently, acquired Colonel Grisha, his aide, machine guns, grenades, and all that vodka.

She seemed to have been spending a lot of time with my husband. At least she wasn't one of those tall blondes he seemed to attract like flies. Too, I was reassured by the fact that Brad seemed, if anything, slightly afraid of her. There was one incident involving some thermite grenades that I never did get the full story on.

Over potato soup, butter-laced tea, and vodka, Jennifer McAusland and Colonel Grisha bickered over his use of grenades. "They were of no tactical use," she told him, "and look what you caused! An avalanche that trapped this entire village behind a wall of snow!"

That was when Rukshana explained that the avalanche had merely started the snowed-in season a bit early. I'm not sure that Jennifer and Grisha took in the full explanation; he was arguing that one of his grenades had done for

Hormuz Rakhim, and she told him the grenade wouldn't have been necessary if he had ever been taught to *aim*, not to mention learning to cease fire occasionally so that his gun didn't overheat and jam. He replied that the machine-gun fire alone would probably have set off the avalanche and what did she expect him to do, sneak up on the terrorists one by one and kill them with his bare hands?

"Any woman who's so casual with thermite," Brad put in, "shouldn't be too critical of anybody who merely used a few traditional frag grenades."

They ignored him in favor of continuing their argument. Grisha insisted that he *could* have killed them all bare-handed, only it might have taken too long given that they were armed and on guard.

"I'm sure you could, big boy," Jennifer said. She ran one hand up his arm and squeezed his biceps. The big Russian gave her a silly smile.

Over *plov*, a rice casserole seasoned with shreds of meat, and more vodka, a white-bearded man stood up and recited a rambling tale about dragons, treasure, and the ruby mine in these mountains that had once made Shaimak village wealthy. When he paused, Rukshana nudged me. "Now it is your turn to tell some stories. You repay hosts by giving us new tales."

"Uh – somebody? Help? I really don't want to stand on this ankle," I pointed out to the others.

Alternating English and Taklan, Jennifer McAusland told them about the Massacre of Glencoe. The Campbells came in for vigorous condemnation; hospitality was a sacred thing to the Pamiris.

Colonel Grisha contributed a severely truncated version of *Anna Karenina*, edited to fit the Pamiris' world knowledge. I thought the substitution of a dragon for a railway train at the end was brilliant. I got the feeling that a couple of the younger women sympathized with Anna but most of the others thought she got exactly what she deserved.

Even Brad came up with something, though it wasn't exactly literature. With Rukhshana translating sentence by sentence, he told the story of the Center for Applied Topology, the discovery of paranormal abilities, and our first clash with the Master of Ravens. That was definitely a breach of the CIA's rules, but it wasn't like they were ever going to find out. And he did have fun telling the story to people who actually believed it.

By the end of that last tale, Jennifer McAusland and Colonel Grisha were getting very cozy indeed. Well, it's a cold climate; people huddle together for warmth, right? I was certainly huddling pretty close to Brad, although warmth wasn't the only factor here.

Over apricot-stuffed flat bread and even more vodka, one of the old guys brought out a thing that kind of resembled a lute, and another one came up with a long tube that made a shrill windy sound. Rukshana and a young woman in her twenties darted out of the house and came back with tambourines. Another woman stood up and began a long, plaintive song that kind of wound in and out of the instrumental music. When she finished, the music changed to a quicker beat. Rukshana put down her tambourine and began dancing with a young man who'd been eyeing her throughout the feast. In one sense it was totally innocent: they never touched. They'd probably have been shocked could they have seen Lensky and me waltzing. But in another sense it was the most suggestive thing I'd ever seen. They mirrored each other's hand gestures as if they were animated by a single brain, swooping and stooping and returning to the face-to-face position, then moving their hands down as if tracing one another's bodies, and... well. The tango had nothing on those two. I began to understand why Rukshana had been told to stay with her aunt even after the school in Tireza closed for the year – and why she'd been so eager to return. She couldn't have been more than fourteen; even in this remote village, surely that was kind of young to marry?

That performance was broken up by the white-bearded man who'd told the first story. He yelled something at the musicians that inspired them to switch to a different melody and tempo. And something in that new melody inspired Colonel Grisha to stand up and demonstrate a Russian dance that involved a lot of jumping up and down and slapping his boots. Mr. M. had rejoined us by then, and *he* was inspired to fly around the colonel's head buzzing out the rhythm of the dance.

Or maybe it was the vodka that inspired them. Hard to tell. Everybody was pretty happy by that time.

We were ceremoniously escorted to a smaller house to sleep off the feast.

(Brad carried me.) Rukshana showed us how to keep the central fire going and how to encourage the smoke to go up into a kind of skylight construction of narrowing box frames terminating in a tiny opening.

I think we were supposed to separate, women on one side of the house and men on the other, but that didn't work out at all. First to break the rules was Brad, who wasn't about to let me out of his sight. Bedded down on a couple of rugs and covered by felt blankets decorated with bright red and yellow spiraling patterns, we were perfectly warm and comfortable. On the other side of the fire, I noticed Colonel Grisha's aide looking very... Oh. TheSila had fully manifested, and he was a happy man with an Oriental beauty twining about him. Naturally, she didn't need clothes to keep warm; the smokeless flame from which she was created took care of that little problem. And from what I could see by firelight, she wasn't wasting any energy on manifesting unnecessary clothing.

Colonel Grisha and Jennifer McAusland were at the far back of the room. I heard slaps, giggling, and the rustle of clothes, and decided not to look.

In the morning I woke to a cold, empty room. Where had everybody gone? I made my way to the door, doing my best to ignore the stabs of pain from my ankle, and shouted for Brad.

He showed up holding a piece of timber and a very long knife. "Borrowed the knife from the old guy with the beard, and Rukshana's boyfriend donated the wood," he said cheerfully. "You're going to need a crutch for a few days until that ankle heals." He sat on the threshold and resumed shaping an arm rest from the thick end of the wood.

"Where's everybody else?"

Mr. M. undulated between us. I was surprised that the cold hadn't inspired him to hibernate; perhaps he was hoping that the party would resume. "TheSila has returned those three, as well as the hostages at Tireza, to what you people refer to as civilization. The precise destination was some border outpost—"

"Gundiz?" Brad asked.

"I believe that was the name, yes."

Brad laughed. "Colonel Grisha is going to have fun explaining what happened to a jeep, a box of grenades, four machine guns and all that vodka!"

"Wait a minute," I interrupted. "When is TheSila coming back for us?"

"She made no mention of that."

"And she's a free agent again," Brad told me. "I had to break the bottle to persuade her to find you."

Well, that had pluses and minuses. On the good side, if the charms of the colonel's aide had distracted her from us, we would no longer have to put up with her manifesting in our midst and making highly inappropriate comments. On the bad side, of course, we still needed transport out of this village. And I did not exactly feel able to teleport all the way to Merzadeh. Altitude, exhaustion, and pain were all draining me.

"Just as well," Brad said, "it might not be smart to go to Merzadeh until we can check the news. If the fighting's still going on… I don't know if State can exfiltrate us."

"Trouble is, I haven't got any closer locations I can teleport to… even if I take some time to recover and build up my strength."

I thought about the problem for a while.

"I bet Adjdaak can fly us out of here to some place on the far side of that pass. Maybe even to Gundiz."

"Who?" Brad asked.

"Oh. Right. In all the confusion of the fight, I guess you weren't formally introduced. Um. Breakfast?" I'm not really all that greedy, but I felt the need to stoke up before trying to teleport myself and Brad even the little distance from here to Adjdaak's lakeside home.

Breakfast was bits of yesterday's bread soaked in tea with salt and butter. Yes, butter tea sounds disgusting, but just now it was delicious. Brad said our bodies needed more fats because of the altitude. Also, given that the only sugar in the village had come up on yak-back and was strictly reserved for preserving fruit, the butter was my next best source of quick energy.

Teleportation sometimes leaves us a few inches above the destination, resulting in a lot of falls. Just now I *really* didn't want to fall, so after wrapping Mr. M. over my shoulders I took a firm hold of my improvised crutch and asked Brad to put an arm around me for extra stability.

We landed on the lake shore without difficulty, and for a moment I had a feeling of *déjà vu*. The huge pile of rocks was still there! Had I dreamed its destruction?

Then a leg curled up, a wing moved, a bright golden eye opened, and I recognized that the "rock pile" was now, literally, the Dragon of Shaimak.

Adjdaak had been growing since yesterday. The effect of roast, um, meat? I hoped he hadn't been growing so fast that he was hungry again.

"Adjdaak, this is my husband Brad. Brad, this is Adjdaak."

The dragon opened his mouth and made a rather unfriendly sound like a rock-crushing mill.

"You should address him by his title," Mr. M. advised me.

"Oh! Dragon of Shaimak, meet my husband Brad. Brad, this is Adjdaak, the Dragon of Shaimak."

Adjdaak replied with another series of hard consonants interspersed with rock noises. Mr. M. didn't translate, so I trusted this meant the dragon was satisfied with my manners now.

With Mr. M.'s help, I humbly requested the Dragon of Shaimak to transport Lensky and me over the closed mountain pass and to a village accessible to the rest of the world. One with a good road and some vehicles would be nice.

Adjdaak responded with one short clash of breaking rocks, or something that sounded like it.

"He might refuse," Mr. M. told me. "I think that means, he *does* refuse."

"What? He can't do that! How will we get out of here? Why did he help us yesterday, if he meant to stick us in this village for months?" Okay, I can't stay humble for long. I admit that it's a bug, not a feature.

The dragon spat out consonants and rocky noises for some time before he fell silent and left Mr. M. to translate.

"In the first place, he was not helping *you* yesterday; anything he might have done would have been to protect his lake. In the second place, he wishes to know what could be the hardship of spending a few days in *his* birthplace? And in the third place, it might be good for your *khngl* if you were to rest and reflect upon his lake for some days. Also," Mr. M. added, "to give your ankle time to heal."

"Uh, what's a…" There was no way I could pronounce the word he'd used, but I tried anyway. "What's a, a kungel?"

"*Khngl*," Mr. M. corrected me with a disdainful sniff. Easy for him to say! "It means something like soul, something like heart, a blend of both."

"Well, my kungel is doing just fine without any lakeside meditation, thank you!" But that was just my argumentative instincts taking over. When I actually pictured myself sitting by the lake, possibly leaning against one of those great silvery wings, possibly holding Brad's hand, I felt… well, peaceful. I could stand to feel that way more often. So I subsided fairly quickly when Mr. M. refused to translate on the grounds that it was unwise to give dragons grief.

I did feel guilty, though, that we were giving the villagers two extra mouths to feed for who knew how long, in winter when every mouthful of food was precious. We didn't even have any gifts with which to repay their hospitality – or so I thought until we returned to the village and Brad formally offered the headman four machine guns, a supply of ammunition and the rest of the vodka in the Russian jeep.

"Why didn't you give them the jeep too?" I asked.

Brad gave me the same are-you-retarded look that I'd observed Jennifer McAusland giving to him. "The Russians will probably want it back."

"And they won't want the rest of their stuff back?"

"They won't get it. I have confidence in the Pamiris' ability to make any portable property 'disappear' before the passes are open." He thought that over for a moment. "Actually, I think the vodka is going to disappear well before that. It's too bad they don't have any potatoes to spare; I could spend this enforced vacation building them a still, while we wait to see how the civil war is going to shake out."

Brad bound my ankle up with a strip of cloth he found in the back of the Russians' jeep. It only smelled very faintly of gun oil.

The village *khalifa*, who combined the functions of healer and cleric, made him untie the cloth so he could smear my ankle with a pungent green paste before tying it up again. He also wrote several charms which he inserted into the folds of the fabric as Brad wrapped it around my ankle. I don't know how much good the charms did, but the green paste was certainly useful. My bandage no longer smelled like gun lubricant. It smelled like mint, garlic and several other very aromatic plants which I didn't recognize.

And I have to admit that my ankle got better remarkably fast. Within a couple of days I was able to teleport to the lake without borrowing Brad to steady my landing, and the day after that I actually hobbled down to the natural rock seat overlooking the water where I'd imagined myself sitting when Adjdaak talked about my *khngl.* The next day I walked the entire way instead of teleporting, to strengthen my ankle.

This short walk to sit and look at the lake became a daily ritual, with or without Brad. When the sun shone, my lakeside perch was almost warm; when it didn't, Adjdaak opened the lowest fold of his left-hand wing and draped it over my shoulders. When Mr. M. came along to translate, Adjdaak talked about his own interests, which were mainly centered on the rubies that used to be mined close to this village. He considered all the rubies his but had been willing to allow the miners a small share of them in return for their labor in dark, enclosed places where he preferred not to go.

That was where the jewels for that necklace of Aunt Alesia's had come from, then.

When the avalanche that created the lake occurred, Adjdaak had closed the entrances to the mine for fear that instability from mining activity would topple the rock mass into the lake and set off the disastrous flood that everyone feared.

"Didn't it ever occur to you before that you could destroy the rocks by heating them?" I asked.

"That would have been unnecessarily complicated. Closing the mine would have been simpler," he said dismissively through Mr. M. I don't know why he couldn't just say, "*Was* simpler," but his language didn't seem to work that way.

But now, I gathered, he might consider allowing the villagers to mine for rubies again. Even if the yield was poor, even if Adjdaak claimed eighty percent of it, this mining would vastly improve the economic position of people who could only survive by cultivating every teaspoonful of arable land in their valley.

On the days when Brad wasn't helping to fix up houses and terraced gardens in Shaimak, he came with me to the lake and Mr. M. stayed behind, saying he needed to catch up on his hibernation. On at least one occasion that I know of, "hibernation" involved some of Colonel Grisha's vodka and a whole roomful of Pamiri teenagers roaring out "Rock Around the Clock," to the lead of a croaking turtle-snake mage. But we decided not to ask any questions. It was nice for us to have some privacy. Learning rock and roll lyrics would be good for the kids' English. And it was nice for Mr. M. to meet some people who actually liked his singing.

We were staring into the milky blue of the lake one afternoon when I finally got up the courage to apologize to Brad about Hormuz Rakhim and all the trouble that my ill-considered belief in him had caused both of us. As I might have expected, he brushed aside my apology with his usual generosity of spirit. "You're not exactly the first person to be taken in by a charlatan, Thalia, and you won't be the last. I expect it's because you get so uncomfortable when you're lying. You're just not equipped to recognize somebody who lies as naturally as he breathes. I should have taken the time to go through the evidence against him with you, instead of dropping hints and pushing intelligence analyses at you and, well, shouting. Not to mention… well, I've been hoping *you* wouldn't want to mention it… the, er, the handcuffs incident. Not exactly my finest moment. I realize that now." His face reddened.

I snuggled into his shoulder. "Consider it forgotten. We were both somewhat overwrought. Have you noticed, we haven't yelled at each other once since we came to Shaimak? And I haven't thrown anything. Maybe we're entering a more mature phase of our relationship."

"*You* may be maturing," Brad said. "Me, I'm just afraid of starting another avalanche if I raise my voice."

"Well, *I* think this place is good for my kungel. Yours too."

"*Khngl,*" grated Adjdaak.

"And," I said without acknowledging the interruption, "I'm actually okay with not having any more adventures for a while."

Brad hugged me. "You know what, so am I. This tour in Taklanistan has been like five years of covert ops condensed into a month. I could stand not to have to shoot anybody for a few years."

I leaned back into the curve of his arm and we contemplated the lake in mutual amity.

But Brad wasn't with me on the day when Adjdaak dropped his little bombshell.

What he said, of course, sounded like everything else he said to me: "Dz [crack] kshaadyb [smash] khngl [crush]." If anybody ever studies that language, they're going to have to invent half a dozen new consonants for the variety of rock-noises. And it would be a good deed if they'd donate some vowels, too.

But I did think I'd picked out the only word of Dragontalk I sort of knew.

"Mr. M., what's he saying about my kungel now?"

"*Khngl*. He says that it might be divided."

"What?" I felt fractious. All that peace and serenity, not to mention making up with Brad here at the lake, *plus* making up with Brad somewhat more enthusiastically in the privacy of the tiny house they'd loaned us, and my kungel was *divided*? I'd thought it was in great shape! I was even getting less argumentative... I thought.

"It might not be a bad thing," Mr. M. said. "It might be part of the natural order of things. You should stop flouncing like that. If you could sit still and gaze into the lake, he might show you."

I followed orders. It was a most peculiar lake; when you just looked at the surface it was an opaque milky blue, but when you tried to look through that blueness there were depths upon depths to be seen. And after a long time, I did see what Adjdaak wanted me to see.

Shaken, I drew a deep breath. "Is that – uh, like, something that could happen in the future?"

"It is something that has begun to happen now," Mr. M. said, for once dropping the subjunctive nonsense, "and that is why your *khngl* is now divided. Part of it is still with you, and part – "

I waved him silent. "Yes. I... I get the idea." For some reason, my eyes filled with tears. Adjdaak snaked his head out, turned to look at me with one golden eye, and said something that sounded like stones crashing into a heap.

"You might be unhappy?"

"No – no, tell him I am *not* unhappy. Not in the slightest! Mr. M., can you ask Brad to come here? I need to talk to him."

Mr. M. grumbled about people who would use a great mage for their errands, but he rose into the air and sped back towards the village in his finest flight mode.

Brad, of course, had to walk down the path to the lake, so I had a few minutes to decide how to tell him. It was the kind of news you wanted to break gently. And I had a lot to think about. I thought about certain supplies that hadn't been available since I got taken hostage, and about the glorious reunion with Brad here in Shaimak. I thought about Penny Nicholson, and I remembered the curly-haired toddler who kept trying to escape the restaurant in Barcelona.

"Sorry you had to walk," I said when he finally joined me.

He brushed that aside. "Doesn't matter. Actually, I like to walk."

"That's good," I said, "because there's going to be a lot more walking in your near future. I won't be able to teleport you around for a bit. In fact, I won't even be teleporting myself. Or doing any other fancy stuff."

"Thalia? Did you somehow lose your abilities? Not that it matters to me, I don't love you for your applications of topology, but can *you* handle it?"

"I didn't lose them," I told him, "I just… I'm going to put them aside for a while. Fortunately, we don't need me to teleport us anywhere right away. Adjdaak says he's willing to take us to Gundiz." Interesting, how he'd suddenly decided that we could go back to civilization now. Had this whole stay in Shaimak been a setup? And – how could my mother have suborned a dragon she'd never even met?

"Is this some kind of penance you're imposing on yourself for having trusted Rakhim?"

"No. It's more… caution."

"About what?"

"Well, nobody in my condition has ever teleported before. And I don't want our baby to be the first test case. So I'm benching myself for the next nine months."

From the way he hugged me and picked me up and spun me around and generally carried on, you'd think we'd just won the lottery.

Come to think of it, I feel rather like that myself.

Keep reading for a preview of *Salt Magic: A Regency fantasy romance*

# Salt Magic: A Regency fantasy romance

Despite my family's concern, my marriage to the March-Lord was perfectly happy until mainlanders troubled our island, seeking to use the magic of Faarhafn and bringing death and destruction upon us.

In truth, my mother and aunts had considerable responsibility for my marriage, even if they did not realize it. Between them they did not have nearly enough children; worse, my nephews and nieces were so much younger than I that they did no chores and raised no deep concerns. As I grew to womanhood, I benefited from so much concentrated attention that I feared my beloved family would drive me mad. They could imagine no man good enough for me; they feared that I would develop an unsuitable attachment; from morning to night they kept me busy with household chores, or tried to, all in the name of loving and protecting me.

Under the circumstances, I feel that I took the only action possible.

I ran away with an older man.

Granted, I did not run very far away; only to the island of Faarhafn, my family's ancestral home and almost within sight of their present dwelling place. But he was a much older man, my dear lord Kosta Greenmark, March-Lord of Steinnland and the Isles – having seen sixty-seven winters to my seventeen – so on average, it was a more than adequate gesture.

Steinnland had been more than good to me ever since we met by chance during one of my brief escapes from the incessant demands of my family. He understood the hungers and desires that were nameless torments to me; he named and satisfied them and opened a new world to me.

In short, he taught me to read, and gave me the run of his library. And I began to understand that my mind had been starved for learning and for knowledge of the wider world – for my family keeps to the old ways of our people, and sees no call for overmuch learning beyond knowledge of the tides and the deep currents of the sea.

Steinnland offered what they call a marriage of convenience, though to give credit to his generosity, the convenience was mostly for my sake. Not only was I finding it increasingly difficult to find excuses to spend as much time as I wanted reading in his library or simply talking with him; other people were beginning to comment on our association. "That strange child Sabira" was, in the view of landfolk and seafolk alike, now a woman grown and marriage-ripe, and nothing honest could come of her spending so much time alone with Kosta Greenmark.

"They give me too much credit, and you too little," Steinnland said with a smile when he first mentioned marriage. "Lovely though you are, Sabira, I trust you will not be insulted when I say that at my age I feel no temptation to do more than enjoy your beauty with my eyes. As for you, I know, if your family and the islanders do not, that you spend time with an old man out of kindness and intellectual curiosity, and not for any other reason."

"Kindness! That is all your virtue, and none of my own," I said. "Nothing in my life means so much as the hours I have spent here with you. If you accuse me again of visiting you out of kindness, I'll leave your library and find my friends among the waves breaking on the shore, as I did when I was a child."

"But you are no longer a child, Sabira, and the time you spend here, for whatever reason, is causing unpleasant talk." Steinnland regarded me steadily, his pale blue eyes piercing like shards of ice under his shaggy white brows. "My dear, I have no desire to beget an heir, and I cannot bear to hear your name smeared over with tavern jokes. If we marry, we shall go on just as before, except that you will no longer have to lie to your family and no one will see any impropriety in our association. Otherwise...."

He paused, and I could see by the twist of his thin lips that the words he was about to speak pained him deeply.

"Otherwise, I must ask you, for your own sake, to come here no longer. I have not so many friends that I would willingly lose one such as you, Sabira."

It came to me that it was not just my name, unimportant that it was, that was stained by smutty tavern jokes about our friendship. It was the name of Kosta Greenmark, March-Lord of Steinnland and the Isles, who all his life had been a byword for integrity among both the sea folk and the subtle politicians of the land.

"Of course I'll marry you," I said on a breath, "and I am honored to do so. If you are sure that is what you really want?"

That was a foolish question; Steinnland never said anything that he did not mean.

Our marriage was a quiet affair, attended only by the cleric who came from the mainland to speak the words over us, Steinnland's factor Hendrie, and two of his tenants for witnesses. Once the agreement was made, he was urgent to see it done, and would not wait to send word for any of his friends from the city to attend. As for my family, I felt it would be easier to reconcile them to my marriage after the fact and so it proved.

Indeed, forgiveness was much easier to gain than I had ever imagined.

"So that's where you've been slipping off to all these hours!" exclaimed my aunt Maarit when I bore the news to my family. "Oh, yes, my girl, don't think I haven't noticed. You've grown sly and underhanded. I told Norin some disaster would happen if she didn't keep a closer watch on you."

"Perhaps we kept Sabira too close, so that she felt she had no way to get any privacy except by lying to us," said my aunt Eliina, the youngest and gentlest of the sisters.

"And I am not sure that I would call marriage to Kosta Greenmark a disaster," said my aunt Seija. "With his fortune, not to mention the estate of Steinnland and the Isles – including Faarhafn," she added pointedly.

"Which will pass to some distant male relative on his death," snapped Maarit. "That is the way of the great lords; they call it an entail, and it is a law made to ensure that the lands stay together and under some man. A wife has little or no rights under that law. What good does it do Sabira to marry the man who rules the Isles, if none of the power passes to her?"

"Kosta Greenmark is a strong man and healthy, for all his age," mused Seija. "He might live for many years yet, and who knows but he might be persuaded to relinquish Faarhafn to its rightful owners?"

At this my entire family perked up, even my father, whose custom was to sit quietly in a corner lined with a mosaic of iridescent shell bits and compose his poems while the seven sisters argued everything out.

It was a long-held tradition of my people that Faarhafn was rightfully ours, that it belonged to all our people together and not to one man from distant Din Eidyn. During the long winter nights when Teran churned the waters into a fury, stories were told of how Faarhafn was lost to one of Lord Steinnland's ancestors in a game of riddles and trickery where my lord's forbear cheated. During the summer evenings when the Mother of the Sea kept Teran's fury in check and the waters were calm, we would look with longing on the fair island that had once been our summer home.

"If Lord Steinnland could be persuaded to say the words that give us back the island…." Seija reflected.

"If anybody can talk him round, Sabira can," my mother said. "Look at what she's gotten away with while I thought she was tending the outlying gardens and hatcheries!" Her tone was half irritated, half proud. It had been wrong of me to lie to her and evade my chores, very wrong to marry without her permission – but if my wrongdoing won us back our island home, how could she be angry with me?

"He would not even have to know what he was doing," said Seija. "The power is in the words; Sabira could tell him anything, perhaps that they are an old charm to calm the waves. After all, his ancestor cheated to get Faarhafn. I do not see anything wrong with using a little misdirection to get it back."

"And what about this entail?" snapped Maarit.

Seija gave a graceful shrug that made her whole body undulate. "The power of all law is words – just words. If the right words are said by the one who owns it now, Faarhafn is ours – entail or no entail."

I was not so sure that the law of the sea would override the law of the land, but I was not being asked for my opinion in this discussion.

"And what about the risk to Sabira?" Aunt Raonaid asked. "We all know what marriage to one of Steinnland's sort can lead to."

"If she does not let him use her body, there is no risk," said my mother, "and she says he has promised there will be nothing of that sort. When he's said the words and the island is ours again, she can come back to us as pure as she went."

They decided, without even asking me, that I had married Steinnland solely to trick him into giving up his rights over the island, and that once this was done I would return to being the patient, obedient, and submissive daughter of the house and niece of six aunts.

It would have been rude to contradict them, and in any case they probably would not have listened to me.

I could have told them, for instance, that one small island was a only trivial part of my lord's estate, and that he would probably give us back Faarhafn for the asking. Indeed, we had already discussed the matter. There were only two small problems hindering the return of the island. Among the folk who looked to him as their lord were a number of fishers and crofters who had made their homes along the sand of the smooth southern shore, or in the western cove where the cliffs reached out from the land like cupped hands to form a natural harbor. These people would have to be settled on some other part of his estate; it could have been done by a single order from my lord's factor, but he loved persuasion better than force, and wished for time to make the transition gentle for them.

The other matter was Steinnland's own home. He had other places to live – the Greenmark manor house on the northern coast, not to mention his town house in Din Eidyn – but like his ancestors before him, he loved the island from which his family took their title. The first Greenmark to win title to the island, the one who had been given the title of March-Lord in view of his service in making Faarhafn part of Dalriada to serve as a resting place for the boats that plied between the mainland and the Isles of the North, had built himself a modest home atop the western cliffs of our island. Every generation afterwards had added a room or a gallery to this summer home, until it had become a great, strange, rambling maze overlooking the sea. There were rooms that leaned perilously out over the cliffs, all lined with panes of clear glass whose greenish swirls transmuted the air and sea beyond into one swirling mass, so that you could almost imagine yourself living beneath the waters. There were deep cellars cut into the rock to store the wines laid down by men long dead. There were rambling halls that had been built on and on, piecemeal, to display things that had caught some Greenmark's interest, from a device to track the stars to a piece of twisted and sea-polished driftwood – for all his family had a bent towards the study of natural philosophy, though perhaps none took it to such lengths as my own dear lord. And best of all, there was the library, a high round tower with a spiral stair that carried you past his shelves of books so that you could select at will and take your chosen book to the little round room at the top where windows alternated with deep, soft leather-covered divans. Stone shelves holding lamps jutted out at either side of each divan, so that day or night, you could sink into your seat and immerse yourself in your book as long as you wished.

My lord knew that his title to the island rested on a chancy transaction involving some trickery (although in his family's version of the tale, it was our people who sought to cheat his ancestor and so deserved to be cheated in their turn) and he might have given back the island willingly – but his home on the western crest? It would have pained him deeply to leave that strange, twisting, many-windowed house in which he had taken root after his retirement from public affairs in Din Eidyn, and he could hardly have continued living there after the island was ours again.

And, after our marriage, there was a third obstacle which I could hardly explain to my family. They might have convinced themselves that I married my lord in order to trick him into relinquishing the island, but as you already know, that was not even in my mind at the time. I married him because I loved him for the new worlds he had opened to me, and because I loved to come to his house and choose a new book as I mounted the spiral stairs to his reading room, and because I was tired of inventing stories to explain my absences from home. And after we were married, I loved our peaceful life together and had absolutely no wish to end it by manipulating him into giving up Faarhafn.

We met as we chose during the day, by appointment or by accident. I was free to wander the shores and watch the storm clouds driving across the sea, or to read for hours in the library, or to visit those few of the fisher folk who did not feel uncomfortable in my presence. If I did miss my family, they were close enough for me to visit whenever I felt so inclined.

Although my lord somewhat deplored my frivolous tastes, he allowed me to send for all the latest romances from Din Eidyn to lighten the serious fare of his library of scientific and historical tomes. He laughed to see me ensconced on one of his leather divans with a three-volume tale of the perils of some virtuous heroine toppling into my lap and colliding with a treatise on the movement of the stars. We dined together every evening, and our meals were spiced by incessant, lively talk, the more so as I learned enough of his world to question and even debate his assertions. Though he had long since lost interest in the social and political life of the capital, he said that he intended to take me there one day, if only to convince me that the streets were not lined with silver and that every house did not contain a poet-swordsman languishing over a fair lady or an heiress masquerading as a kitchen-maid to escape the machinations of her wicked guardian.

As I may have mentioned, he did not altogether approve all my choices of books. But how else was I to learn what life among his people was really like? I knew nothing but my family home and this isolated hold on the cliffs. And while that life pleased me well enough, I felt it was only my duty to learn something about society so that I should not disgrace him, if ever we did go to the capital, by acting like a simple country girl. Besides, the stories were compelling in their own right. Once I had fairly begun a novel, I could hardly bring myself to stop reading until the ending was achieved and the lovers united.

Not that I was in any hurry to deal with Society as evidenced in Din Eidyn. We were happy enough as we were; I felt in my smug ignorance that Society could wait.

It was an unpleasant shock to find that Society was coming to us instead.

It happened that one of my visits to my family was marred by another fight with my Aunt Maarit over this question of getting back Faarhafn for our people, a fight in which I found myself alone against all six aunts and even my mother. After returning home I lay long awake that night, and so I slept late the next morning and woke to find Steinnland breakfasting without me – and talking to someone! There was a low deep laugh that made me shiver to the backbone, a strange voice that I had never heard before, followed by both voices dropping so low that I could not make out what they were saying.

Not that I was some servant girl to listen at doors, you understand. I was Steinnland's lady, and he would never conceal anything from me that I needed to know. If I paused before opening the door to the breakfast room, it was only to make sure that my hair was smooth and my overdress and petticoat arranged as foreigners from the mainland would think proper.

Steinnland rose to greet me when I entered, smiling his welcome, and yet I had the sense of some urgent conversation broken off, of dangerous words hanging on the air. That feeling, or something else, so troubled me that I could scarcely concentrate on what he was saying; all the air seemed stirred and quivering about the person of his visitor. Unlike the stunted fisher-folk of the island, this man was tall enough to look level into my eyes, and he had about him all the town-polish that I had read about in my books but had never seen in person: black hair artfully cut and brushed about a lean, narrow face, a white stock creased into intricate folds, a coat that fit as if it had been stitched upon his body, boots as glossy as a black seal's coat all wet from the sea, and closely fitted knit breeches that left nothing to the imagination. Not, you understand, that I was unaware of how a man is built, but we simple country folk are either naked or clothed. It had not occurred to me that clothing might be used to emphasize what it pretended to cover.

Steinnland was introducing the man as his dear friend Viscount Iveroth from the mainland, come to bring in person some important papers from Steinnland's advocat in Din Eidyn, and all I could think, like some simple country girl indeed, was, "But he's young!"

Oh, he was not of an age with me, this fellow from the mainland; he might have lived thirty winters or a few more. But I had somehow assumed that all Steinnland's friends would be of his own generation, that I would be able to deal with them as I did with my own family – keeping the mask of patient, obedient, quiet Sabira, there to run errands or do small tasks or to keep herself out of the way.

There would be no quietly keeping myself out of the way of this Iveroth, not if he wished otherwise. Young and dark and dangerous, he was, with a vital force that breathed about him in a quivering aura so bright I was surprised that even his own people, blind as they were, were not disturbed by the flash of his dark eyes under slanting black brows. *I* was disturbed. The peace of my lord's house was disturbed. In that instant I knew that change was upon us and that I had been simpler than any country fool to think it was in my power to delay it.

In the next instant, of course, I made my curtsey to him – without disturbing the arrangement of my petticoat – and welcomed him as Lady Steinnland should receive any good friend of her husband's. Whatever Steinnland thought, I had not read all those novels from Din Eidyn for nothing!

"My lady." The man was all but gaping; had he assumed, then, that Steinnland had made a mésalliance with some peasant? "I – I – Rumor had not warned me," he all but stammered, making a leg with some grace at last.

Actually, to be fair, he did it far more gracefully than I had imagined possible. There are some nuances you cannot learn from studying literature. Naturally he could not achieve the full *grande révérence* as performed by my people, but then, such a gesture would have been more than I was entitled to.

Steinnland beamed as if showing off one of the treasured possessions that filled the rambling halls of his house. "Rumor told you that I was wed at last, did it, Iveroth? But no tales could prepare you for the beauty and grace of my Sabira."

"Indeed," Iveroth agreed, and it seemed to me he stared at my petticoat a little harder than was proper. "Lady Steinnland is indeed – beyond all expectation." He did not sound one bit pleased about it. "I can quite understand your happiness."

It hardly appeared that he shared that happiness. Perhaps he was just generally displeased with the world around him. If so, he would make a good match with my aunt Maarit. For some reason I found that thought distasteful.

"My dear," Steinnland went on, "I fear Lord Iveroth has brought news that will disturb the peace of our house for some days."

It is already disturbed, I thought wildly, it is already destroyed. Can you not see that this man is a raven of ill omen? But I had just enough sense to keep those words between my teeth. The folk of the land have only one sight; Steinnland could not have been expected to read the dangerous blaze of this Iveroth's soul-force.

# Also by Margaret Ball:

## Applied Topology series:

### A Pocketful of Stars
*A quiet math major has to fight in the magical realm for her life and those of her friends after the CIA decides to make use of her paranormal abilities.*

### An Opening in the Air
*When a rival mage attacks, Thalia needs wits as well as magic to save the Center for Applied Topology. And the defense may cost her the man she loves.*

### An Annoyance of Grackles
*It's bad enough when a rival mage tries to destroy you. When he turns out to be a god, that's worse. And when the god teams up with the most notorious contract bomber in America? If Thalia can't outwit the duo, she may wind up scattered across the campus in tiny pieces.*

### A Tapestry of Fire
*Saving her best friend from life as a fish is difficult. Rescuing the man she loves from a past era of fire and fury ought to be impossible, so it may take Thalia a little longer.*

### A Creature of Smokeless Flame
*When CIA officers' children are kidnapped for revenge, Thalia and her colleagues follow the trail across the continents to an African terrorists' camp whose leader has the help of his own personal genie.*

**Harmony series:**

Insurgents
Awakening
Survivors


**Earlier books:**

Disappearing Act
Duchess of Aquitaine
Mathemagics
Lost in Translation
No Earthly Sunne
Changeweaver
Flameweaver
The Shadow Gate